In the thistles where they hid, J.D. felt Mari and Amy draw closer

The gesture filled him with a fierce protectiveness he'd never experienced before. It was almost like having a complete family at Christmastime. Except that Mari wasn't his wife and Amy wasn't his daughter....

Amy watched him, gauging his reaction to the danger they were in. He winked and squeezed her shoulder. Then Mari looked up and gave him a reassuring smile. J.D. felt the impact all through his body. He could feel the warmth, even in the frosty December dawn.

But they were still in grave, life-threatening danger.

And that bitter knowledge suddenly wrapped itself around J.D. like an icy wind....

Dear Reader,

At Harlequin Intrigue, we all agree—nothing is better on a cold winter night than cozying up with a good romantic mystery. So we've asked some of our favorite authors—and yours—to entertain us with some special stories this month, which are set around the holidays.

We hope you'll grab some cider and cuddle up with *Bearing Gifts* by Aimée Thurlo—a Christmas mystery that we know will warm your heart!

Sincerely,

Debra Matteucci
Senior Editor & Editorial Coordinator
Harlequin Books
300 East 42nd Street
New York, NY 10017

Aimée Thurlo
Bearing Gifts

Harlequin Books

TORONTO • NEW YORK • LONDON
AMSTERDAM • PARIS • SYDNEY • HAMBURG
STOCKHOLM • ATHENS • TOKYO • MILAN
MADRID • WARSAW • BUDAPEST • AUCKLAND

To Peggy Chauvet, the best friend anyone could ever have. And with special thanks and acknowledgment to Glenda F. McCary-Moos, Philip N. Moos, Mary Elizabeth Allen, Bill Blohm and Rita McLaughlin for their help and support.

ISBN 0-373-22304-8

BEARING GIFTS

Copyright © 1994 by Aimée Thurlo

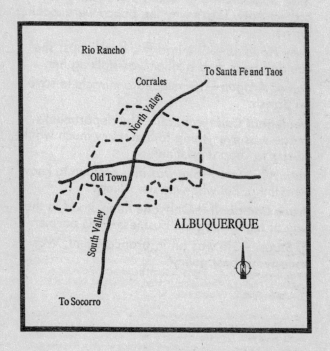

CAST OF CHARACTERS

J. D. Hawken—Who was he out to protect, his sister, Amy, or his business?

Mari Sanchez—She would do anything to protect Amy. That's why the police were looking for her.

Amy Hawken—She had two handicaps: she couldn't hear, and a killer was stalking her.

Father Aragon—He needed a miracle to save his parish.

Lieutenant Colin Randall—The department's image was everything to him. How much would he risk to keep it pristine?

Ruth Whitmore—She was in a position to know everything. But who was she telling?

Bruce Campbell—Only one thing stood in the way of his owning the business—his partner.

Al Stuart—He was an insurance agent. Was honesty his best policy?

Prologue

Elizabeth Hawken walked across the sheriff's department evidence room, hating the claustrophobic feel of the place. Huge gray metal shelves crammed with labeled boxes of evidence loomed ceiling high against the four walls. Long folding tables occupied the center, leaving almost no walking room. As far as she was concerned, there were only two bright spots here. One was the huge bin of donated toys, part of the Toys for Tykes Christmas drive she and her best friend, Mari, were sponsoring. Elizabeth placed her handwritten I.O.U. inside the large packing crate, then retrieved a small potbellied polar bear.

Holding the plush toy up at eye level before her, Elizabeth smiled. It was just like the one she'd had as a child, down to the red-and-green plaid bow. The bear would make a perfect gift for her eight-year-old daughter, Amy. Not that she intended to keep this particular one. The soft, cuddly fellow would go to some needy child who deserved the joy the stuffed animal would bring. Elizabeth was only going to borrow the bear long enough to stop by the toy store so they could order one just like it for her. Then, tomorrow morning, she'd return the borrowed bear to the bin.

Elizabeth was certain no one would mind. As she looked at the bear's ever-cheerful grin, pleasant memories of long ago crowded her mind. At one time, the stuffed animal like this one had been her constant companion. Now she'd be able to share in the wonder and the fantasy a special friend like this one would bring Amy.

Elizabeth glanced across the room, her gaze resting on the small statue of the Madonna resting on a shelf between two small cardboard boxes. This figure was the second bright spot in the room. Its jewel-encrusted dress sparkled in the light of a single bulb directly overhead. The Madonna, a religious treasure over one hundred years old, belonged to a parish in one of the poorest communities of northern New Mexico. The statue was said to bring a special blessing to each child who worshiped at its church on Christmas Day. Elizabeth whispered a prayer of thanks. Perhaps heaven was working overtime. The blessing to her own child had come early.

Elizabeth walked toward the two-foot-tall figure, entranced as always by the very human features on the Virgin's face. In order to publicize the much-needed toy drive, Father Aragon had reluctantly agreed to allow the Madonna out of the church. Every day, the Madonna was placed for public viewing in a special secure glass case behind the station's front window. Afterward, she was returned to the evidence room, where she was kept under lock and key.

Mari Sanchez had spent a week assuring Father Aragon that the Madonna would be safe in Elizabeth's care. The priest had even come to inspect the place where the Lady would be kept after hours. He hadn't been thrilled with the bleak surroundings, but he'd finally acknowledged that she couldn't be any safer, surrounded as she was by the police. Toy donations had in fact doubled since the Madonna's arrival, which had helped ease the burden of his decision.

As Elizabeth stood before the statue, she suddenly noted something that made her blood run cold. Some dried paste edged the bloodred ruby that adorned the figure's dress, and part of the fabric was damaged, as if cut by the silver circle that kept the jewel in place. Elizabeth's heartbeat quickened. The cherished Madonna had somehow been damaged. She ran her fingers over the cloth, assessing the damage to the rest of the dress. Suddenly another problem caught her attention. The sapphires that formed the petals of a tiny flower in the back of the dress seemed too small for the setting. Elizabeth leaned forward for a closer look and saw the faint white of drying paste there also.

Elizabeth stepped back, a queasy feeling in her stomach. No such flaws had been there before. In fact, when the Madonna had first arrived, the priest had pointed out to everyone how extraordinary the workmanship was.

Elizabeth picked up an instant camera kept in the evidence room for official use, snapped a close-up photo and stuck it in her pocket. She had a feeling the picture would come in handy. She'd taken another snapshot as a souvenir weeks ago. She'd compare the two when she remembered where she'd put the first one. With one last worried look at the statue, she exited, closing the door behind her.

The clerk at the desk, Deputy Ken Gonzales, chuckled as he saw the bear in Elizabeth's hand. "What's this? Grand bear larceny?"

Elizabeth smiled and explained, "I left an I.O.U. Don't try to stop me. I'm a desperate woman. I've got to get the toy store to order one just like this for my kid. It's exactly like the one I used to have."

Ken, a lanky deputy with eyes as dark as coal, chuckled. "Okay. But I want to see it back here tomorrow. Now empty your pockets and let's finish the drill," he said.

Elizabeth was patted down. Ken looked at the photo she'd taken of the Madonna. "What's this for?" he asked.

"For my scrapbook. Do you mind? She's really special, and since my best friend and I were the ones who initiated this drive, I'd like something to remember it by."

He pursed his lips, considering her explanation. "I suppose it's okay. Couldn't do any harm."

"Thanks, Ken." Elizabeth pocketed her possessions and the photo and rushed down the hall.

She couldn't discuss what she suspected with just anyone yet. The very first order of business was to notify the division supervisor. Though she was part of the civilian staff, she still had to follow the chain of command. Elizabeth strode to Lieut. Colin Randall's office, scarcely aware of the people who were passing down the busy corridor. She'd had trouble with Randall before and wasn't looking forward to this meeting. She knew only too well how he received bad news.

Elizabeth hurried past Ruth Whitmore's desk, brushing against a tiny ceramic Santa and reindeer, then stopped, seeing the door to Colin's office was shut. Elizabeth felt Ruth's gaze. She was a formidable woman whose toned physique and six-foot frame managed to intimidate half the cops on the force, though she was a civilian employee like Elizabeth.

Ruth stood and moved to block Elizabeth's path. "The lieutenant's in a meeting. Can I help you?"

"When will he be free?" Just then the door opened, and a businessman in a gray suit hurried out. Elizabeth darted around Ruth and slipped inside the door. "Colin, I need to talk to you. This can't wait."

Her boss managed a raised eyebrow. "With you, it never can."

Elizabeth struggled to keep her temper in check. He was baiting her. She held his gaze, refusing to look away. Colin's face was tanned and pleasant enough, but his eyes betrayed an unmistakable lack of warmth. "I don't want to waste your time," she said, "so I'll get right to the point." Elizabeth told the lieutenant what she'd discovered, then waited as silence stretched out between them.

Colin finally shook his head. "Let's not go off half-cocked, okay? You and I have been through this before. Remember a year ago when you came in claiming some evidence had been lost? We couldn't even find a record of its existence in the first place."

The sting of his words was almost like a physical blow. She'd been so certain something was missing. To this day, she still didn't know if Colin had somehow covered up just so he wouldn't look bad.

Colin met her gaze dispassionately. "Okay, here's what I'll do. Maybe you noticed something wrong, and maybe you didn't. *I* couldn't tell, that's for sure. I haven't been in there for a week. I'll have the insurance appraiser come in tonight and check the gems on the dress. Just keep this between us until tomorrow morning, clear? Let me find out if there's been a theft first. I don't want anything leaking to the press, only to find out the story's all in your head. The figure is in our care, and if anything's happened to it, our careers will be on hold soon enough without jumping the gun."

"Okay. I'll check with you tomorrow," Elizabeth added, letting him know she wasn't prepared to let the matter drop. She'd find the other photo, then show him the differences she'd detected.

Elizabeth returned to her office, sick at the prospect that the statue had been tampered with. The consequences of such a crime would go a lot further than just the bad press the sheriff's department would receive. Touched by scandal, the children's toy drive would be dealt a harsh blow, and the entire parish would then suffer. The Madonna represented hope and stood for a faith that kept the community together through hard times.

As much as she hated the thought, Elizabeth had to admit that she would appear a likely suspect. She had almost limitless access to the evidence room. Possible scenarios, from being fired to going to jail, flashed through her mind.

And Amy! How would she protect her daughter from the accusations, veiled or otherwise, that could be made?

The current situation—and her own past experiences—made Elizabeth realize she had no choice as to her course of action. The lieutenant would cover his own backside first and throw her to the wolves. She had to start her own investigation immediately. Recalling the names that had appeared on the sign-in sheet for today, she wrote them down on a piece of paper. The remaining pages for the week were in a three-ring binder in her desk.

Taking the book from its drawer, Elizabeth walked to the copy machine and made duplicates of the past week's records. Although she had no way of judging the authenticity of the stones, there was something else she could do tonight to gauge what damage had been done. She'd get to that part of her plan as soon as she left the office.

Whatever decisions she made in the next few hours would affect everyone she loved. Mari, her dearest friend, would share in the disgrace of failing to carry out a promise to Father Aragon. And her brother, JD, would be torn apart by the dishonor of having their family name dragged through the mud.

She picked up her tote bag and started out the door. Elizabeth suddenly remembered where the other photo was. It was in her tote bag among the dozens of receipts and the clutter at the bottom. Resisting the temptation to verify that right now, she kept walking. She'd place the photocopies and the snapshots of the Madonna in a safety deposit box, then call the only two people she trusted. Among the three of them, she was sure they could sort out this mess. Then, by tomorrow, she'd be prepared to face whatever came her way.

One thing gave her the edge, truth was on her side. That would be enough, she hoped.

J. D. HAWKEN SWIVELED around in his chair and stared out his window. His company's parking lot was almost empty, and his view of the snowcapped Sandia Mountains to the east was unhindered. The New Mexico weather, always unpredictable, was cooperating. Though it was December, the temperature was in the mid-fifties, and the sun was shining brightly. That meant his crews, unhampered by snow or chilling rain, could continue working.

He could hear the sounds of "Jingle Bell Rock" drifting out from someone's radio. The office manager and her staff were busy, but the atmosphere was relaxed. Things couldn't have been going better for him. He could afford to be generous with year-end bonuses this year, too. His employees would have a good Christmas! After years of scrimping and saving and fighting to hold on to a dream, he was finally on solid financial ground. JD felt in control of his life and his future.

The intercom on his desk buzzed. "Yes?"

"It's your sister, Elizabeth, on line two," his secretary informed him.

"I'll take it," he said, drawing a deep breath. Leave it to Elizabeth to unsettle what should have been the best time of his life. He loved her. She and his other sister, Pat, were his only blood relatives. But he often wished she wasn't around so often to remind him of the past. It never ceased to amaze him how a brother and sister, raised in the same household, could be so different. They'd lived through the same miserable childhood, shared memories neither could ever forget, and yet they were as different as night and day. "Hello, Elizabeth." He toyed with a pencil on his desk, passing it from finger to finger like a magician with a coin.

"I've got a big problem, JD."

"What's going on?"

"I think someone has taken property out of the evidence room. But it's more than that. What's been taken . . . well, it's irreplaceable. We have to talk. Can you meet me tonight? I need your advice."

It was the forced evenness of her tone that frightened him most. The one trait they shared was that the more scared they were, the more detached and logical they tried to become; it was a survival lesson they'd both learned early on in life.

"I'll be over this evening. Is that soon enough?" JD asked, his tone guarded.

"Yeah, and thanks. I'll see if Mari can come then, too."

Hearing Mari's name, JD's muscles tightened. Mari's face flashed before his mind's eye in vivid detail. There had always been a very special chemistry between them, but her friendship with Elizabeth had led to disagreements that stood in their way, forming a barrier he could never get past. He wasn't the kind of man to dwell on a woman he couldn't have. There were others who wanted his attention, enough to keep his limited social calendar full. Still, he'd never managed to put Mari completely out of his mind.

Elizabeth's voice cut into his thoughts. "You've always wanted to have our family name spoken with respect. Well, it's going to be mud unless we fix what happened. Then our name will never be forgotten and you'll get what you've always wanted."

JD tried to banish the sudden chill that ran down his spine. As he put down the receiver, an old adage repeated itself in his mind in a mocking singsong: *Be careful what you wish for. You just might get it.*

Chapter One

Mari Sanchez drove down a lonely rural stretch of Albuquerque's South Valley, bordering the Rio Grande. Cottonwoods with their bare branches lined the Bosque area astride the wide, shallow river, and fenced bottomland held livestock trying to graze on dried rabbitbrush and thin desert grasses. It was warmer than normal for mid-December this year.

Long quiet drives down narrow New Mexico roads always helped her unwind, but today nothing short of talking to Elizabeth Hawken was bound to do that. They'd been playing phone tag all day, but the fact that Elizabeth had tried three times to reach her at work meant that something was seriously wrong. She'd never done that before, not in the six years Mari had taught at Alice Anaya Elementary School.

Mari nervously drummed her index finger on the wheel as the Spanish radio station continued to play "Feliz Navidad." Liz was her best friend, more like the sister she'd never had. The one sure thing they'd each counted on through the years, no matter what challenge they'd faced, was the strength of that friendship. The mutual intuitions the two women had developed after sharing their most intimate thoughts now left Mari certain that something was terribly wrong.

The southwestern sun was in her eyes, blazing crimson and orange near the horizon when Mari slowed down. The long dirt track leading to Elizabeth's home was just around the bend. Mari raised her hand, shielding her eyes from the glare as she rounded the curve. There was something just ahead on the road, perhaps an accident victim, but she could barely make it out. She slowed down even more, her uneasiness growing. A heartbeat later, as the shapes became more distinct, her breath caught in her throat. She could see someone wearing a thick dark jacket and a blue baseball cap going through the purse of a woman lying on the edge of the road. Mari spotted Elizabeth's van parked nearby and a pickup she didn't recognize skewed across the road behind it.

Mari rolled down her window. "Get away from her!" she yelled. When the person ignored her, Mari honked her horn, accelerating at the same time. The man in the jacket jumped to his feet. As Mari's gaze shifted to the body on the ground, she recognized Elizabeth's battered navy peacoat. Thoughts raced through her mind too fast for her to register anything except raw fear. The apparent thief broke into an uneven run and crossed the street. He took a quick glance inside the van, then ran to the pickup and jumped inside.

Mari braked to a stop a dozen feet from Elizabeth. As she opened her door, the other driver pulled out onto the highway, tires squealing, and sped down the road. Mari tried to focus on the license plate, but the place where it should have been was covered with mud.

Mari's gaze immediately shifted to Elizabeth's face. She was pale and so very still! A thin ribbon of blood ran from the corner of her mouth and down her neck. *Oh, God, don't let her be dead!* Mari crouched and placed her hand over Elizabeth's. Relief flooded through her when Elizabeth's eyes opened slowly. "I'm here," Mari said, quickly taking off her coat and covering Liz. "Hang on. I've got to go get help." Hearing the sound of an approaching car, she turned

her head. "Here comes someone now. I'll be right back."
Mari raced to the center of the road and flagged down the
driver. After asking her to call the police and an ambulance, Mari ran back to Elizabeth's side. Taking her hand
again, she tried to assess her injuries without moving her.
"What happened? Was it a hit and run?"

Elizabeth's eyes mirrored the pain that had to be wrack-
ing her body. "Take...care of Amy. It wasn't...an accident!"

A paralyzing thought stabbed through Mari. Was it a
kidnapping? "Where's Amy?"

"The...van. Don't let JD...have her. She needs *you.*"

"Don't talk anymore," Mari said quietly. "Just save your
strength." She couldn't stand seeing the agony on Elizabeth's face knowing there was nothing she could do to abate
it. Much of the damage to her was obviously internal. "I'll
take care of Amy. Just hang on."

"Hide her. She might have seen..."

"I'm going to be right here. Nothing will happen to her."

"Don't trust...department...." Liz managed, her voice
thready. "They're in this...."

"Liz, who did this to you?"

"I...couldn't see his face. Mailbox...take key...take
Amy...." Elizabeth's voice drifted off and her eyes closed.

Mari's throat tightened until she could barely draw in a
breath. She slipped her hand down and felt for Elizabeth's
pulse. Liz was still alive, but where were the paramedics?
She stared down the empty road, then back at the van. Amy
must be terrified!

Leaving Elizabeth's side, she ran across the road, knowing that calling out wouldn't do any good. Amy had been
born deaf. Mari peered inside and, for one agonizing minute, didn't see any sign of her godchild. Then she heard a
low sob. As she pinpointed the location of the sound, she
saw movement beneath an old wool blanket at the rear of
the van. She reached out gently, so as not to frighten the

child beneath, and started to pull back the blanket to let Amy see her.

The child shrank back with a mewling cry that tore at Mari's heart. Instead of pulling the blanket completely off Amy, Mari reached beneath it. She fingerspelled her own name slowly. American Sign Language was a visual language that required many gestures. Fingerspelling, under the circumstances, was the easiest way to reassure Amy fast.

It worked. Amy touched her hand and stayed still as Mari pulled the blanket away. No child deserved to have that look of fear on her face, especially so close to Christmas. "It's okay," Mari signed, and gathered Amy against her. The thought that Amy might have seen Elizabeth's assailant sent a flash of panic through her. But there was no time for questions now. If Liz had uncovered police corruption, then Mari had to protect her godchild at all costs.

She remembered the day Amy had been born. Elizabeth, unmarried and alone, had asked her to be there. Mari had not only stayed but had even helped in the delivery. Determination fueled Mari's resolve and boosted her courage. Nothing would harm this child, not while she was there to protect her. Mari signed quickly, asking Amy to come with her. Wrapping the blanket around Amy's shoulders, she urged the child toward her own vehicle across the street, but Amy resisted.

Breaking free, she ducked back inside the van and reached beneath the seat for a white teddy bear with a bright red-and-green plaid bow. Clutching it tightly against her, she emerged a moment later. Amy looked up as if worried Mari wouldn't understand. "Mom left it for me. It was under the blanket. With me, it was less lonely," she signed.

Mari smiled at her quickly. At the moment, she wouldn't have tried to prevent Amy from taking anything that would comfort her. Mari had no illusions about what was yet to come. The next few hours were bound to be extremely difficult for all of them.

Moving quickly toward her own car, Mari kept Amy from running toward her mom as she urged Amy into the back seat. The child's wide brown eyes looked even larger against the pallor of her face as Mari signed, asking Amy to hide again. Amy nodded once, then huddled down onto the floorboard, cuddling her bear and pulling the blanket over herself. Hearing the wail of approaching sirens, Mari closed the car door quickly and turned around. As she looked searchingly down the road, she spotted a solitary figure standing at the top of the mesa a few hundred yards away. Her flesh prickled with fear. Surely Elizabeth's assailant wouldn't come back, now that help was on the way.

Mari shielded her eyes from the last rays of sunlight with her hand, trying to get a better look. Two patrol cars and an emergency vehicle came speeding around the curve. Her attention shifted for only a few seconds as she ran across to Elizabeth, but by the time she looked back, their watcher was gone.

A pair of khaki-uniformed sheriff's deputies approached her as the paramedics rushed to examine Elizabeth. "I'm Officer Perea. What happened here?" the barrel-chested officer asked.

She recounted what she'd seen, most of what Elizabeth had told her, and mentioned the figure who'd been watching. She deliberately omitted any reference to Amy or police involvement in anything criminal. Remembering Elizabeth's warning, Mari made up her mind to avoid giving out any more information about her friend's activities than was absolutely necessary.

Officer Perea nodded to the other deputy, a slender redhead, who ran to his patrol car and quickly drove down the road toward the mesa on which their watcher had stood. Officer Perea retrieved a small notebook from his shirt-front pocket. "Can you describe the person you saw and the vehicle he was driving?"

Mari detailed everything she recalled, trying to keep her voice steady despite what had happened. "I think there was something wrong with his leg," she added finally. "He ran stiffly, as if he'd been injured at one time."

The officer penciled the information into his notebook. "What brought you here tonight?"

"Elizabeth Hawken and I are good friends. She invited me over." As the paramedics continued to work on Elizabeth, Mari cast a quick, furtive glance toward her car. She had to get Amy away as soon as possible. With a little bit of luck, Amy wouldn't peer out or decide to run to Elizabeth's side.

"We'll have to treat this as a hit-and-run until we get more information. We don't have any evidence to list this as an attempted murder."

"Elizabeth told me this was a deliberate attempt on her life."

"We'll take that into account, miss. Now I have to call this in." Office Perea went to his car, and Mari stepped over to see how the medics were doing. They were working intently, so she didn't interrupt them with questions. Before she could figure out a way to check on Amy, the deputy returned. "I need to ask you some more questions."

"I've told you all I know. Why aren't you checking for tire tracks or setting up a roadblock or something? Don't waste time talking to me when the man who hurt Elizabeth is getting away." Fear and anger fought for control of her voice.

"Just relax, ma'am. There's an officer looking for the person you described. In the meantime, you can help by providing some background information for a possible motive."

Mari hesitated for a fraction of a second, wondering what she should tell him. She was about to reply when she saw a shiny red pickup approaching. A few seconds later, it pulled to a stop behind the police cars amid a cloud of gravel and dust.

She watched curiously as the driver stepped out. As the failing rays of twilight revealed his features, Mari recognized him instantly. Her body responded to his presence as naturally as a parched rose to water. J. D. Hawken had a presence few men ever achieved. He was at least six foot three, with a lean, strong-looking physique. He took in the scene before him at a glance and strode toward the paramedics who were tending his sister.

"JD, I'm so sorry," Mari said, stepping into his path. "Liz has been hurt. Somebody ran into her."

"Is she—" JD nodded, then made his way over to the paramedics. "I'm her brother. I won't waste your time. What's her condition?"

Both paramedics looked up at the same time. Something about JD's tone had secured their undivided attention. "We're attempting to stabilize your sister now, sir. Then we'll transport her to a hospital. After that, it's up to the doctors. And to her."

"Take her to Saint Agnes's Hospital. And notify Dr. Lenore Freedman. She's Elizabeth's physician." The paramedics both nodded and returned to their work. JD stepped over to where Mari waited with the officer. Ice-cold azure eyes registered her presence, then focused on Officer Perea. "I'm J. D. Hawken. Do you have the person who did this to my sister in custody?" His clipped tone revealed his deep concern for Elizabeth.

"Not yet, but we will. At the moment, we only have one witness," Perea noted, indicating Mari with a glance.

JD's eyes were as unfathomable as a mountain lake. For a moment as he held her gaze, Mari thought she saw some emotion flicker in his eyes. Like a pool disturbed only briefly by a pebble tossed into its center, his expression quickly stilled, leaving no traces to mar its outward calm.

JD was about to ask Mari what she'd seen, but hearing the paramedics lift the stretcher, he quickly stepped forward to help them shift Elizabeth into the emergency vehicle. "I'll be in shortly to sign her admittance papers." He signed the release form the paramedic handed him, then caught the man's eye. "I know you'll do your best."

Mari saw the medic's expression, and knew Elizabeth would receive exactly that. Charisma was hard to define, but it was a quality all natural leaders had; it made others want to follow them and commanded instant respect. That's the way it was with John Daniel Hawken. JD mingled toughness with persuasiveness and this combination naturally drew people to him.

For a moment, she couldn't help but wish that she had someone like him in her life, a man who'd watch over her and protect her. She banished the thought quickly. There were no Prince Charmings left in the world.

JD returned to her side after the ambulance raced down the highway. "Now, Officer, do you need anything from me? I have to get to the hospital."

"I've got all the information Ms. Sanchez can give me. If you could also tell me what brought you here tonight, that would be a help."

Mari tried desperately to catch JD's eye, but there was nothing much she could do to warn him, not with the officer standing less than five feet away. To her relief, JD's answer was vague.

"Why do you ask?" JD countered brusquely. "Do you think this was a deliberate attempt on Elizabeth's life?"

"I don't have enough evidence yet to make that judgment, sir. But, according to Ms. Sanchez, your sister thought it was."

JD shook his head slowly. "My sister's conclusions aren't always supported by facts."

Mari suspected that the criticism was only meant to force the police to dig deeper for answers, but she didn't like him speaking that way about Elizabeth, especially now. Remembering what she disliked most about JD, she gave him an icy glare. There were times when he was too stone-cold logical.

As the officers moved toward Elizabeth's van, JD turned to Mari. "You and I can discuss these events later. Right now, there's only one thing I need to know. Where's Amy?"

Chapter Two

Mari fought the urge to answer him honestly, knowing Officer Perea was close and might overhear. Instead she shrugged casually. "Amy's probably at a neighbor's house. I'm sure she's fine. I'll take care of finding her. Don't worry."

JD glanced toward the officer, who was several feet away searching the dirt road and studying the tracks. "I should have been here sooner."

"How could you have known this was going to happen? There was no way you could have been here sooner."

"I'm not used to listening to excuses—especially my own." JD shook his head. "Forget I brought it up. Listen, I hate to drag you into my problems, but I really need your help locating Amy. She's a kid who needs special handling. There's no telling how much of this she'll be able to understand. I'll have to present things to her a little bit at a time."

Had she not heard all of it, Mari would have sworn he was referring to a horse instead of a little girl. "JD, I'm Amy's godmother. I'm *very* aware of her needs." Mari bit back the urge to remind him that she undoubtedly knew Amy better than he did.

JD stared down at her, obviously surprised by her abrupt change in tone. "I need to go take care of Elizabeth. I'll trust you to find Amy."

Mari watched JD as he went to say something to Officer Perea, then hurried back to his pickup and drove away. Elizabeth had frequently said that ice water flowed through her brother's veins. She'd warned Mari not to get involved with him, noting the obvious attraction between Mari and JD the few times they'd been together. Still, Mari had always suspected that there was much more to JD than just his toughness and self-sufficiency. There had been times she'd glimpsed pain in his eyes, like someone who'd shouldered too much responsibility and too much sorrow as a child. Her yearning to communicate with him had surprised her. He was a tough businessman with a reputation for getting the job done. He certainly didn't want or need her help.

Officer Perea interrupted her thoughts. "You're free to go, ma'am. We have your address and telephone number and will let you know if we need anything else. I appreciate your cooperation."

As she hurried to her car, Mari offered a silent prayer of thanks that Amy had done as she'd asked and stayed hidden. She slid behind the wheel and drove away quickly before Amy could look up. Once she was certain that no one was following her, Mari pulled off the road and stopped.

After opening the rear door, she crouched beside the seat and took Amy gently by the shoulders. The little girl threw her arms around Mari in a mighty hug, trembling violently. After a while, Amy released her hold and reached for the teddy bear with the bright Christmas bow, clutching it to her chest. Mari wiped the little girl's tears and then signed to reassure her.

Mari had expected Amy to ask about her mother, and the fact that the little girl hadn't done so, frightened her. Amy was an active, intelligent child, but at the moment she was very still, watching Mari passively. Mari signed, simultaneously speaking slowly. "Stay down. We're going to my house. We'll be there soon."

Settling the child more comfortably on the back seat, Mari fastened Amy's seat belt and wrapped her in the blanket, then quickly drove home. It was completely dark by the time they arrived at her modest, two-bedroom adobe home. Red chili pepper Christmas lights lined the windows facing the street, and pine boughs formed a wreath upon the door. She'd spent last weekend decorating for the holidays, something she enjoyed that never failed to get her into the right mood for the season. But now, under the circumstances, the season of miracles and love seemed more an illusion than reality.

Mari inched the car into the garage, then after the automatic door closed, led Amy into the house. She kept the lights at a minimum. Amy walked directly to the Advent calendar that Mari had placed on the coffee table, and stared at the tiny open doors as if entranced.

Mari walked over to Amy, knelt on the carpeted floor and gently turned the girl around to face her. For a brief moment, Mari studied Amy's expression. The child seemed more relaxed now, but there was a sense of waiting, as if she wanted Mari to answer the questions she didn't dare ask.

As a special education teacher, Mari knew there was particular danger when a deaf child withdrew, shutting the world out and keeping any hurt at bay. The isolation in their world of silence could be seductive. She'd have to tread carefully if she was going to prevent that withdrawal from happening now.

Using speech and signing, she assured Amy once again that they were both safe. Mari waited for Amy to ask about her mom, but the little girl just stood there. "Talk to me," Mari signed.

Amy stared at Mari, then using her voice as she'd been encouraged to do, and signing, asked, "Will Mom come back soon?" Her words were high-pitched and faint. Although it would have been hard for some to understand, Mari had no difficulty. She knew the effort Amy's speech had taken. She'd sat with Amy for hours on end as she'd tried to emulate sounds made visible on a computer screen through a series of waves and jagged lines. "I don't know when she'll be back, but the doctors will take care of her. What happened? Can you tell me?"

Amy shook her head. "The car came too fast. Mom fell," she signed. "Danger." Tears ran down Amy's cheeks and she stopped signing, hugging Mari hard around the neck instead.

The silence of Amy's crying made it all the more heart-rending. Mari knew that in an effort to be accepted, despite her disability, Amy had taught herself not to make sounds, since the quality of her speech would mark her as different. It was impossible for her to gauge degrees of loudness or enunciate as clearly as the hearing, and Amy had always been particularly sensitive to the stares of people who didn't understand. It had taken her teachers a very long time to coax Amy to speak at all, and she was still shy around strangers.

Mari gathered Amy in her arms and carried her to the master bedroom. After putting her down near the bed, Mari signed and spoke slowly. "You need to get some rest. Sleep."

Amy stared around the room and shook her head. "Don't leave me alone," she signed rapidly.

"You won't be. I'll be right outside. And besides, that's my bed," Mari expressed with a smile. "I'll be sleeping there, too." Mari tossed back the covers and then helped Amy take off her shoes. "Rest. I'll be right outside the door." When she tried to take the bear from the little girl's hand, Amy recoiled, hugging it all the more tightly. "Okay, you can keep it with you," Mari signed with an accompanying smile.

Amy settled back, the bear under one arm, and signed, "Stay."

"Sure." Mari lay next to Amy and cuddled the little girl close to her. Although Mari needed to find out what Amy had seen, she couldn't bring herself to subject Amy to that kind of questioning yet.

When she felt Amy crying again, Mari held her, trying to provide some comfort. Amy had fought hard to establish herself in the world of the hearing. The isolation that came from deafness transcended the silence the condition imposed. She understood that type of situation well, but perhaps it was easier for her to empathize. She knew what it was like to be different from the rest, to lack an ability that the world took for granted.

MARI HELD AMY LONG AFTER the child had fallen asleep. In the dimly lit room, she tried to remember the details of the message Elizabeth had left for her at school. It had been brief and very simple. She'd just insisted on a meeting this evening.

After a while, Mari disengaged herself from Amy. For the first time, the girl looked at peace. Kissing Amy's forehead gently, she pulled the covers up over her and left the room.

Now that Amy was settled in, Mari had to do something to make sure Elizabeth would be equally safe at the hospital. Mari picked up the receiver and dialed. The security firm that had worked for her family for years would provide bodyguards for Elizabeth for as long as needed. Although she normally didn't deal with them—the trust took care of everything—she knew that they'd comply with her orders. Coming from one of New Mexico's most prominent families had advantages at times, though it was something that she didn't let make much of an impact on her day-to-day life.

Once assured that Elizabeth would have full protection, Mari allowed herself to relax a little. If she could only figure out what to do about Amy now! The thought of turning her over to JD didn't feel right, especially after

Elizabeth's request. But that probably wasn't going to stop JD from insisting on it. Mari was certain of that, and opposing him was going to be like trying to stop a flood with a sponge.

Through the crack she'd left in the curtains, Mari noted approaching headlights. She stood to one side and peered out. A moment later, she saw JD's red pickup. When her pulse quickened, she told herself that it was only a reaction to the confrontation about to take place. Yet deep down, a small voice whispered a warning against lying to herself. Frustrated with her own lack of good sense, she opened the door as JD walked up.

He looked like a man who'd been working for twenty-four hours straight. His black hair was disheveled and his brown leather jacket was unzipped despite the cold. Still, his expression was determined and his jaw was firmly set. Her heart went out to him.

"How's Elizabeth?" Mari asked, stepping aside and inviting him into the living room.

"She's been stabilized, but she's still unconscious and in guarded condition, whatever that is. The doctors are doing all they can." He glanced around the room. "Where's Amy? Did you manage to locate her?"

"She's here. You don't have to worry." Mari paused. "No, that's not exactly true." She hesitated, trying to figure out the best way to tell him what she'd learned. After a moment, she opted for the direct approach. "Amy might be in a great deal of danger." Mari explained that the child might have seen Elizabeth's assailant.

"Amy's a handicapped little girl. That's no secret to people around here. She's no threat to anyone," JD concluded flatly.

"Amy's physically challenged, but she's extremely bright. And I have no idea how much she may have seen, or more importantly, if Elizabeth's assailant saw her," Mari added, telling JD about the man she'd seen glance inside the van.

JD sat down in a chair and leaned forward to speak. "As I was leaving the emergency room, I met some security people. They claimed you hired them to protect Elizabeth."

"Yes, I did. I figured that it wouldn't hurt, and Elizabeth might need them."

"You had no right to do that," JD snapped, his blue eyes flashing with anger. "I can take care of my own family. That's my responsibility."

Mari glared at him, suspecting this was masculine pride at its worst. "Look, can't we settle this later? Right now we've got other things on our hands."

"No. This argument isn't over." JD stood up and paced. "Have you thoroughly checked out the firm you hired?"

She rolled her eyes. "No, I flipped a coin," she countered sarcastically. "Get over it, okay?"

"The bill's mine."

"Fine. Now what are we going to do about Amy?"

"Not 'we.' *Me.*" JD returned to the chair. "I'm almost certain I can talk my sister, Pat, into taking her for now. I'll support Amy financially, of course, but staying with Pat and her family is the best solution. Amy will have a stable home life until Elizabeth's back on her feet. You can help if you'd like. Find someone for me in Phoenix who'll be able to teach Pat to sign or communicate in some other way with Amy. Maybe the school system here will be able to get you in touch with someone."

"You can't just send Amy away from everything that's familiar to her, particularly now. It's almost Christmas and her mother is in the hospital. She needs to be with someone she knows, someone who understands her special needs—me."

"Pat's a fast learner, and Amy can talk, though it's hard to understand her at times. In the long run, this will be the best course of action, believe me. I can't take care of her here, and you have a job and your own life. If you'll tell me which room she's in, I'll take her with me now."

He was talking about Amy as if she was nothing more than a responsibility without her own needs or feelings. Anger began to build within Mari. JD seemed as cold as Elizabeth had said. "She's sleeping, and you're not taking her anywhere," Mari said flatly. "She's finally stopped crying, and I want her to get whatever rest she can."

Hearing a door creak, Mari turned around. Amy came out of the bedroom and looked around absently. The sleepy, vacant expression in her large doe brown eyes suddenly vanished as she saw her uncle. Smiling broadly, Amy launched herself into his arms.

Mari stared in muted shock. In view of JD's attitude, she'd never expected Amy to feel any closeness to her uncle at all. Then Mari got a second surprise. JD had come alive in his niece's presence and was showing more sensitivity than she'd ever suspected he possessed.

He pulled away a little so Amy could see his face. "Don't be afraid. I'm going to take care of you. I love you." His cold rationality seemed to have suddenly vanished. He reached out to stroke Amy's shoulder-length brown hair, then tried to sign something, but it was more like pantomime than any specific sign language.

Amy didn't seem to mind or notice. She fingerspelled the word *Mom,* and looked questioningly at him. JD hesitated, clearly uncertain how much, if anything, to say. Amy signed the word *afraid.* The gesture was clear, but seeing the uncertainty on her uncle's face, Amy spoke in her halting voice. "I miss Mommy."

A flood of tears suddenly started down Amy's face. JD took out his handkerchief and, wiping her tears, lifted her chin until she looked at him. "No, honey, don't cry. I'll take care of everything." As he glanced across the room, he saw the Advent calendar. He took Amy by the hand and led her to it. "By the time Christmas Day comes, your mom will be back again."

Mari stared at JD, aghast. How could he have made such an irresponsible promise? There was no way he could guarantee that! It was clear that Amy loved him and trusted him; the little girl's face lit up at his reassuring response.

Amy looked up at Mari and signed, "May I keep the calendar?"

"Of course you can," Mari answered, trying desperately to think of a way to soften the impact of JD's reckless promise.

Mari was still weighing her options when a familiar, yet uncomfortable, sensation suddenly hit her. Someone nearby was watching them; she could feel it. She peered cautiously out the window, certain she'd spot whoever it was. Only the red and green Christmas lights twinkling in the distance interrupted the blackness of the night with signs of life. The street seemed deserted, but her uneasiness grew even more persistent and she continued watching.

Her neighborhood was typical of the South Valley. Houses were acres apart, and the graveled roads were noisy and saturated with dust. But it wouldn't have been hard for someone to approach on foot and remain undetected. No neighbors were close enough to notice and sound an alarm.

Finally, ready to conclude it was only a case of nerves, she released the edge of the curtain. As it billowed back against the wall, she caught a glimpse of a shadow. Quickly she pulled the curtain back a fraction and looked again. She saw a vague outline about twenty yards away take a step.

"I'll take Amy with me now," JD told her as he lifted the girl into his arms.

"No, I don't think so," Mari countered, moving to block his way to the door.

JD's face hardened. "Don't fight me on this. I'm her next of kin. Legally I'm responsible for her. If you make trouble now, you'll only frighten Amy all over again. I know that's not what you want."

"You don't understand," Mari said, forcing herself to appear casual for Amy's sake and making sure the child couldn't read her lips. "Someone's out there, watching the house."

Chapter Three

JD set Amy down and gave her a reassuring smile. "It'll be a few more minutes, honey." As Amy walked to the sofa, apparently having lip-read his words, JD stepped casually over to the window and peered outside. Turning to face Amy, he pantomimed shivering. "Looks cold outside." He didn't want to frighten Amy, but Mari was right. There was someone watching the house. No way he'd take Amy out there now and expose her to danger.

"Can we stay?" Amy signed to Mari.

Mari nodded. "Hungry?"

Amy shook her head and indicated she was sleepy.

JD looked at Mari as she took Amy back to the bedroom. Maybe it wasn't such a good idea sending Amy to Pat's. He loved his niece, but Mari at least understood something of that silent world the little girl lived in. The problem, however, was becoming more complicated by the minute. It was no longer just a matter of finding someone to take care of his niece. Now he had to pick someone who could also protect Amy from whatever trouble Elizabeth had inadvertently dragged her into.

He recalled when Elizabeth had told him that her illegitimate child had been born deaf. He'd suggested, for the good of the child, that she give up the baby for adoption. Despite Elizabeth's good intentions, he'd believed that the child would need far more attention than his sister alone could provide. He'd been wrong; Elizabeth had been an excellent mother.

At first he'd limited his visits with his sister and her child, not wanting either of them to become too dependent on him. It was Elizabeth's life, and he hadn't wanted to interfere with her decisions. But he hadn't counted on Amy. There was something gutsy and appealing about the little kid. She refused to acknowledge any form of rejection and always came at him with a smile and a hug.

The more he'd seen Amy, the more his affection for her had grown. She never gave up. On the occasions he'd visited during the past few years, he'd seen her struggling to learn to read. Up to that time, he'd never stopped to think that reading words without correlating them to sounds required a Herculean effort. Much of Elizabeth's toughness was in Amy. He'd never once seen Amy frightened. Maybe that was why seeing her crying now had bothered him so much, though he'd managed to hide most of his reaction.

On the other hand, he'd noted the expression on Mari's face when he'd promised that they'd all be together for Christmas. She'd obviously wanted to throttle him. He realized it was a promise he never should have made. But at the time, he'd been unable to think of any other way to make Amy stop crying.

When Mari came out of the bedroom, her expression was as frosty as a February morning. "Did you discuss Amy or her possible whereabouts with anyone?"

"No. I came straight here from the hospital." Mari's opinion of him had always been jaded for some reason. He was attracted to her, and she knew it, but she'd never even given him a second look. It wasn't as if she was just playing hard to get, either. If anything, he always sensed disapproval rather than mere indifference. Her attitude reflected Elizabeth's own reservations about him. As his sister's friend, perhaps he shouldn't have expected Mari to act any differently.

"You'll have to leave Amy with me, JD. You can't take her out of this house now and expose her to whoever's out there."

"I wish Elizabeth had told me more on the phone. All I know is that she was upset about a theft—something, I think, from the evidence room."

"Wait—did you say the evidence room? That's where the statue of the Virgin Mary is being kept when it's not on display." Mari fought a sudden surge of panic. "Elizabeth and I convinced Father Aragon to let us take it from his parish. It's the focal point for the Toys for Tykes drive. Since donations were down, we needed something special to help us publicize the needs of the kids." She paused. "But the Madonna figure was our responsibility, a sacred trust in every sense of the word. If anything has happened to it—"

"I doubt it. If it was missing, half the state would know by now. And don't tell me it would be easy to fence that statue. It's too high profile to suit most crooks."

Mari paused, then nodded. "You're right." Mari bit her bottom lip, worried. "But if Elizabeth uncovered a crime, there's no telling who's outside the house. Is it a bad cop, or someone else entirely?"

"I have to find a way to smuggle Amy out of here, preferably soon," JD answered. "I need to keep her safe. I'm going to leave alone now and drive toward my house, so we can see if he follows me or stays with you. If he goes with me, I'll ditch him, come right back and sneak Amy out the back door." He paused. "If our watcher stays with you, call the police and report a prowler. *Insist* they come out to check. At the very least, it'll buy some time for you to make arrangements to leave town for a few days or stay with a friend."

Mari shook her head. "I can't turn Amy over to you, JD. Elizabeth specifically asked me not to. And after that promise you made Amy, I think she was right."

JD stared hard at Mari, obviously disturbed by her words. "I may have made a mistake...."

"May have?"

"Let's get to what really matters right now, Mari. Elizabeth isn't here to make decisions. If someone is after Amy, keeping her here will just make her a target. Given enough time, they're bound to spot her, if they haven't already. But we could be jumping to conclusions. Let's see if it's Amy they really want. Maybe the cops think I know something about the accident and it's me they're tailing."

"I suppose that is a possibility," Mari answered hesitantly. "Or the cops might think I know more than I've said and they're watching me."

"There's only one way to narrow down the possibilities. I'll go. Let's see what happens."

MARI WATCHED the country road from a narrow slit in her curtains. Red and green lights twinkled from rooftops in the distance. Two hours had passed. Although their watcher was no longer out there, JD hadn't returned. Tension and uncertainty made her hands clammy and her mouth dry.

She'd called the hospital, hoping for some good news, but had learned little. Elizabeth had made it through surgery, but her condition was listed as critical, though stable. Things could still go either way.

Mari turned her head toward the bedroom. Amy was sound asleep, which, at least for now, was for the best. Mari didn't want to have to explain to Amy where and why her uncle had gone. She sat down on the sofa and took another sip of her tea. Pulling her knitting from the basket, she began working on the sweater she was planning to give Elizabeth for Christmas. The minutes slowly ticked by. In the distance, thunder rumbled ominously. A storm was approaching. The gloomy weather matched her mood.

The mantel clock had just chimed midnight when she heard a soft tapping at the back door. She bolted to her feet and ran to the kitchen. She could see JD clearly through the window over the sink. Mari automatically reached for the porch light, but JD's warning stopped her in time.

"Don't switch on any lights. The guy is no longer around front, but I don't want to take any chances."

"What happened?" she asked, letting him in.

"I don't know. I'm sure I wasn't followed, but he's not there now. I watched the house for an hour before approaching. I figure this is the perfect time for me to take Amy and get her out of here."

"You're not still thinking of sending her to your sister in Phoenix, are you?" Mari asked angrily. "No one there is going to understand her. Unless you're used to the way she speaks, it can be hard to make out what she's saying. Amy can sign, but if they can't, that won't be much good."

"Amy can lip-read," he countered slowly. "She won't have to feel all alone."

"Oh, come on! That's not much of an advantage. It's incredibly difficult in the best of circumstances. Try it yourself. Look in the mirror and see if you can tell the difference between 'I made the bed' and 'I baked the bread.'"

JD ran a hand through his hair. "I can't leave Amy here, so I'll have to take her with me until I can figure out what's best. You'll have to accept my decision." JD stepped past Mari and went directly to the bedroom door. Before Mari could stop him, he was inside, fumbling for the light switch. Then he tripped on the wastebasket and fell heavily against the bed. Before he could regain his balance, a small figure dashed right past both of them.

Mari reached out, trying to grab Amy's arm, but her fingers connected only with air. In a flash, Amy reached the kitchen and bolted out the back door. Mari was only seconds behind, but once she stepped into the night, she had to stop. The darkness was almost total because of the thick cloud cover. Even the Christmas lights in the distance seemed like crimson and green pinpoints lost in an endless expanse of black velvet.

JD was at her side a second later. "Where'd she go?"

"I don't know," Mari snapped. "Why couldn't you listen to me? You scared the hell out of her," she added in a whisper, afraid their stalker might be nearby.

"Amy couldn't have heard me come in," he countered angrily. "Why did she run?"

"She must have felt your steps on the hardwood floor, then when you fell, she probably thought you were lunging to grab her. Your footfall is very heavy, and she's attuned to vibrations. She couldn't see who it was, but she saw a dark shape coming toward her and did what any kid would do— ran as fast as she could! You must have scared her witless!"

"Okay. I blew it. Is that what you wanted to hear? Now help me find her," JD answered softly. "That's all that matters now."

Regret filled her, overcoming her anger. "You're right."

Mari began feeling her way through the dry stalks of the vegetable garden wishing she'd placed Christmas lights all around the backyard. If only she'd thought of grabbing her flashlight before leaving the house. A thundering blast cracked through the air. It sounded like a peal of thunder, only the earth failed to shake and there was no lightning. Before she could turn her head to see what it was, JD pulled her down to the ground.

He drew her tightly against him, shielding her with his own body. "Don't move. Someone's using a high-powered rifle."

"Amy! She won't even know she's in danger! She can't hear the shots!"

"Stay here!" JD rolled away and rose in a crouch, but before he'd gone three feet, Mari was beside him. "You know this place," JD whispered harshly, tacitly agreeing to her action, his eyes darting around. "Where could Amy have gone?"

"The elm ahead? She likes to climb it," Mari suggested. The moon edged out from behind the clouds, giving them a brief respite from the all-encompassing darkness, but also exposing them to the sniper. As the silver moonbeams dappled the ground, Mari spotted Amy huddled against the trunk of the elm, looking toward the house. "There!"

As JD sprinted toward Amy, another shot rang out, this time blending in with a rumble of thunder. Mari stood and waved her arms frantically. Maybe the shadows or the motion would capture Amy's attention. If nothing else, maybe the gunman's attention would be temporarily diverted.

It didn't work. The next shot was almost on target. Mari saw where the bullet impacted just inches above Amy's head. It sent a shower of bark down over her. The little girl glanced up curiously, then brushed some of the wood splinters from her hair.

An instant later, JD threw himself down beside Amy and rolled with her in his arms until they disappeared into the cover of a nearby hedge. Hearing Amy's terrified cries, Mari ran forward in a crouch, zigzagging to evade the sniper's aim. As she neared the hedge, he fired again. Mari felt something tug at her arm, then she dived over the hedge. When she finally looked down at her sleeve searching for blood, she found only a jagged hole going completely through a fold of her sweater.

JD grabbed her shoulder with one hand as he held Amy close with the other. "Do something! I can't make her stop crying!"

Mari drew Amy against her, fingerspelling against Amy's palm, their way of whispering in the dark. As she looked at JD, she caught a glimpse of the strong, fierce boy who'd shared Elizabeth's past. Love and concern filled his expression, to be quickly replaced by a mask of cold neutrality. She realized then that somewhere along the way, he'd become a master at hiding his true feelings. Hearing a car engine start up, Mari gathered Amy closer.

"I'm going to take a look," JD whispered, then rose to his feet and dashed around the end of the hedge, staying in the deepest shadows and crouching low.

Mari looked over the top of the brush and caught a glimpse of a battered, muddy pickup fishtailing wildly down the drive. It looked like the one she'd seen Elizabeth's attacker drive away in, but she couldn't be sure in the darkness.

JD returned to her side moments later, breathing hard from exertion. "I didn't catch a license plate. It was covered with mud, probably to hide it."

Mari nodded, unable to trust her voice. Fear greater than any she'd ever known pounded through her. She'd failed herself and another child once, and no matter what, she would never allow that to happen again. But, God help her, she didn't know how to keep Amy safe!

"Come on. Let's get back inside the house," JD said. "We've got to call the sheriff's department."

Mari shook her head. "We can't. Elizabeth told me they may have a part in this, remember?"

As they hurried back to shelter, JD kept his eyes peeled on the yard around them. His muscles were tense, and he seemed ready for action. Mari felt surprisingly reassured by his stalwart presence. There was an expression on his face that told her he would master any challenge that endangered them, even at the risk of his own life.

Mari hurried Amy into the house, but it no longer seemed the safe haven she'd thought it to be just minutes before. Amy quickly disentangled herself from Mari, anger clear on her face. For a moment, Mari was afraid that Amy would blame them for the events that had buffeted her life in the past few hours. Amy flung a series of signs at Mari at lightning speed, not bothering to speak.

"Dumb," Mari translated and was forced to smile. "All of us."

"Amen to that," JD answered quietly.

"We should stay together," Mari translated again.

JD dropped down onto the sofa, his expression thoughtful and vigilant. He looked at Amy and patted the seat next to him, a hopeful look on his face. Mari felt the tug of his unspoken apology and waited for Amy to make the next move. She seemed to consider it, then finally went to his side. She cuddled up against him, settling beneath his arm.

"You don't seem to like any of my suggestions, so what do you recommend we do next?" JD asked Mari wearily.

Mari took a deep breath, then let it out again slowly. "I'm not sure, but I'll tell you what I *do* know. If we call the sheriff's office and tell them everything, the child welfare department will step in. They may want to take Amy away from both of us, and that could be even more dangerous for her."

"Agreed." JD glanced down at Amy, then looked back at Mari. "You've got to find out exactly what she saw and what she knows."

"There's no way she's ready to talk about it. Look at her." Amy was curled up against JD, her face buried against his chest as if she was trying to block out everything.

"Yes, precisely. *Look* at her. She's depending on us to protect her. Only we can't even protect ourselves. If we don't find out who's behind this and what's going on, someone else is going to keep holding all the cards."

Mari knew he was right, but one look at Amy made her stomach sink. The little girl was exhausted. Mari didn't want to put her through any more trauma.

"Can you think of any other way to protect her?" JD insisted.

Mari stood up, crossed the gap between them, then crouched before Amy, touching her shoulder to get her attention. "Feel okay?" Mari signed, hating herself, hating JD and most of all, hating the situation they'd been forced into.

Amy sat up reluctantly. "I want Mom," she signed.

Mari hesitated. It was so unfair to press Amy now. She glanced at JD and realized he didn't want to do this any more than she did. But he was right. They had to know. She couldn't back away now. "It's time to talk," Mari signed, speaking as she did, mostly for JD's benefit.

Amy's expression changed. The weariness was replaced in the blink of an eye by a wariness that bordered on panic. "Do you know what happened to your mom?" Mari signed, speaking simultaneously.

Amy shrank back into JD's arms and averted her gaze.

"No," Mari said, reaching for her chin and gently forcing Amy to look at her. "You're okay now, and we have to know."

"The car came by fast so I hid," Amy signed.

"Did you see anything besides the car?" Mari asked.

Amy shook her head. "I was scared so I hid. I didn't see. I want to go home," she added emphatically.

"No. You have to stay here. With us. Home isn't safe right now."

JD turned Amy to face him. "Did you see anybody else before you hid?"

Amy shook her head and shrank away from them both. "No. I'm tired. No more questions." She began to sob, the distorted, heart-wrenching sound coming from the depths of her being. Mari tried pulling Amy close to comfort her, but Amy shook free, and when JD reached for her, Amy ran into the bedroom instead.

JD stared after her for a long moment. "Lord, what else could we have done? We had to ask her!"

"Amy can't cope with this right now, and if we badger her, there's no telling what harm we'll do."

JD went after Amy. "I've got to fix this somehow. Can you come with me, in case I need someone to interpret?"

Mari followed JD as he went carefully into the bedroom and quickly turned on the light. Amy sat on the bed, hugging the Christmas teddy bear with both arms.

JD sat on the edge of the bed. "I'm sorry, Amy. Neither of us meant to upset or scare you."

Amy nodded, then shrugged. "I'm tired."

"All right. Why don't you try to get some sleep?"

Amy turned on her side, facing away from them. JD stood, turned the bedside lamp on low, switched off the main lights and left the room.

He walked slowly to the living room sofa and sat down heavily. "I always thought that Elizabeth shouldn't have kept a child like Amy. Being a single parent is hard, and Amy's father made it clear he'd never accept responsibility for the child." He shook his head sadly. "Amy deserved better than she got all the way around. Yet, even in the worst-case scenarios I envisioned for Elizabeth and Amy, I never dreamed something like this could happen."

Mari sat on the love seat opposite the sofa and regarded him thoughtfully. "Even if Amy had been adopted and had had two parents to look after her, her life would never have been like that of hearing children. Elizabeth is unconventional in a lot of ways, true, but no child was ever loved more unconditionally than Amy is."

"Maybe, but love isn't always enough." JD shrugged, then held up a hand, anticipating a protest. "It doesn't matter now. The only thing that does is my responsibility to see this situation through."

Mari watched Elizabeth's brother carefully, trying to figure him out. He was like an intricate puzzle whose pieces all seemed close enough to fit where you thought they belonged yet never quite did. Was it love or simply a sense of obligation that kept him here now? Before tonight, she'd been ready to believe he wasn't capable of love. "You and Amy aren't in this alone. I'm going to be right there with you. Amy is going to need us both, especially if your Christmas promise about her mother isn't kept."

JD nodded slowly and looked pained at the thought. "I know I should turn down your offer of help, but I can't. I need your support, Mari. I sometimes have a very difficult time understanding Amy. And I wouldn't dare rely on my signing skills in an emergency."

"We have to find out what Elizabeth was involved in and why someone would want her dead. But I won't question Amy again." Mari bit her bottom lip, remembering vividly the child's sobs of distress.

JD crossed the room and went to Mari's side. He sat down beside her and placed his hand over hers. "I know how much you love Amy and how difficult it was for you to have to upset her. I'm sorry you had to be the one to do it. If I could have spared you that, I would have."

Mari met his gaze and knew that the grief they'd caused Amy had burned into them both. "I've never *not* wanted to do anything so much in my entire life."

"I know," JD whispered. "It hurt us all." For a brief eternity he held her gaze and they were completely in agreement. Emotions too raw to conceal flickered in the blue depths of his eyes. A heartbeat later, he gently drew her into his arms.

His embrace was so natural, Mari never thought to resist. The warmth of his body and the hard feel of him against her was comforting and exciting all at once. She'd been alone for such a long time! And she didn't want to feel alone, not now.

They held on to one another for a long time. Her heart was pounding frantically, reminding her of needs she didn't dare acknowledge. She could sense the tension coiling inside him, too, and knowing what she was doing to him made a thrilling shiver course through her. Vividly aware of everything about him and about herself, she reluctantly drew away. She meant to caution him, to remind them both that this was not the right time for them.

Unexpectedly, as she looked up at him, something entirely different happened. Understanding more primal than she'd ever known sparked to life between them, drawing them together with a force all of its own. At that breathless moment, she wanted him to kiss her more than she'd ever wanted anything.

She'd never know exactly what compelled him, whether he'd sensed her need or was driven by his own. But at that moment, nothing mattered except the whispers urging her heart and hearing the sound of her name on his lips.

JD's kiss was hard and hungry. His arms, tight around her, pressed her to him as his tongue explored her mouth. Almost as if he was suddenly aware of his own roughness, or perhaps sensing her surrender, his kiss slowly gentled.

His tenderness was practically her undoing. Realizing what was happening, Mari struggled for the courage to pull away. She wanted him but this shouldn't be happening. Sanity fought against the fires raging inside her. They weren't meant for each other! She wasn't meant for anyone. They had to stop!

Mari forced herself to move away, trying to pretend what they'd done had never happened. She was, in her own way, as much of an outsider as Amy was, separated by circumstances over which she had no control. She wouldn't bring him into her world just to share a new pain that could never be resolved.

"Let me get us both something to drink," she said, needing something to do. "I don't have coffee, but I do have hot chocolate. Would you like some?"

"Sure," he answered, a bit unsteadily. He followed her into the kitchen and leaned against the counter while she poured some milk into a saucepan. "The old-fashioned way?" JD sounded as awkward as she felt.

"Never cared for those mixes," she replied with a trace of a smile, trying to relax, but not yet succeeding. Her lips still throbbed from his kiss. As Mari reached for the chocolate, JD moved to stir the milk. She smiled. "Good. Keep it from scorching while I get the rest of the stuff."

"I like your kitchen," he said as she continued gathering ingredients. "It's ... homey."

Mari thought of the way it might have been for her once. A home filled with children and held together by love. "It's comfortable," she answered, choosing another adjective to avoid the memories.

"Hey, why don't you let me finish this? If you've got a whisk, I make a mean cup of hot chocolate."

Mari returned to the kitchen table. "By all means, be my guest."

JD worked in silence, lost in thought. A few minutes later, he poured the cocoa into the mugs decorated with holly sprigs she always used this time of year. "We've got to go back to Elizabeth's house," he said at last. "The answer has to be there."

"Elizabeth did say something about her mail, but there was so much going on at the time, I didn't pay much attention." She stared pensively at the reindeer along the edges of the Christmas tablecloth. "There's another problem to consider though. The police might still be there. The last thing we need is to run into them, end up answering more questions and losing Amy."

"The police should have sealed off the house and the driveway leading to it, but by now I'm sure they've gathered all the evidence they wanted from the scene. I really doubt they would keep the entire area under surveillance. They seemed convinced it was an ordinary hit and run." He lapsed into a thoughtful silence. "I could go and check it out but I don't like the idea of leaving you two here alone."

"I don't think any of us can stay here. Not anymore," Mari observed. Hearing a soft cough, she turned her head. Amy stood in the doorway. There was no way to tell how long she'd been there and Mari worried how much of their conversation she'd made out through lipreading. "Are you okay?"

Amy signed, drawing her index finger across her lips, her palm facing left.

"Oh, honey." Mari gave her a hug then drew back so Amy could see her face. "Don't be, okay?"

"What did she say?" JD asked as Mari went to get Amy some cocoa.

"That's the sign for 'lonely,'" Mari said past the lump in her throat.

JD crossed the space between them and lifted Amy into his arms. "You never have to be lonely," he said, his voice quiet and determined. "Not as long as I'm around." Something in JD's voice captured Mari's attention; it rang with genuine empathy.

Not bothering to speak, Amy signed, "Where will we go?"

Mari smiled. So she had eavesdropped in her own way. "We haven't decided."

Amy considered. "Home? I need more clothes," she signed, speaking the words for her uncle's benefit.

"She's right," Mari agreed. "If we're going to stay on the move, we'll all need warm clothing. I can pack a few of my own things here, and then we can go get some for her and you."

JD smiled at Amy, then turned away, making a show of putting his cup in the sink. In reality he needed to say something he wasn't eager to discuss openly in front of Amy. "Do you think she can really handle going back there?"

"We're all in this together. No one has to feel alone," Mari answered vaguely, seeing Amy's eyes on her and not wanting to reveal too much. "Let's get ready to go."

Chapter Four

JD drove past the lane that led to Elizabeth's house. "I'm going to park farther down the road in case there's anyone hanging around. Wait in my pickup while I walk over and check the mailbox. If there's any trouble, drive off and get the police."

Mari signed to Amy, explaining, and asked her to sit low in the rear bench of the extended cab so any passersby wouldn't notice her. Betraying only a hint of nervousness, Amy obeyed. Maybe she was beginning to feel safe with them. Mari hoped so, but it was hard to tell for sure what was going through the little girl's mind.

JD parked about a hundred yards from the turnoff. There were no streetlights or Christmas decorations on this stretch of highway, miles from the metropolitan area. Only the moon, when it occasionally peered out from behind a cloud, illuminated the surroundings with its glow. "Well, at least no one else will be able to see any better than we can away from the headlights," he muttered.

Mari glanced back at Amy. She had Mari's Advent calendar and the teddy bear on her lap to remind her that Christmas was only five days away. Despite her tight grip on the stuffed toy, Amy appeared to be handling the pressure and the tension remarkably well.

"I don't see anyone in the neighborhood," JD said. "I better go now. While I'm here, I'm also going to take a walk up the driveway and check out the house."

Mari watched him stroll casually toward Elizabeth's barn-shaped mailbox with tinsel wrapped around it. To anyone passing, he would be mistaken for any of the half-dozen residents whose brightly decorated mailboxes lined the country road. Soon he became only a faint, darkened outline. She saw him stop at Elizabeth's mailbox then disappear down the driveway. Finally, several minutes later, he reappeared, heading their way. Out of the corner of her eye she saw Amy peer over the back of the seat. Mari's gaze remained on JD as Amy touched her arm. "What is it, honey?" Mari signed and spoke softly.

Amy pointed down the road a half mile ahead. Lights flickered then vanished. They were headlights of a car traveling down the country road, being partially obscured by the trees.

Mari's heart lodged in her throat. "Duck down on the floorboard," she signed quickly. "Pull the blanket over you." As JD reached the pickup, she threw open the door. "Someone's coming."

"We've done nothing illegal. If it's the police, don't let them intimidate you," JD said, looking down the road at the approaching car.

"Amy," she reminded him gently. "We can't afford to attract any undue attention no matter who it is." As the vehicle approached, the outline of a police car became obvious.

"Too late. We can't drive off now. We've got to play it out."

Before she could move, he pulled her against him. He tangled his hand in her hair and slanted his mouth over hers in a searing kiss. Mari started to pull away, wondering if he'd gone crazy, but he held her fast, his mouth hard over hers. Her body turned to fire, yet despite the blaze raging through her, she realized what he was doing. No one would think anything of two lovers sharing stolen moments under the cover of darkness on a deserted country road.

JD drew his fingers down her cheek and traced an imaginary line down the column of her neck. Her thoughts became muddled, his caress weaving a spell that robbed her of breath and reason. Her insides seemed to be melting.

Mari's fingers were coiled around the fabric of his shirt. When it parted slightly, straining against the buttons, she unintentionally slipped her fingertips inside and touched his chest. His masculine body felt hard and solid. And wonderful. When he groaned with passion, she felt the vibrations ripple through her. His hold intensified, becoming more urgent. It was as if he was determined to pull everything he could from that one stolen moment.

Though her eyes were closed, she saw the flash of a spotlight as it illuminated their pickup. The police car had stopped. She heard someone coming across the road.

"Don't get nervous," JD whispered, his breath hot in her ear. "And don't stop now. Make it look real. Two lovers carried away," he murmured in a tortured voice. "You're doing great so far. Trust me," he groaned, then left a string of moist kisses at the base of her throat.

As his mouth covered hers once again, the sweet impossible ache growing within her made Mari gasp. JD took full advantage of the opportunity. Deepening his kiss, he devoured her with a fierceness that battered her sanity.

She didn't mean to whimper but the sound escaped her lips before she could stop it. Oh, dear heaven, they were supposed to be just acting! Why couldn't her heart and body understand that?

Then she heard a sharp rap on the window behind her. "Move along now," she heard the officer say.

JD released her mouth and, looking slightly dazed, nodded to the officer. As JD drew away, Mari felt a crushing sense of disappointment. Although he no longer held her, the ache and the longing he'd created remained.

The officer returned to his vehicle and headed up toward Elizabeth's driveway. Hearing Amy stir behind them made Mari's thoughts focus back on the crisis that had brought them there.

JD drew in a long, unsteady breath. "It worked."

"What?" she asked, realizing in surprise that they'd even fogged up the windows on the driver's side.

"He's gone."

"Oh, right," Mari managed. "Our act convinced him." What would he think of the way she'd responded to him? Would he assume that she was a love-starved spinster? Amy peered up from behind the front seat and touched Mari's shoulder. "We're okay," Mari signed.

Amy's smile made Mari wonder if she'd peeked out earlier. Raising herself off the floor, Amy sat on the back seat and pulled the blanket up around her, waiting.

"I took everything that was in the mailbox." JD patted his jacket pocket. "I think we'd better get out of here before the officer returns. He's probably going to check out Elizabeth's house since they know it's vacant. But he'll undoubtedly come back by here soon and we don't want to be around."

"Which brings us to an interesting question. Where are we going to hide out? We can't stay with friends. If that gunman finds us, it would be too dangerous for them. Staying at a motel is just as bad. It would make us too easy to trace. Of course, we could check in separately, then try to sneak Amy in, but..." She let the sentence trail off and shrugged.

"I've got a better idea, though it's still risky."

"Let's hear it."

"My company's been refurbishing an apartment complex in the South Valley. It's less than ten miles from here. I know which units are vacant and I have a master key to all of the complex."

"That'll be a great hiding place!" Mari said.

"Maybe not," he countered hesitantly. "A lot of people could see us."

"Best place to hide," Mari assured him, "as long as we act normally."

"That's true," he admitted, "but some people may recognize me. And if they see us going into an apartment they know to be vacant this late at night..." His tone reflected his uncertainty.

"It's a chance we'll have to take." She glanced back at Amy who'd lain down on the rear bench and fallen asleep still clutching her Christmas bear. "Well, at least she's finally resting."

THEY ARRIVED at the modest-looking apartment complex less than half an hour later. "There aren't that many people currently living here," JD explained. "Maybe twenty or so units are occupied out of a hundred, and those people are here only because of the break they're getting on rent. The rear of the building is practically empty. The units back there are either being remodeled or scheduled for work."

"Then that's the safest place for us to go tonight."

"If it works out, we may stick around here longer than that." JD glanced back at Amy, who was still sound asleep. "I'm going to carry her in. She's zoned out."

He lifted Amy carefully. Mari tucked the blanket around her, protecting the girl from the frigid air.

"Take my keys," he said, holding them in his open palm. "The one you'll use is the shiny nickel one with three holes in it." He glanced around, noting the red chili pepper lights blinking from an apartment window that faced the front. The other windows that surrounded it were barren of decorations. No one seemed to have noticed their arrival. "We'll take the apartment at the end, bottom floor."

JD led the way, watchful and vigilant. He'd always been a loner, preferring that over the alternatives life had offered him. What a time this was to question the habits of a lifetime. His gaze drifted over Mari beside him. She'd make a good mother someday. His thoughts drifted momentarily, and he envisioned her naked in his arms, wanting him, her belly swollen with his child.

He shook free of the thought abruptly. It was just a holdover from the hormone blast of having her in his arms. The wildness of her response, the fires she'd stirred in him, had torn through him with the force of a tornado.

Mari reached over to cover Amy with the blanket where it had shaken loose. He'd never realized how seriously she took her role as Amy's godmother. He'd always suspected that Mari was the type who needed to be needed, who saw herself in the role of rescuer, particularly of children. But there was more to it than that. She really loved Amy.

An emotion he couldn't quite identify stabbed through him. If only Elizabeth and he had met someone like Mari, someone who cared enough to get involved, when they'd been children!

But maybe something good had come of that time. It had made him stronger and more determined to meet his goals. He'd sworn to himself back then that the day would come when the name Hawken would no longer inspire pity or represent failure and poverty. He'd achieved that much, but he still had a long way to go to truly claim success. He wanted the community to look up to the name Hawken.

Crossing a dried patch of grass, they made their way along a narrow sidewalk running the length of the complex. Discarded building and packing materials made their footing hazardous.

"Let me lead the way," Mari said. "I can clear the path for you."

"At least none of the tenants is likely to hear us moving around back here. It's going to be impossible to walk through this mess without making some noise."

Mari leaned down and pulled some cardboard boxes to one side. "Be careful here. There's a lot of debris scattered around." She used a small pocket flashlight to light the way. "You chose the right apartment. We'll have a good view of the parking lot."

"Harder for anyone to sneak up on us that way."

Mari walked ahead, systematically clearing the path of obstacles that might trip JD. Suddenly a bright beam spotlighted her. "Stop right there!" came a disembodied voice from somewhere up ahead.

Mari halted immediately. "You failed to mention security guards," she muttered.

"I didn't expect to run into them. They inspect all of our sites every night at random intervals," JD whispered, his voice taut.

"I've got an idea. Unless he knows you, we can pull this off," she answered.

As the guard approached, JD stayed in the shadows holding Amy. As soon as the man stepped out into the open, Mari shielded her eyes and launched an offensive.

"What on earth do you think you're doing? I'm trying to get home after a very long shift at work. My daughter's so exhausted she's finally fallen asleep and she still hasn't had dinner yet. Then you shine that beacon directly in our faces, waking her up. This is our home and we pay our rent. Why are you hassling us?"

"Calm down, ma'am. I was told that no one lived in this section. When I saw people back here, I thought maybe some transients—"

"I am *not* a transient!" Mari said angrily. "I have an apartment and a job. Now, if you'll kindly let my family by, I can fix dinner and put my daughter to bed." She strode past him as if in a huff and stepped up to the apartment door.

JD watched her put the key in the door with a confidence that would have been the envy of any poker player. She was a great ally. Too bad they weren't much more. Before he had time to savor that thought, she spun around and faced him.

"What are *you* waiting for? Let's go," she snapped. "If you had fixed that casserole for dinner like I asked, I could put Sandra to bed right now!" She transfixed the guard with a withering look, known to every student she'd ever taught. "And I'm sure you have locks to check and windows to peek in somewhere else."

As he stepped past the guard, JD muttered something vague about nagging wives and quickly went inside. Mari closed the door as soon as he was past the threshold and flipped on the light switch. The low-wattage bulb in the overhead fixture flickered but stayed lit. The place wasn't much, furnished with just a battered vinyl couch, a chair and a cheap dinette set occupying the combination living room and kitchen, but it would do.

JD went to the adjacent bedroom. It was empty except for an old twin bed with a striped mattress. He laid Amy down on it gently then tucked the blanket around her. The little girl stirred but didn't waken.

At last he joined Mari in the other room. "You're a good partner in crime."

"A *great* partner in crime," Mari corrected with a trace of a smile. She walked to the window and glanced outside. "Well, at least the guard's gone."

"You scared him off," JD said as he turned up the thermostat, causing the gas furnace to come on. The apartment was cold.

"It's the teacher in me. You learn to bluff effectively or the kids walk all over you." She looked at the threadbare, tattered covering that had once passed as a curtain. "Well, this place isn't much, but it'll do for now. We probably shouldn't stay here after tonight, though. That guard may put things together."

"Yeah, I think you're right about that." JD reached into his pocket for Elizabeth's mail and handed Mari the stack. "There was also this small-change envelope," he added, sitting on one of the four metal-legged dinette chairs. "I found it taped inside the mailbox. I would have missed it if my hand hadn't caught on it when I pulled everything else out."

Mari sorted through the mail. "These are mostly circulars and Christmas cards so I think we'd better find out what's in that envelope you're holding."

JD opened the envelope and pulled out a small piece of paper folded lengthwise. A long, double-cut key had been taped inside. Below it was the signature of someone he didn't recognize, and a four-digit number. "This is a safety deposit box key, but who is Vanessa Vanderstoop, and why did my sister have a copy of her signature?"

Mari stared at it for a second, thoughts racing. "Now I know why she said something about the mailbox. It seemed like such an odd request at the time. Vanessa doesn't exist."

"How do you know that?" he asked.

Mari smiled. "Elizabeth and I made her up." She stared at the signature, shaking her head. "It was just a silly game we played when we were roommates in college. When someone ate the last piece of pie or a casserole dish broke, it was always Vanessa's fault."

"Well, someone signed this. And this isn't Elizabeth's writing," he said, handing it to Mari.

"You're right. That's her best forgery of *my* handwriting."

JD stared at Mari in surprise. "It seems she was going to get you involved one way or another. But, then again, that's not surprising. Elizabeth trusts you implicitly."

"We're very good friends. We have a lot in common."

"Like what?"

"The way we are," Mari answered and shrugged. "Elizabeth doesn't like to let people get close to her. That's why her job is so important to her. It gives her a sense of purpose and keeps her from feeling too alienated. Her acquaintances at the station stay at a distance. Yet there, she can reach out and become part of the group, while contributing something useful."

"And that's the way you reach out, too?" JD asked softly. Like his sisters, he'd learned not to let people get too close. No one could hurt him now, but that wall he'd erected so long ago still kept him separate and alone. Perhaps one of the things that had attracted him to Mari was the intuitive recognition of having found another of his own kind.

"We're getting off track here," Mari warned, shaking her head.

"Working partners need to get to know each other."

"In this case, it's our knowledge of Elizabeth that'll be the biggest help. She's at the heart of what's happening." Mari leaned back against the wall and closed her eyes for a second. "She's trying to tell us something important but what does all this mean? I'm so tired I can't make sense out of anything anymore."

JD rubbed the back of his neck. "I think we've both had it. Why don't you take the couch while I sleep here on the carpet? The place is warm enough now that we won't need blankets. If we can just get a few hours' sleep," he said, bundling his coat and positioning it beneath his head.

Mari walked across to the couch, which looked as if it had seen better days, twenty or more years ago. She settled down into it, surprised that she didn't feel any lumps. Resting her head on her arms, she closed her eyes.

JD WOKE WITH A START. He hadn't really meant to do much more than rest his eyes. Hearing a sound behind him, he jackknifed to a sitting position and turned his head quickly.

Amy stood there, the Advent calendar in her hands and a sheepish look on her face. One thing his niece wasn't, was quiet. Of course, she couldn't hear the racket she made, only other people's reactions to it. He smiled at her, reassuringly.

Amy gave him a hesitant smile in return. "Sorry," she signed, mouthing the word. "Didn't mean to wake you," she added. "I wanted to open the new door on my calendar. There's only four doors left. There's no door for Christmas Day. See? It's a toy drum," she said, turning it so he could get a clear look. "Mom will like it."

"It's pretty," he said, avoiding the question she hadn't quite asked.

Amy glanced around. "Will we stay here?"

Her words stirred up memories of his own childhood, his longing to stay in one place and hating the shabby places that were all they had. His stomach knotted. "No, honey, we can't," he answered, shaking his head.

Hearing the couch rustle and creak, JD glanced over at Mari, who was yawning. "Good, you're awake, too. Let's get going. I want to be out of here before my crew arrives." He looked at his watch. It was almost seven.

"Where can we go? Any ideas?" Mari asked.

"Our first stop will have to be Elizabeth's house. Amy still needs clothes and we could use some more answers," he said, choosing his words carefully, knowing that Amy was looking at him. He met the child's gaze and held it. "Is that okay with you?"

Amy shrugged and looked at the floor.

JD glanced at Mari for help. "Maybe you two should stay here," he suggested.

Amy touched Mari's arm and signed quickly. "No. All of us will go."

Mari looked at JD. "I think she's right. We should stick together for the time being."

JD hesitated, but seeing the determined and frightened look on Amy's face, relented. "Okay."

"Good," Amy signed. Then, as if to make sure JD understood, she spoke the word.

TEN MINUTES LATER, they were on their way. Amy hugged her teddy bear and studied the Advent calendar on her lap.

Mari turned to face Amy and said, "My grandmother had an Advent calendar like that. That's why I bought it. I hope this one will leave you with as many pleasant memories as hers did me."

"I'm glad you gave it to me," Amy said. "It'll help me keep track of the days until I can see Mommy again."

Though her speech was thick, JD understood it perfectly. His gut knotted. As he glanced in the rearview mirror, he realized Amy would be using it to lip-read anything he said. He could move it so she couldn't see him, but JD knew that would make Amy feel left out and even more isolated. He tried to ignore the tug of recognition that touched his soul. He knew very well what it was like to feel that way.

JD slowed down as the truck approached the turnoff leading to Elizabeth's house. "I'll hide the pickup behind the cluster of junipers down by the mailbox."

"Smart move," Mari answered, looking around. "Can't hurt to be cautious."

In the predawn light, everything looked fresh and filled with the promise of a new day. But JD wasn't expecting miracles or easy answers; life had taught him how fruitless that could be. As he pulled off the road, Amy sat up and leaned forward. Mari turned in her seat and signed for the girl to wait in the pickup. Amy shook her head adamantly.

"What's wrong?" he asked.

"Nothing. She's just a little scared," Mari replied.

"So am I," JD muttered under his breath.

Amy signed again. "I'll go, too."

"Okay. We'll all stay together," Mari said, and glanced at JD. "You can't blame her. When she hides, she can't see, and then she's even more vulnerable. She can feel vibrations and smell and sense things most of us never even bother to think about, but still, it's got to be scary for her."

Deliberately turning his head so Amy couldn't see his face, he said, "It's what she may not even realize that she knows that worries me the most."

Mari nodded, then opened her door and started to get out, reaching back for Amy's hand. "What can we do?" Mari asked, not really expecting an answer.

"We're doing it. Let's go," JD said.

JD stayed close beside them, hurrying Amy and Mari along, making sure they all stayed out of sight from the highway. Though JD had always hated the sloppy way Elizabeth kept her yard, he had to admit that the thickets of weeds and brush Elizabeth had allowed to grow out of control, were now their allies.

Minutes later, he reached the front door, unlocked it with the key Elizabeth had given him months ago and hurried them all inside. "Let's move fast," JD said, glancing at Mari. "Help Amy get some clothes. I'll go check Elizabeth's answering machine and her desk and computer in case she made any notes to herself."

JD went directly to the study, trying hard not to look at Amy. The patient determination etched into her expression, transcended any a child her age should have known. It broke his heart to see the miniature adult she was quickly becoming.

Elizabeth's study was small, barely the size of a large walk-in closet. It was Spartan, as opposed to the homey atmosphere she'd created with plants and old photos in the other rooms. There were a few family pictures and some Christmas cards propped on a mantel. An unopened box of cards waiting to be addressed and mailed lay on the desk along with Elizabeth's Christmas card list. As JD sat at his sister's desk, he heard a car engine and the crunch of tires on gravel. He went quickly toward the window but before he reached it, Mari rushed in, pulling Amy along by the hand.

"Did you hear a car?" she asked.

He nodded. Pushing aside the curtain, JD peered out. A chunky-looking sheriff's deputy had parked his vehicle about twenty yards from the front of the house. His face was hidden by dark glasses and the bill of his cap.

JD watched, wondering what had prompted the officer to stop. He couldn't have discovered the pickup unless he'd gone looking for it on foot. As the man strode up the driveway, JD realized his speculations would have to wait. "He's coming inside and I didn't lock the front door."

Amy gestured to them, pointing toward the back door. "Hurry," she urged. When they hesitated, she rushed up to JD, grabbed his hand and tugged him along. "Hide," she said.

Mari followed them out. "Any idea where she's taking us?" she asked.

"I was about to ask you the same question," JD answered.

Amy led them past the oak tree and the garden plot where Elizabeth had grown vegetables. Finally she took them down into a dry arroyo that edged the north side of the property. It was hidden in a maze of dead Russian thistles.

JD felt the sharp stab of tumbleweed barbs piercing through his jeans. Not exactly a hospitable place, but they were certainly hidden from view. He strained to listen. By not locking the door, he might have inadvertently invited the cop inside. But what the heck was he doing there anyway? From where he'd parked, it was clear that he wasn't exactly eager to advertise his presence to anyone passing by on the highway.

JD felt Mari and Amy draw closer to him. Their gesture filled him with a fierce protectiveness he'd never experienced before. They seemed like a family; he'd never truly had one. He liked the feeling.

When Mari looked up and gave him an encouraging smile, he felt the impact all through his body. Even after all they'd been through she still managed to look beautiful. Her pale skin was even paler, contrasting sharply against the inky blackness of her hair. She was so near he could feel the warmth of her body in the December dawn. Yet, in reality, Mari was as far away from him as everyone and everything he'd ever wanted in his life. The bitter knowledge wrapped itself around him like an icy wind.

Then he saw Amy watching him, too. She was gauging his reaction. Sometimes he was certain that she could understand far more than an eight-year-old should. He gave her shoulder a squeeze and winked.

Minutes ticked by. It seemed to him that they'd been crouching in that infernal arroyo for an eternity when he finally heard the cop slam the front door shut. JD's nerves had been stretched to the limit and he was eager to leap into action. The purr of a car engine fading away suggested the cop was leaving.

"Wait here," JD said, and hurriedly climbed out of the arroyo. He jogged to the back door and turned the handle. As he stepped inside and got his first good look at the rooms beyond, a black rage engulfed him. Just then, light footsteps sounded close behind him. He glanced back quickly.

Amy stood by the door, her face pale, her eyes wide with fear.

Chapter Five

JD watched emotions ranging from fear to anger flicker across Amy's face as she stared at the living room beyond. Concerned, he crouched in front of her, turning her face toward him. "Honey, no, don't come in. Just wait outside."

Amy shook free and walked around him. "No, Uncle JD. It's my home."

JD glared at Mari, who arrived a split second later. "You shouldn't have let her come in here."

"It wasn't a matter of letting her do anything. She bolted right after you."

Amy stood inside the door to the living room, her shoulders slumped. The Christmas tree lay on the floor, ornaments smashed. Water spilled from the base, spread in an expanding pool that soaked into presents that had been torn open. Amy turned to both of them. "Why did he do this?"

"I don't know," JD answered.

Amy knelt by the Christmas tree. "Everything's broken!" Tears overflowed down her cheeks.

"Don't cry, honey." JD gently pulled Amy to her feet then stood the tree upright on its stand. "We'll fix it later when we come back. But right now you have to get your clothes so we can leave." JD turned to Mari. "I'm going to check out the rest of the house. Keep her here with you."

"I think it's better if she sees what's happened. Otherwise her imagination will work against her."

JD glanced down at Amy and saw Elizabeth as a child. Elizabeth would have come up with a picture in her mind far worse than any reality. "Okay. You're probably right. But let me lead the way."

"You'll get no argument there," Mari replied.

"About time, too," JD muttered, going across to the den. Houseplants had been overturned leaving soil all over the carpet, and a chest of drawers had been emptied onto the floor. The hall closet's contents were strewn everywhere, including a few gaily wrapped presents that had been ripped open, impeding their passage farther into the house.

He picked his way past Elizabeth's study, casually glancing inside and noting the chaos there. He'd check it out later. Right now he wanted to take a look inside Elizabeth's and Amy's bedrooms. He wanted no more surprises today.

JD stopped at Amy's room first. The closet and toy box had been emptied. Clothes and toys were tossed everywhere but there was no major damage. He studied the scene, lost in thought. It made no sense. What could anyone have expected to find here?

He continued on to Elizabeth's room. Broken perfume bottles, their contents still spilling onto the carpet, confirmed that the deputy clearly had a penchant for destruction. Elizabeth's closet had also been ransacked. Her purses lay all over the floor, as well as shoe boxes overflowing with receipts—Elizabeth's random method of keeping track of tax deductions. The pockets in all her clothes had been turned inside out, too. Despite the seeming senselessness of the search, the cop had been thorough. JD couldn't imagine any hiding place that had gone unnoticed.

JD stopped by the door then turned back around for one last look. That cop had been risking his badge by conducting what was obviously an illegal search. What did he believe Elizabeth had hidden in her home that would have been worth his career?

JD returned to the hall and called out to Mari, "Help Amy get her clothes, then let's get out of here."

Mari accompanied Amy down the hall to her room. JD watched them for a minute as they stuffed clothes into Amy's school backpack and a blue duffel bag. They were asking a lot of Amy. He really wasn't sure how much more she'd be able to take.

JD hastened over to Elizabeth's study and looked around. This room in particular had been searched from top to bottom. A small three-shelf bookcase stood empty, all the books in a heap on the floor. The metal file cabinet lay on its side, assorted folders and their contents scattered everywhere. The drawers had been completely pulled out and upended.

He went to Elizabeth's desk and after a cursory look, decided he was wasting his time. Any useful notes Elizabeth might have left were long gone or hopelessly buried in the scattered papers and right now there were other priorities. He picked up the phone, handling it only at the top of the earpiece, and called the sheriff's department. After identifying himself and giving the dispatcher a brief report, he was transferred to Elizabeth's boss.

"This is Lieutenant Randall," a voice thundered over the line. "I've checked the roster and I assure you, none of our officers has been in that area. Are you sure it was someone wearing our uniform rather than a security guard's?"

"There was no mistake," JD growled. He'd used up all his patience by now. "Check off-duty personnel. I'm certain of what I saw."

"We *will* check into this matter immediately. Stay right there and we'll send one of our officers over to meet you. While I have you on the line, could you tell us where we might find Mari Sanchez? We've been unable to locate her.

We'd like both of you to come down and help us with our investigation."

Recent events did not put JD in any kind of mood to cooperate with the police, at least until they cooperated first. "Try Ms. Sanchez at her school. If she's not there, I don't know where she might be," JD snapped.

"One of our officers will be there to meet you shortly. He'll give you a lift to our office."

"I don't have the time right now. I have to leave."

"We need to speak to you."

"I'll come to the station as soon as I can. In the meantime, you'll have a chance to find out which officer was responsible for this mess."

"Could you tell me what damage—"

JD hung up. He had a feeling the lieutenant was trying to keep him on the phone until his officer arrived. He went to Amy's room and found Mari and Amy still stuffing sweaters and jeans into the duffel bag. "We have to go right now." JD recounted his conversation with Randall. "We can't afford to place ourselves in the hands of the police—particularly not after what happened here and back at your house."

"We got what we needed," Mari said, handing JD the duffel bag. She carried the backpack by its shoulder straps.

A few minutes later, they were back in the truck and underway. JD stared at the road ahead, grateful for the silence that had descended between them. He needed time to think. So far they'd done little beyond reacting to the threat. He had to find a way to keep them safe, yet go on the offensive. He hated running from anything.

"We need to find an apartment in a busier part of that same complex we used last night. The work crews should be there by now, so the security guards will be gone and no one will notice us in the bustle. Let's get settled in." And in the meantime, he'd have a chance to figure out their next move.

"Finding out what's going on isn't all up to you," Mari said, interrupting his thoughts. "Being in this together means more than just geographical proximity. We share the risks and the decisions."

He blinked, focusing back on the road. "My family is my responsibility."

"You may want to see it that way, but you're wrong."

"Taking care of Elizabeth and Pat is a longstanding habit with me," JD said with a wry smile. "We may not always agree on methods, but I've never let her or Pat down. I may not have the answers we need yet, but I'll find them. I've always done that. It's how we survived."

"They were there for you, too, weren't they?" Mari observed tautly. "You didn't do it all alone. So don't be so quick to discount my help. I'm a survivor myself," she added, her tone distant, reserved.

There it was again. That hint of something that attested to secrets and another side of Mari he could only guess at. "You say things like that, then you shut down. It's almost like drawing the curtains closed and putting up a sign that says No Trespassing."

"That's exactly the way it is. Right now we have other things to worry about."

"We're doing all we can. We're on our way to the complex. We've got time. Talk to me."

"I am talking to you," Mari snapped.

"No, I mean really *talk*. I'd feel much more comfortable in a fifty-fifty partnership if I thought my partner trusted me."

She paused for a long time, and JD wondered if he'd pushed her too far. The frigid silence stretched out. Then he heard her take a deep breath.

"Money isn't the shield you think it is. Life brings pain and there's no way to run from it. Sometimes that pain is so great it can destroy you inside. The difference between those who find the strength to go on and those who curl up inside and retreat isn't dependent on how much money they have."

"Then what is it?" he prodded softly.

"It's the ability to dream, to hope, and when all else fails, to accept and make the best of what life has handed you."

"Is that what you've done, made the best of things?" JD asked, eager to learn more about her.

"I went through some hard times and a lot of heart-break. It took me a long time to put things back together afterward. Eventually I learned how to create new hopes and dreams."

"My own dreams sustained me for years," he admitted. "Sometimes they were all I had."

"And had those been taken away, you would have found new ones. You said you're a survivor."

JD pulled into a parking area of the apartment complex that hid his vehicle from view of the street. "Let's do this quickly. We have to find a place that'll work, and then get going." He led the way along a road of apartments but none of them proved to be suitable. Either their locations gave them no privacy, or they held no furniture whatsoever. "Once we find a suitable place to return to, we'll go see Elizabeth and find out for ourselves how she's doing," he said. "So far, all we've heard is a lot of medical double-talk. Even her doctor won't give me any specifics on the telephone and I need answers. I want to know what the doctors think, not just what they're saying. I figure that this is going to be our only real shot at it. The longer we avoid the police, the more they'll be looking for us. It's now or never."

"If all three of us show up at the hospital, we'll stick out like sore thumbs," Mari warned.

"We won't be there long, so Amy can stay in the truck. You and I will go in separately. Since you hired the security people, they'll talk to you. While you're doing that, I'm going to scout around, see what I can learn from the nurses, and check any records on Elizabeth I can get hold of."

"Since you're family, you'll be allowed to see her and be given whatever information you want. It shouldn't be a problem," Mari said, feeling Amy's eyes on her.

"Maybe, but if the police are as eager to talk to us as they seemed to be a while ago, they may anticipate my move. I'm going to do my best to avoid them."

"I want to see my mom," Amy said, determination punctuating each syllable and gesture.

"You will," JD assured her, turning to face her squarely so she could lip-read more easily, "but not this time. Trust us to find out how she is for you, okay?"

Amy looked as if she was about to argue, then averted her gaze, staring at the Christmas decorations on one of the windows. JD knew her gesture was the equivalent of shutting them out. Amy was letting him know that she was angry at being excluded, but at least she wouldn't fight him.

It took them fifteen minutes to decide upon another apartment in the complex. JD insisted on one facing an overgrown hedge of thorny pyracanthas. "Not exactly scenic, but no one can approach here except on foot."

"They would get all scratched up," Amy said.

Mari laughed. "She's right."

While Mari and Amy returned to the truck, JD went inside to drop off Amy's and Mari's clothes and a few spare blankets. He turned up the heat and checked to make sure the apartment's appliances were hooked up. A few minutes later, they left for the hospital. A somber mood settled over all of them.

JD watched Amy furtively in the rearview mirror as they drove north toward Albuquerque. She was leaning against the side window, her white teddy bear with the Christmas bow clutched tightly in one arm. The Advent calendar lay flat on her lap. She wouldn't be separated from either of her treasured possessions.

"Amy must be exhausted," Mari said, glancing back. "She hasn't slept much these past two days."

"None of us has," JD answered. "I don't know about you, but it's the uncertainty that bothers me the most. I lived with that for too long when I was a kid."

"What do you mean?"

"Elizabeth must have told you how often we had to move as kids. We lived from one month to the next. Landlords weren't always understanding when the rent was late."

"Elizabeth told me a little but she doesn't like talking about the past. She told me once that she couldn't change what happened back then, and going over it didn't help."

JD pulled into the hospital parking lot. "I want to find a spot where we can keep an eye on the truck from inside."

Five minutes later, after circling back and forth down rows of cars near the side entrance, Mari signed to Amy, letting her know the plan. Amy's grip on the teddy bear tightened but she nodded calmly.

"Come back soon, okay?" she asked.

"We will," Mari assured her with a confident smile and wrapped the blanket snugly around the little girl.

JD went in first. The lobby was crowded. A large Christmas tree stood in the center of the room and decorations lined every wall interspersed with posters for the Toys for Tykes drive. There was a nearly empty toy drop-off bin against one wall. Christmas carols played low over the speakers, interrupted sporadically as doctors were paged. JD noticed a uniformed policeman standing near the information desk. He watched the officer for a few seconds. Something wasn't right. The cop wasn't doing anything, just hanging around as if waiting for something—or someone. Uneasiness spread through him.

Mari came in a moment later and joined JD near one of the janitorial closets. "What are you still doing down here? Elizabeth's on the second floor."

"Did you notice the cop?"

"The one checking out the receptionist?" she asked.

"Is that what he was doing?"

"Looked like it to me," she answered.

JD considered her reply, then shook his head. "I'm not so sure. Let's play it safe and avoid the elevator. We're not as likely to run into as many people on the stairs."

"The stairwell is straight ahead. As soon as we reach the second floor we'll split up."

JD watched Mari as she strode quickly down the hall, looking as if she knew precisely where she was going. She had guts, there was no denying that, JD thought admiringly.

They reached the second floor a few minutes later. "Let me go first," Mari said, opening the door and ducking out. "Give me five minutes or so before you step out. It won't hurt if I scout out things a bit," she called back softly.

The time seemed to go by slowly while he waited. JD glanced at his watch. As he was about to leave, she returned to the stairwell.

"There are at least two more cops lurking in the halls. I met one of the security guards for just a second. Seems the department believes that Elizabeth's assailant will come to finish the job. They know she has protection, but they want to be in a position to act in case something goes down."

"Just what we needed," he grumbled. "They may not be looking for us but you can bet they *know* about us."

"Agreed. So let's get out of here. We'll have to postpone checking any further on Elizabeth's condition for now."

"Right." JD nodded.

They went down half a flight of stairs and Mari spotted a double door. "Depending on where this leads, this may be a safer place to exit."

"Take a look."

Mari peered through a glass window in the door. "It's the cafeteria. It'll be easy to cut through here. We can blend with the crowd and cut down our chances of being spotted."

"Let me go first," JD said, handing her his keys. "If I get stopped, find another way out and take my truck. I'll meet you two back at the apartment as soon as I think it's safe."

"All right."

JD opened the door and stepped through into the noisy cafeteria. Garlands were strung from wall to wall and bright Christmas balls hung from them. It was nearly one-thirty, and the lunch crowd was in full force. He walked at normal speed, as if on a break, and passed through the room, trying to avoid making eye contact with anyone. He'd just passed the line of people waiting to fill their trays when he saw a familiar face at a table near the main entrance. He recognized Pearline Gutierrez from the times he'd stopped by the station to take Elizabeth out to lunch. JD forced himself not to increase his pace.

Before he could walk past, Pearline stood and greeted a middle-aged uniformed sheriff who'd just come in. JD slowed and looked away. A moment later, they'd both disappeared out the door. JD stood in the doorway for a second then hurried toward the front. The hairs on the back of his neck were standing on end. What about Amy? They'd taken too long in here trying to duck the cops.

As two uniformed deputies passed by, JD strolled casually toward the window. Peering through the openings between the taped-on paper snowmen and Christmas angels that adorned the windows, he managed to get a clear look down at the truck. Amy was still in the pickup. That was one less worry.

As he reached the lobby, JD spotted a hospital security guard standing beside the doors. JD quickly stepped up to a public phone, trying to assess the situation. Then he felt a hand on his shoulder.

Turning with a start, he stood face-to-face with Mari. "What the heck are you trying to do? You scared ten years off my life," JD whispered.

Mari gestured toward the guard. "He wasn't there before. What's going on?"

"I don't know but I don't like it. Look at him. He barely notices the doctors or nurses who go by. But he seems really interested in everyone wearing street clothes."

"We're in trouble then. We're stuck in these clothes—that is, unless you want to streak past him," she observed wryly.

"There's a thought. You go first. You'll create a diversion and give me time to get to the pickup." Seeing the smirk on her face, JD laughed. "Just kidding. I have another plan in mind. What do you say we borrow some hospital whites?" JD gestured behind them and across the hall. "There's a linen closet."

"Let's go."

When they emerged moments later, JD wore a wrinkled white lab coat some doctor had left inside on a hook, replete with a name tag. Mari hadn't been quite so lucky. The best she'd been able to find were scrub greens.

She glanced at him. "Whadda ya think?"

"It'll do."

"Okay. I might as well put it to the test." Not giving him a chance to object, she walked directly toward the exit.

JD used the Christmas tree to screen himself from view and watched. Mari walked confidently, her back straight, head held high. As she reached the doors, JD saw the guard staring at her. Mari must have noticed him, too, because some of her confidence seemed to fade. She slowed down slightly, approaching the guard with a wariness that hadn't been there before.

Chapter Six

Mari saw the guard looking over at her. *Smile at him. Do something. Act natural.* Possibilities zipped through her mind as her heart leapt to her throat and lodged there.

The young man's gaze wandered over her. He was looking for hospital ID, she just knew it! If he asked, she'd claim she'd left it in the operating room. By then she'd be close enough to the door to make a run for it.

As she reached the guard's post, Mari half expected him to make a grab for her and hold her for the police. Instead he winked. The security guard was flirting with her! He'd only been giving her the once-over. Mari was so relieved her knees wobbled. With a tiny smile, she continued past him.

As she cleared the doors and stepped outside, Mari breathed again. She hadn't realized until now that she'd been holding her breath. She hurried over to the truck. How could she *not* have known the difference between a man ready to arrest her and one who was flirting? She was losing her grip; that was the only possible answer.

As Mari reached the truck, Amy glanced up and smiled. The relief on her face was so evident, guilt assailed Mari. Amy's face revealed the signs of the tension and fear the little girl had struggled with during their absence.

Mari brushed Amy's cheek with her hand. "I'm sorry we left you for such a long time. We had a few problems. Your uncle should be here any time now."

Hearing footsteps, Mari turned and saw JD approaching. "Let's get out of here. It's like a policemen's convention in there," he muttered.

They were underway seconds later. Amy leaned back in her seat and refrained from asking questions or trying to lip-read. Noting that withdrawal, Mari shifted in her seat and signed, letting Amy know that they'd been unable to see Elizabeth.

"Mom's okay," Amy answered. "We'll be together for Christmas. Uncle JD promised." She stared at the Advent calendar on her lap and counted the four doors that remained to be opened.

Mari glanced at JD and saw the lines around his face tighten. If only he'd never made that promise. Mari shifted and faced front, unable to think of a reply that would prepare Amy for disappointment. "What's next on the agenda?"

JD shot her an icy look, then, as if deciding she hadn't meant that as a criticism, relaxed. "The safety deposit box. We'll head there next."

JD lapsed into silence. After fifteen minutes, curiosity got the better of Mari. "You seem to be a million miles away. What's on your mind?"

"My business."

Mari blinked. Was he telling her rudely that she was intruding? "I didn't mean to pry, but it wouldn't hurt to discuss things, particularly if something's bugging you."

JD nodded absently. "I *was* telling you. I'm worried about Bruce Campbell. He's a good partner, but I'm not sure he can run the business by himself. Unfortunately this is the worst possible time for our profits to drop. I'm going to need every last dollar, what with security guards to pay, the costs of Elizabeth's injuries and us on the run with Amy."

"We haven't exactly used truckloads of money so far to evade the police and whoever's gunning for Amy. As far as I can tell, our investigation shouldn't entail a lot of money, either, just time. And Elizabeth's insured for medical care. So why are you worried about your company's profit margin?"

"It's only realistic to be concerned," he said, shrugging. "People depend on my company for their livelihoods. I don't want anyone to lose their jobs over this. Don't tell me you haven't thought about your teaching position—whether it'll be there when you return."

Mari felt her temper rising. "To be perfectly honest, that hadn't even occurred to me. Job security isn't a priority right now."

JD gave her an incredulous look. "Oh, come on, admit it. You're human. Personal concerns must have crossed your mind."

Mari shrugged. "Well, I do worry about my students, but that's scarcely the same thing."

"In a way I don't think it's that much different. I love Thunderbird Construction. I built that company from the ground up. It has been my family, my companion and my dream for a long time. My employees depend on me like your students depend on you. My presence or absence affects their future." JD dropped his voice and in a barely audible tone, added, "And I'm in control there."

Mari managed to hear most of his words. Was he focusing on his company as a way to avoid dwelling on matters that were beyond his control? If only he was a little easier to understand! Half of the time she wasn't sure whether she liked JD or not.

"You know, the way the cops were acting in the hospital has made me pretty nervous. Let's cover ourselves just to be on the safe side. The bank we're going to is only a few blocks from the station," Mari said.

"What do you have in mind?" JD's eyebrows rose slightly.

"We need some disguises."

Even though Mari's nerves were stretched taut, she managed to make a game out of shopping for Amy. The little girl treated it as a Christmastime expedition, enjoying the displays with their bright multicolored lights. The fresh scent of pine trees filled the shops and the minimall. Amy stared, fascinated at all the holiday decorations as they purchased the disguises they needed, and Mari added a few Christmas ornaments to make their borrowed apartment seem more homelike for Amy.

Mari held the child's hand as they headed back to the truck, glad they'd been able to spend this time together. Amy had needed the chance to enjoy herself. From this point on, things would get tense and very, very strange.

AN HOUR LATER, their disguises completed, they drove to the bank. Mari bit her bottom lip to keep from laughing each time she glanced at JD.

"I should have been the one to choose these disguises," he grumbled.

"I did the best I could with what was available," Mari protested.

JD brushed back the bangs of the blue-white shoulder-length wig that seemed to have been sprayed into paralysis. Catching a glimpse of himself in the rearview mirror, he flinched. "It's obscene."

"There's nothing obscene about a little old lady, even one wearing sexy jeans. That blouse with the lacy collar really gives the disguise a great touch, too, I might add. And the makeup's perfect, if I say so myself." Mari saw Amy put a hand over her mouth to suppress a giggle. She had to struggle not to smile. "You really should be more appreciative. No one would ever recognize you."

"I can't possibly tell you how grateful I am for that," he said sarcastically. "But did you have to get so carried away with the lipstick? And I think you put enough powder on my face to rival New Mexico's best ski slopes."

"Maybe, but your whiskers won't show through."

"And this eye shadow? This goop is really thick. It feels like paste on my eyelids."

"But it makes your eyes look so pretty," Mari answered.

JD glowered at her, then caught a glimpse of Amy in the back seat. "And I wouldn't laugh too hard if I were you, little girl. You look just as awful."

"I look like an old lady," she said with a grin.

"You don't have enough wrinkles," he retorted.

"Aren't we lucky that *you* do," Mari countered smoothly.

JD looked at her coldly. "Another week of this and we won't need this wig. Gray will be my natural hair color."

Mari laughed. "Look at the bright side. While you two wait for me outside the bank, you won't have to hide. I really think that would have looked too suspicious in a bank's parking lot."

"I still want to hide." JD studied Mari in her reddish brown wig. "You don't look too bad in that." His gaze took in all of her.

"Gee, thanks. But if you're complimenting my wig, why are you looking at my legs?"

"I've never seen you except in jeans or slacks," he answered.

JD's awareness of her touched Mari like an electric shock, leaving her tingling in some very inappropriate places. There was something so virile about the way he'd looked at her, everything feminine in her responded. She willed away the warmth his words had created. This wasn't the time for distractions.

JD parked near the entrance to the bank and shut off the engine. "You ready?"

Mari took a deep breath, then let it out again. "I better be, 'cause it's show time."

"If anything goes wrong, get back to the truck as fast as you can and we're out of here."

"Nothing will go wrong," she said, for his benefit as well as her own. Mari checked inside her purse for the safety deposit box key she'd tucked inside, along with the piece of paper with the box number. "I'd better go now. This will only get harder the longer I put it off."

Mari stepped out of the pickup and with one last glance back and a smile for Amy, went inside the bank. Her hands were sweating as she approached a woman seated at a desk draped in red and green tinsel. Since it was a small bank, there was an even greater risk that they might remember Elizabeth. That's why she'd chosen this wig. It was the closest she could find to Elizabeth's hair color.

As the woman went to retrieve a set of keys, Mari signed the fictitious name on the bank's signature card. "I'm ready now, Miss Vanderstoop," she said, leading the way to the safety deposit boxes.

"Thanks," Mari answered, keeping her words to a minimum. Then the young woman left her to examine the contents of the box in private. Mari took out a large envelope and put it in her purse. She resisted the temptation to open it and look inside. There'd be time later. Right now, she had to get out of here.

After going through the closing procedure quickly, she left the vault. She was on her way out when she saw Elizabeth's boss, Colin Randall, coming into the bank. They'd met several times as the Toys for Tykes drive got underway. Her breath caught in her throat.

As she crossed the lobby, passing by the aluminum Christmas tree, her heart hammered against her ribs. She was going to be caught in here; she just knew it. Pretending to be interested in the Christmas cards hanging from ribbons on the far wall, she looked away, hiding her face.

Randall headed toward one of the tellers. He glanced over at her casually as he walked by. For that one brief moment, Mari's blood turned to ice, and she studiously avoided making eye contact. It seemed as if time had suddenly stopped. Then he turned away to make a transaction at the counter.

Mari forced herself not to rush for the door and somehow kept her pace steady. A moment later she was outside. Her hands were shaking and her stomach felt queasy. She just wasn't cut out for this cloak-and-dagger business. She was a teacher, not an undercover detective. Even as a child, her make-believe worlds had never included anything like this.

Amy's face lit up as Mari rejoined them. "You okay?" Amy signed.

"Yeah. It was a little crazy in there with the Christmas rush and everyone needed a check cashed."

Amy nodded, then satisfied, turned her attention to the bag of decorations they'd bought. She carefully picked up the small ceramic Christmas tree and set it on her lap.

Noticing that Amy's attention was diverted, Mari continued. "Actually, I'm a little rattled," she said and explained about seeing the lieutenant inside as JD started the truck.

"What was he doing there?" JD asked, immediately alert. "I was watching the main entrance. Randall must have come in the side door." He put the truck in gear and pulled out into traffic.

"At first, I was afraid he'd followed me here somehow, but then he went to a teller. He had to cash a check or something, I suppose."

"Okay, now tell me what you found in the box," JD said, pulling into the crowded parking lot of a large grocery store.

Mari extracted the envelope from her purse and opened it. She then placed the contents down between them as Amy watched over the top of the seat.

"They're close-up photos of the Madonna," JD said, surprised. "I don't get it. What's that supposed to tell us? And why two identical photos?"

Mari studied the snapshots. "The gems look a little different in the one on the right, but that could be the lighting."

JD brought the pictures closer and studied them in silence for several seconds. "You're right. It's just not clear enough. What's in the other papers?"

Mari unfolded the first then glanced at it. "It's a copy of the sign-in sheet that shows the people who've gone into the evidence room. Their addresses and telephone numbers are listed here, too." Mari felt her throat tighten as a terrible sense of foreboding filled her. "Something's wrong with the Madonna. I can just feel it."

"There's writing on the back of this," JD said, bending down as she held the paper up.

Mari set it down between them and they both tried to decipher Elizabeth's hastily written scrawl. "Jewels—not right."

"What's that mean?" JD asked, perplexed, studying the photos again. "Think these are before-and-after photos?" JD stared at the pictures. "Wait a minute. This big ruby near the bottom isn't as round here as it is in the other photo." He peered at it closely. "No, maybe it's just the angle."

Mari looked closely at each of the photographs. "No, it's more than the angle." She considered them silently for another long moment. "Maybe the gems were switched." She shook her head. "No, that doesn't sound right. If that's what Liz thought, she wouldn't have kept it a secret. She knows how important the Madonna is to the parish. She's what keeps their hope alive, no matter how tough things get.''

''Normally I'd agree,'' he said slowly, ''but there are extenuating circumstances. She may have wanted to check things out herself before saying anything. You see, about a year ago, Elizabeth reported some things missing from the evidence room. It turned out that there was no record that those items had ever even been in it, and the lieutenant used that point to make her look like a fool. Elizabeth almost lost her job over it.''

''Now that you mention it, I remember her telling me about that.'' Mari sucked in her cheeks and chewed the insides of her mouth nervously. ''Liz may have been in the process of verifying her suspicions. If that's the case, she would have undoubtedly spoken to others. That might explain the attack on her life.''

''I think it's time for me to phone Lieutenant Randall and find out what's going on. There's a phone booth just ahead.'' He glanced down at himself. ''But there's no way I'm using it wearing this getup.''

''You'll be safer in that disguise,'' Mari answered.

''You may have a point.'' He pulled the truck over next to the phone booth then stepped out. ''I feel like a fool,'' he growled to Mari.

''Believe me, even if the lieutenant pulled up beside you, he'd never guess it was you. Actually, you look really sweet.''

''Stuff it,'' JD muttered. ''I owe you one for this.''

Mari rolled down her window to talk as he fished a coin from his pocket. ''Amy's really enjoyed this, you know. It's taken her mind off things, at least for a while.''

''Great. Pile on the guilt. Just what I needed,'' he mumbled, then began to punch in the numbers. Moments later, Lieutenant Randall picked up the phone.

''Lieutenant, I've been trying to figure out why my sister thought the hit and run was deliberate. Going through some papers she's sent me, I've made a few disturbing discoveries," he said.

"What exactly did you find?" the lieutenant asked in a guarded tone.

"She was worried about the safety of the Madonna statue."

The lieutenant drew in a breath then let it out slowly. "Mr. Hawken—JD—do you mind if I call you that?" Randall didn't wait for an answer. "Your sister's worked for me for the past three years, and she's sometimes been...let's say, impulsive. Recently she came into my office claiming that the Madonna's jeweled dress had been tampered with. She thought that maybe the stones weren't real and that someone had made a switch. Before I pushed the panic button, I asked Al Stuart, the insurance man who underwrote the special policy covering the statue, to come in with an appraiser. Everyone has assured me that the stones are genuine. The dress was a bit wrinkled, but we believe someone dropped it on the floor, then put it back a bit hastily."

"What about Father Aragon? Did he come to take a look? No one knows the Madonna better than he does."

"I didn't see the need to worry him. There was no reason to raise an alarm. This isn't the kind of rumor I'm going to risk leaking to the press, especially at Christmastime. The department doesn't need that sort of publicity. Let's face it. There was *no* story, only Elizabeth's overactive imagination. And this isn't the first time she's cried wolf."

Randall cleared his throat then continued. "But there's another problem and it's imperative we speak to you and Mari Sanchez. We've been unable to locate your niece and we've had to put out an APB and Missing Child Alert. You're raising all kinds of questions and throwing suspicion on yourself by not coming in voluntarily. If you push things, I can make this a lot more official."

"We'll be in touch," JD promised, then hung up abruptly without saying when and returned to the truck. "Something's going on. I think they know we have Amy, but they're not saying so, and I don't know why. I had the strongest feeling he was keeping me on the line to have the call traced."

"What happened when you told him about the Madonna?"

JD repeated the conversation, aware that Amy was lip-reading. "Elizabeth was obviously onto something, but what? If those jewels checked out, then she couldn't have been right about that."

"I have a theory. Let's say some deputies are involved. It's logical to assume then that the department would want to keep a lid on the entire thing until it can be straightened out. The lieutenant is right. Leaking this to the press would be disastrous for the department and for the toy drive. I'd hate to be the one responsible for spoiling Christmas for all those needy kids. Or maybe there's more to this than Elizabeth ever realized. Maybe the cover-up is being engineered by someone actually involved in the scam."

"You mean the lieutenant could be lying about the gems being authentic?" JD asked.

"It's one possibility. Or maybe they've been put back, at least temporarily. I think we should pay that insurance underwriter a visit. We'll play it safe and go in disguise."

"Not this one," JD answered flatly. "No way."

"Okay. I'll come up with something else." She stepped out of the truck and looked up the address in the phone book inside the booth. "The insurance guy's office is downtown," Mari said, joining them again in the truck. "Let's go. I've got an idea. We'll say we're representing the bishop's office and we're writing a report on church treasures around the state, for release to the public. We'll tell him we need the net worth of the Madonna and descriptions of the jewels."

"What if he asks us for ID?"

Mari grinned and pulled out a business card from her purse. Across the center was printed, "Archdiocese Media Liaison." "I served in that capacity while a friend of mine was on vacation. I kept the ID as a memento."

"I'll find someplace more private to park. Then I'll take off the wig and makeup."

Mari smiled. "The red lipstick might be tricky."

JD glowered at her. "Find a way."

She laughed. "I was only teasing. It's almost all gone now."

JD pulled into the back parking lot of an empty warehouse and removed his disguise. Mari worked on Amy, changing her appearance again. In jeans and an oversize sweater, she'd pass for a scruffy little boy. Amy wrapped her hair in a knot then held it in place on top of her head using JD's baseball cap.

"Good," Mari signed. "You don't look at all like yourself."

JD wore a black shirt and inside it was a strip of white cardboard that looked amazingly like a clerical collar. "From a laundered shirt I had in the back," he explained.

Despite his new look, there was a tightness around his eyes and a dangerous calm about him that made her mouth go dry. He looked like trouble about to happen. "Try to relax, JD," she said softly. His expression softened a little and he smiled but it never reached his eyes.

Despite her apprehension, Mari responded to his nearness as naturally as a flower to the sun. He was pure male. He exuded quiet strength, confidence and power. Yet, despite that dangerous edge, he had the uncanny ability to make her feel protected. A pleasant warmth coursed through her.

Aware she'd been staring, she forced her gaze away. "We're as ready as we'll ever be. Let's go."

They drove directly to Al Stuart's office. The building was a one-story adobe structure in a recently renovated section of downtown. JD insisted on circling the block first. It was just past four-thirty, and a cleaning crew had propped the rear door open as they brought in their equipment and supplies.

JD parked at the front. The lobby was aglow with a ceiling-high Christmas tree that sparkled in the gathering half light. Amy signed to Mari that she wanted to go in and look at the tree.

Mari started to object but then nodded. "Be careful, all right?"

JD looked at Mari in surprise. "She should stay in the truck."

Mari shook her head. "She'll be safer inside. The city's beautification project aside, this is still a rough section of town."

JD glanced around then relented. "Amy, don't let anyone approach you, okay?"

"I won't. I can't hear but I can see people coming. No one will get close enough to talk to me, I promise. If anyone tries, I can go back inside the truck and lock the doors."

JD stepped out of the vehicle and handed Amy a spare key that he usually kept in a magnetized holder in the tire well. "This is in case you want to come back to the pickup."

Mari hurried inside the building, leading the way. As Amy went over to see the tree, Mari checked for Al Stuart's office number. It was right down the hall. "We're cutting it close. Let's hope he's still there."

Finding the door was still unlocked, they walked inside. A young man in his late twenties glanced up from the front desk of the two-room office. "Hello. May I help you?"

"We're looking for Al Stuart," Mari answered.

"I'm sorry, but he's on a conference call right now. Perhaps I can help you. My name's Larry Wright. I work with Mr. Stuart."

Mari pulled out her ID. She sat down on the chair across from the young man's desk and went through her cover

story. "I know it's almost closing time, but if you can photocopy the information I need from your files, we'll be on
our way. It shouldn't take you long."

He regarded her thoughtfully. "Well, our files would list
the net worth of the statue, but a complete description of the
gems is a bit harder to find. What we keep are the ways we
use of identifying the pieces through inclusions in the
stones."

"Okay, that'll do. We can get the other information using historical sources."

He stood and retrieved a file folder from a large cabinet
behind his desk, almost knocking over a large poinsettia in
the process. "I can give you a copy of the appraisal, of
course, but the parish already has one on file."

She smiled indulgently. "It's a long drive, and I *am* on a
tight schedule. I'm sure the bishop would appreciate your
cooperation. Call his office if you like," Mari bluffed,
hoping the man wouldn't take her up on the suggestion.

"No, that won't be necessary," Wright answered, glancing at JD's clerical collar before going to the copy machine
in the corner. As he placed the first original down onto it,
the door to the adjacent office opened, and a middle-aged
man with salt-and-pepper hair and carrying a cane emerged.

He stood, favoring his right leg, nodded at Mari and JD,
then glanced at Larry Wright. "What's going on?"

Larry explained briefly as he continued to make copies.
"It won't take long," he said, gathering up the copies and
originals as he spoke.

Stuart's gaze fell on Mari, then he looked hard at JD.
"Larry, come into my office for a minute, okay?" He
smiled benignly at Mari. "This'll take only a moment."

Chapter Seven

As soon as the door closed, Mari went over to it and listened. "He's calling the police and saying something about fugitives." She paused. "He's reporting us! He figured out who we are!"

"Let's get out of here," JD said, grabbing Mari by the hand.

As they rushed out the door, they heard sirens begin to wail in the distance. "They work fast."

"Or that might be some other crisis. It makes no difference. We've got to leave now."

They found Amy standing by the tree, staring at the star on top as Mari had often done as a child. Mari tapped Amy's shoulder and signed, "Let's go. Hurry."

They kept their pace brisk, just short of a jog. In seconds they reached the truck and pulled out into traffic. "Don't worry. Pickups make up half the vehicles around here, maybe more. We'll blend into traffic and no one will give us a second look," JD said reassuringly.

"I can't believe he figured out who we were," Mari returned. "The police must have put out an APB and warned Al Stuart specifically after you called to ask about the Madonna."

JD switched on the radio. His shoulders were rigid with tension. His hands curled and uncurled around the steering wheel as he drove directly out of the neighborhood and down a busy side street. When the news report came on, he turned up the volume.

The sheriff's department's public information officer was briefing the press at a news conference. According to the sheriff's office, Elizabeth had allegedly been part of a ring responsible for stealing valuables from the evidence room. Mari listened carefully.

"As a civilian in charge of the evidence room," the officer said, "Ms. Hawken had ample opportunity."

A reporter quickly followed with the natural question. "What's been taken?"

"We're in the midst of an investigation right now. So far there are no obvious big-ticket items missing, but we're still taking inventory. We'll have more for you later."

"Is this somehow connected to the hit and run that placed Elizabeth Hawken in the hospital?" a woman reporter asked.

"We believe Elizabeth Hawken was struck down by a fellow conspirator. Some of our own people have reported she'd been seen acting strangely earlier that day. But the purpose of this conference is to ask for everyone's help in locating Amy Hawken, Elizabeth Hawken's eight-year-old daughter. The child is deaf and we believe she may be in danger."

"Do you think the girl was kidnapped to prevent Elizabeth Hawken from testifying when she regains consciousness?" another woman reporter asked.

"It's too early to speculate on any motives, but we're looking to speak with two people in connection with our investigations. The victim's brother, J. D. Hawken, owner of Thunderbird Construction, and a local teacher, Mari Sanchez, are both being sought for questioning. Ms. Sanchez reported the hit and run and knows the Hawken family well. Both refused to assist our investigation and have dropped out of sight."

"He's making it sound as if we're guilty," Mari gasped.

"A statewide search is underway. If anyone has information as to their whereabouts, please give the sheriff's office a call. Photos of Amy, J. D. Hawken and Mari Sanchez are in this evening's newspaper," the officer ended.

Mari stared at JD. As the weather report began, he switched off the radio. "This is going to make it impossible for us to go anywhere without a disguise," she warned.

"You're right." JD paused for a long moment. "Can you cut Amy's hair and maybe dye it?"

"Sure. I'd better restyle my auburn wig, too. But what about you? How do we disguise you?"

"Nobody looks at a guy," JD answered with a shrug. "I mean, what's there to see?"

Mari looked at him, allowing her gaze to drift purposely up and down him. "Don't act so innocent," she answered. "Grow a beard or at least start one, okay? Comb your hair differently. And don't look so neat all the time. Change your image." Unfortunately for her, the rugged look would only enhance his appearance. It would add a wallop to the masculinity that was so much a part of him. Now all she had to do was figure out a way to avoid letting it affect her.

"The first thing we have to do is find another safe house," JD said. "With this story out, the guard at the complex may see the paper and ID us to the police. Once we finish moving, we can go on the offensive. We have that list of people who had access to that evidence room. Let's go check out their homes and see if any are living beyond their means, or way below, which might indicate a gambling problem, for instance. We need to find a motive for the theft."

Amy leaned forward and placed a hand on Mari's shoulder. "We're detectives," she said. "Like on TV. It'll be fun."

Beyond the innocent pleasure that shone in Amy's eyes was another emotion. It was as if Amy was putting on a front for them. In her own way, she was trying to help.

JD pulled into the parking lot of the apartment complex a short time later. "Let's move fast," he said, glancing around. "It's too late for my crew to still be around, and I don't want to run into that security guard again."

IT DIDN'T TAKE LONG for them to pack up their few belongings and steal back out to the truck. As they pulled out, JD looked in the rearview mirror. There was someone sitting in a white sedan. He'd been there when they'd arrived, and he was still there.

Amy was leaning forward, looking from JD to Mari. Finally, when neither adult spoke, she signed to Mari, "Where are we going?"

"Yes, JD, where?" Mari wondered.

"To a grocery store first. We need supplies. Then to another apartment building still under construction about forty minutes from here. We've been working there, but I know it hasn't opened to the public yet." JD glanced in the rearview mirror again as they drove down the road. Though he'd been trying to keep his expression neutral, he felt Mari's gaze on him. She knew something was worrying him. Her eyes seemed to look right through him sometimes. "It's okay. It's nothing," he said.

"I deserve better than that from you," she said calmly.

Maybe it was the fact that she spoke without anger, but he suddenly felt guilty, though all he'd been doing was trying to protect her. "I noticed a white car back at the apartment complex and there's one behind us now. But there's nothing we can do about it on the highway with no turnoff in sight. And, like I said, it may be nothing."

"If we *are* being followed, who do you think it could be? The police?" Mari resisted the temptation to turn around and look.

"I don't know. It's a possibility. But I caught a glimpse of the driver a minute ago, and I think it might be the security guard who saw us the other night." JD took another glance in the rearview mirror.

"Shouldn't we lose him."

"Not yet. I don't think he has a radio in that car. I can't see any antenna. He must not be sure it's us. Otherwise he would have tried to stop us. If I make a run for it, he'll know for sure, and I'd rather avoid that."

"What's your plan?" Mari asked.

JD spotted a supermarket at the end of the next block. "We'll go in there. You two buy the supplies we need. Just act as normally as possible. I'll take care of him."

"*How* are you going to take care of him?" Mari insisted.

JD suppressed a smile. He had a feeling she was one hell of a teacher. Excuses about homework or evasions about tardiness wouldn't work with this lady. "First, I want to identify him. Then once I know for certain that he's really who we think, I'm going to make sure he can't follow us." He paused, then grinned. "Before you ask—I plan to disable his car in whatever way I can without attracting too much attention."

"So you'll need us to act as decoys," Mari noted.

JD nodded. "You have to keep him from ever getting too close to either of you while you're at it. I'm hoping he won't really be sure if it is us or not until it's too late."

Amy smiled, and Mari saw a glimpse of the impish little girl she'd been before all this trouble had started. "Okay," Amy assured her uncle, having lip-read the conversation.

The instant JD parked the truck, Amy and Mari hurried to the store, carefully sidestepping the rows of Christmas trees that lined the outside wall. Fear for their safety nagged at him. He liked being in control—of himself, and his life. Why did he have the feeling those days were over?

He left the truck and pretended to follow them in. Instead he ducked around the side of the building at the last minute and waited. The man stepped out of the white sedan a moment later. JD's suspicions were confirmed as the figure approached. Although their tail was in civilian clothes, JD recognized the security guard. He was now certain that the man was either trying to make a positive ID or trail them to their next hideout.

The threat was to all of them but for now only one thought drummed through JD's mind. He had to protect Mari and Amy; they were his responsibility. In the back of his mind, he knew that in reality neither was his to keep, but it still seemed very right to want to take care of them. There was a genuine sense of family growing among the three of them that he hated to admit would end someday.

Focusing his thoughts on the present, he followed the man but kept well back. Amy and Mari darted expertly through the aisles in a frenzy of shopping. The guard apparently had no idea that he'd been spotted.

JD glanced back at the man's car. He couldn't exactly let the air out of a tire without attracting attention. Then another idea came to him as he passed one of the cash registers. Making a quick purchase, he went outside, confident that Mari and Amy could keep the man running around in circles for several more minutes.

JD completed his plan quickly. He then walked back inside and gestured to Mari. She and Amy joined him outside a few minutes later with two bags of groceries. Out of the corner of his eye, he saw recognition, final and sure, dawn on the guard's face. "Let's go." They hurried to the pickup and jumped inside with their supplies.

The guard ran to his vehicle.

Just before JD pulled out into traffic, he risked a glance in the rearview mirror and saw the man still trying to open the door to his sedan. JD laughed. "Krazy Glue in the locks," he explained.

Mari gave him a startled look. "How appropriate," she teased.

Amy leaned forward and smiled at them. "We did a good job."

"Yeah, we did," JD agreed, and glanced ahead. "There's a convenience store in the next block. I'll stop there and get a paper. Let's find out exactly what we're going to be up against."

AFTER PURCHASING the evening paper, JD continued north. "Have you decided what to do to make Amy look different?"

"Cut my hair short," Amy answered, "and make the color red."

"Strawberry blond," Mari clarified, wondering what Elizabeth would say once she saw the transformation.

Thinking of the day when she'd have to return Amy to her mom, filled Mari with a numbing ache. Amy was hers only temporarily. On loan, nothing more. It had been too easy to surrender her heart to the little girl. It left her acutely aware of the barren emptiness at the center of her own scarred heart. Mari brushed her longings aside with a burst of will. Some problems had no solutions, though the wounds they inflicted cut so deep that an eternity wasn't long enough to heal them.

Mari noted how JD continued glancing in the rearview mirror. She'd been watching, too, but she was certain no one followed them now. She glanced down at the newspaper he'd bought and shook her head. "That's the clearest photo of Amy I've ever seen."

"They must have taken it from Elizabeth's home. I remember seeing it on the coffee table. What's the article say?"

Mari scanned it, knowing that some details were not ones she'd want to speak about in front of Amy. As she read on, her heart felt like a rock. Up to that moment, she could have sworn that things were already as bad as they could get. She'd been wrong. "The police had enough probable cause to convince a judge to issue a court order. They've gone through Elizabeth's bank and personal records. Apparently they discovered that she owed you quite a bit of money."

"So what? I can lend my sister money if I want to. What's the problem?"

"Well, being in debt is one possible motive for robbery. They're speculating you were pressuring Liz to pay you back."

"I don't understand," Amy said.

Mari tried to swallow past the lump in her throat. "The police are trying to find out who hurt your mom. One way they do that is to try to figure out why people do things. Only, in this case, they're getting everything mixed up."

"I'm near the top of the suspect list now. Is that what they're saying?" JD asked.

"For everything this involves," Mari answered obliquely, turning her head to look out the window so Amy wouldn't be able to lip-read. "They did a search of my home and found recent fingerprints they think they'll be able to link to all of us. They now have more evidence to support the theory that we're kidnappers."

"So they've found themselves some very handy fall guys—you and I."

Amy glanced at Mari. "What's happening?"

"Just grown-up talk," Mari assured her, turning around to touch Amy's face in a light caress.

Nodding, Amy leaned back and looked out the window.

Seeing Amy now, Mari suddenly remembered an incident years ago when she and Elizabeth had taken Amy to the playground. The other kids, realizing she was different, had ignored her. Amy hadn't been able to understand why, and had run back to Elizabeth wondering if she'd done something wrong.

Her heart had ached for Elizabeth and Amy that day. Elizabeth had sworn never to take Amy back, but to their surprise, Amy had asked to return. Week after week, they'd gone back with her. Eventually Amy had made sign language into a game and in the process, turned the other children into friends.

Mari watched her now with admiration. Like many other gifted children, Amy had developed an intuitive sense of when to press an issue and when to back off. Instead of insisting that she be made part of Mari and JD's conversation, she'd withdrawn, confident that the people she loved would make things work out just the way they were supposed to.

"She's quite a kid," JD muttered.

"She's special in more ways than one," Mari admitted.

"Listen, Mari, something in that article really upset you. What was it? I saw you digging your fingers into that newspaper as if you wanted to strangle the writer."

"The sheriff's department has intimated we're lovers. We're now prime suspects in Amy's kidnapping. We're also accused of burglarizing Elizabeth's home, since prints they believe are ours were found there on freshly disturbed items."

JD muttered a curse under his breath. "Most people are going to believe that tripe. That means we're now in as much danger from average citizens as we are from whoever's behind this mess. There's an even bigger problem. If the good cops believe you and I and Elizabeth are guilty, then they won't look any further for the real culprits."

"That means the Madonna's jewels, if they're really the thieves' target, could be halfway across the globe by the time anyone discovers what's really going on." Mari pressed her lips together. "The parish may never recover from the loss and the benefit for the needy children will be spoiled. I also glanced at another article asking people to continue supporting the toy drive. Donations are way down." She took a deep breath and let it out again slowly. "Can you imagine what all this will do to Amy? The way things look now,

Elizabeth could go straight from the hospital to a jail cell. We could end up in prison, too."

"We can't let any of that happen."

Mari thought of Amy being left among strangers. The girl's sense of isolation would grow, fostered by a world that wouldn't welcome her. Mari had known that kind of utter aloneness and the ravages it left on the spirit. No, Amy wouldn't go through that, not while she had breath left in her body. "We *won't* let that happen," Mari said flatly.

It was dark by the time JD pulled into the parking lot of a one-story apartment complex. His headlights cut a path through the blackness that surrounded them. It was almost frightening to see so many windows without the usual glow of lights. "This is it."

As her eyes adjusted to the dark, Mari looked at the block-long building skeptically. There were no Christmas decorations or even a spark of life to brighten the gloomy structure. "This place could be the setting for a horror movie."

"Let's take that apartment on the side, directly ahead. We'll be able to see most of the parking area from there. I'll go unlock it," JD said, reaching for his keys.

Mari retrieved some of their supplies from the back of the truck. As she placed a sack down on the asphalt, Amy came over and picked it up. "Thanks," Mari said with a smile. "Please take it inside," she added, gesturing to where JD stood.

Amy nodded. "Sure."

As the girl started to cross the road, a Bronco squealed around the corner of the building. Mari turned her head, but before she could even draw in a breath, the driver hit the brakes and skidded straight toward Amy.

Chapter Eight

The Bronco screeched to a halt a few feet from the child. The groceries fell, unnoticed, from her trembling hands.

JD bolted from the apartment door and rushed toward the Bronco. Rage contorted his features as he yanked open the driver's door. As the light inside the vehicle revealed the man's face, JD pulled his hand away and stopped cold. "What the hell are *you* doing here?"

"Calm down, JD. I didn't see her crossing the road. But I wouldn't have hit her, believe me. I'd have swerved and demolished your truck first," he added in an attempt at humor.

JD glared at him. "What are you doing here?"

"Three of our men are still working in one of the units. We had a problem with a gas line earlier and I came by to make sure everything was being taken care of. Then I saw you guys pull in. I recognized you immediately. Do you realize the mess you're in with the cops?"

JD glanced at Mari as she stepped forward. "Mari, this is my partner, Bruce Campbell," he said.

Mari studied the cherub-faced redhead. "You drive like a jerk," Mari snapped, then impulsively kicked him lightly on the shin. "That's for scaring all of us!"

Hopping back on one foot, Bruce smiled at JD. "Let me guess. That's the woman the police are looking for? Well, she's definitely violent." He put his foot back down, still favoring it. "I thought for a moment *you* were going to try to pound my face in—"

"*Try?*"

Bruce grinned and continued without hesitation. "But I never expected *her* to attack me," he said in a wounded voice, green eyes sparkling. "You're in luck. I take no offense. Good thing, too, 'cause it looks like you really need my help. There are several people around here right now who know you, and it's safer to get going as fast as you can."

JD quickly gestured to Mari. "We can't stay. There's a problem with the gas line and my men are here. Take Amy back to the truck. I'll join you in a minute." He looked back at Bruce. "You already know I'm in some trouble. Helping us out could put you in the line of fire, too."

"You can't believe everything you read in the newspapers," Bruce said, shaking his head good-naturedly. "I know you better than the cops and reporters do. What can I do to help? You need anything in particular?"

"As a matter of fact, I do." JD scribbled on a notepad, tore off the sheet, then handed it to his partner. "It would help if you could pick these up for me."

Bruce glanced down at the note and nodded. "Okay, so where can I find you?"

"I'll have to let you know later. I'll contact you."

"You sure you're safe driving your truck? They'll be looking for it, you know."

JD glanced at it pensively. Maybe some extra precautions wouldn't be a bad idea. "Let's trade vehicles. You can leave mine at the office where it won't create any undue attention, and take one of the company trucks."

"Fine with me. My Bronco's still leased under my ex-wife's name," he said, tossing JD the keys. "It won't be easy to trace back to you."

"Great." JD returned to the truck. Together with Mari and Amy, they moved their stuff to Bruce Campbell's Bronco.

"There's a cellular phone in there, buddy. I know you hate them, but I'm not as technophobic as you. Use it from time to time," Bruce said.

As he moved to open the door for Mari, she noticed his limp. "I didn't kick you *that* hard."

"Well, actually you did, but the damage isn't all your fault. I stepped off a ladder wrong earlier. I'll be fine in a day or so."

As they waved goodbye and pulled back out into the street, Mari gave JD a long look. "Do you think it was wise to switch vehicles with him?"

"Can't hurt. They know my truck and the license number by now. And the Bronco does have a phone. I hate the darned things because I think they distract from driving, but in this case, it's going to come in handy."

"Unless Bruce Campbell decides to turn us in."

"He won't."

"Can calls on the cellular phone be used to track us?"

"Not really. Our conversation can be monitored with the right equipment but it's tricky at best, particularly in a moving vehicle. And the cops don't know we'll be using this truck."

"You're sure you can trust Bruce?"

"He made a lousy first impression, I'll admit, but I've known him for quite a while. He'd never sell me out. Believe that."

"What was in that note you handed him?"

"I wanted him to pick up some things for us." He started to say more when Amy leaned forward.

"Where are we going?" she asked, clutching her Christmas bear in one hand.

"To another safe house," JD answered. "And this time it really is a house. It's in the South Valley, in the middle of a big field surrounded by trees. As long as we avoid the renovation crews during the day, there's no chance of us running into anyone."

"No security guards?"

"Not there. The owners and I both agreed it wasn't necessary."

"Do you think that by now the security guard has reported us to the police?"

"Yeah, I'm afraid he might have. That's why I don't want to risk going to another one of our commercial projects. The house I have in mind is one that Bruce took on personally for a friend of a friend. It doesn't show up on our books at the office. It's ideal."

"Does Bruce know we're going to use it?"

"I didn't tell him. That would have placed him in danger, too."

"So we can settle there. Then during the day, we'll go check out some of those people on the list that Elizabeth photocopied?"

"That's the plan."

BY THE TIME THEY ARRIVED at the old, Spanish-style, turn-of-the-century house, Mari was forced to agree that the location was so remote, this would be the safest place for them. Tall cottonwoods lined the drive, and in the moonlight, the stark branches looked like eerie fingers reaching down to them.

"It's creepy around here," Mari said.

"Not as much as it is inside the house. It's as if the original owners never could make up their minds what they wanted to create. It's a little Gothic, a little Spanish, a little just about everything you can name. It even has a stone turret."

As the trees thinned and the house appeared, Mari stared at the imposing structure. It was shrouded in shadows. Not a single light interrupted the gloom. "That is *one* ugly house."

Amy leaned forward. "A haunted house! We're staying there?"

"It's not haunted," JD said, laughing. "Will you mind terribly if we do stay?"

Amy seemed to consider it then shook her head.

Mari glanced at JD. Tight lines etched his face. She wondered what was on his mind but decided she would wait until later to ask. Sometimes he had a hard time sharing his thoughts. She didn't really blame him. In many respects she was the same way, but as long as they were working together, it was something she'd have to get used to.

They were on the front steps moments later. After making sure Amy would be safe wandering about on the big veranda that circled the building, JD helped Mari unload their supplies.

"I'm going to keep the sack with our disguises inside the vehicle permanently. That way we'll have them with us if we ever need them," Mari said.

"Good idea."

As they stepped through the front door, Mari crinkled her nose. "People live here?" She tried not to inhale too deeply. It smelled stuffy, as if it hadn't been opened in months.

"It hasn't been occupied for a long time. Our men haven't started work on the interior yet. A northern California couple eager for a winter home here in New Mexico bought it a few months ago. They want it revamped from the bottom up."

"I don't blame them. It's like Dracula's hacienda in here."

Turning on a lamp, Mari found they were standing in a small high-ceilinged foyer with pale green wallpaper that was faded and lifting in a few spots. Going straight ahead, she could see a large kitchen on the other side of a perfectly square dining room. A large, dusty, leaded-glass chandelier hung over a dining table covered with a dusty white sheet. The chairs were uncovered, revealing a beautiful mahogany finish coated with a thin layer of dust.

Mari stepped into the canary yellow kitchen, tinted beige by the same New Mexico dust. She brushed aside a cobweb at the edge of the sink and opened the window. A cold breeze wafted inside but at least it was fresh air. For now, it was better than being toasty warm and gasping at the musty smell.

"JD, what was bugging you in the car? I know you were worried about something."

"Are you kidding? My life, yours, Amy's and Elizabeth's are all on the line, and you've got to ask?"

"Yes, because it's more than that," she answered gently. The way his eyes narrowed told her she'd been right. "Sometimes, when you're not so closed off, JD, I think you and I might become friends, but then you pull away. You make me feel off balance, and I don't like it." She held his gaze, hoping to reach past his reserve. They needed each other.

Suddenly, as she saw herself reflected in his eyes, another more primitive emotion flickered to life. Longing, fierce and intense, spiraled though her. His mouth parted slightly, and as he ran his tongue over his lips moistening them, she remembered his mouth on hers, hot and demanding.

"You okay?" JD asked, a ghost of a smile playing on his lips.

She felt her cheeks turn hot as she saw him grin. "Um...sure," she answered.

He grew somber. "Neither of us is a teenager. We're adults, and that means we have pasts and lots of emotional baggage. I'm not sure we're ready for total openness."

Mari nodded slowly. Maybe he was right. She couldn't fault him for protecting himself, not while she was doing the same thing. She would never lower her guard enough to bare her soul to anyone. She knew doing that left a person too vulnerable, and betrayal hurt too damn much. Maybe love belonged to people in their early twenties, when one didn't see anything tainted by the fear of what it might become.

"If you can manage here," JD said at length, "I think I'll go try to find a map of the city. There must be one in Bruce's car. I want to check out the general locations of those addresses on Elizabeth's list."

"Go. I'm fine here. The sooner we get started working on that angle, the better."

Mari watched him leave. Sometimes JD seemed as tough as the Sandia Mountains. But every once in a while, she saw echoes of pain and scars that lay just beyond his smile.

Amy bounded into the room. "Finished?" she signed.

"Yes," Mari replied.

"Can I stay with you?" A cloud crossed Amy's eyes as she asked.

"Is something wrong?" Mari asked.

"Uncle JD is busy," she signed. "I'm bothering him."

Irritated with JD, Mari nodded. Amy was a sensitive little girl. He could have tried harder to be more patient with her.

"I'm bored," Amy signed.

"How about helping me put the ceramic Christmas tree we bought in your room. It'll make it seem homier," Mari suggested, pointing to the paper sack with their supplies.

Amy nodded. "Great."

As Mari reached for the sack, her elbow collided against her purse. It flew off the table and tumbled to the floor, its contents scattering. "Oh, rats!"

Mari bent down to retrieve her things, Amy at her side helping. Even her wallet had snapped open, not much of a surprise considering how many things she kept in it. Notes to herself, grocery lists and receipts—all had been stuffed inside it.

Amy returned the items she found back inside Mari's purse. She then reached for a small photo that had slid underneath the table. Mari spotted it at the same time, and her throat tightened so much that she found it difficult to breathe.

Amy smiled. "Sweet baby," she signed, then picked up the snapshot and handed it to Mari. "Who is it?"

Mari shook her head and as her gaze focused on the photo, felt tears stinging her eyes. Maybe she shouldn't have kept this picture, but it was all she had left. "Family. From long ago," Mari signed.

Amy nodded, then without saying a word, hugged Mari tightly.

Before Mari could gather her wits and sign or say something, Amy moved away, edging past JD, who'd come to the door. Mari looked over at him, unsure of how long he'd stood there or how much he'd seen. But it didn't matter. He wouldn't ask, though a silent question was etched on his face. She averted her eyes. It was surprising how strong the pain still was even after almost nine years.

"I've been thinking that we should go check out some of these addresses tonight. It's the best time. At least we won't be so easy to recognize in the dark."

She nodded, grateful for the chance to have to concentrate on other things. "Let me find Amy."

Mari walked down the hall in search of the child, then saw her in a bathroom in front of a mirror, scissors in hand. She'd cut her hair almost as short as JD's. Seeing Mari, she smiled triumphantly. "A new me," she signed.

Mari somehow managed not to gasp, probably because Amy's new hairdo had startled her vocal cords into paralysis. The little girl's hair was cut almost to the scalp in places. Around her ears clustered a pattern of nearly bald spots. Amy looked as if she was just recovering from some advanced case of mange. If anything, she was bound to attract even more attention in this new incarnation.

"What do you think?" Amy signed.

Mari opened her mouth but could think of nothing to say or sign. JD must have sensed something was wrong because a moment later he appeared by her side.

Mari glanced at him, forcing herself to remain expressionless. "This will take awhile. I'll let you know when we're ready." With a calm smile for Amy, she went inside the bathroom and closed the door.

It took her thirty minutes. First she tried to even out the unusual style Amy had fashioned for herself, but Mari wasn't kidding herself. Her success was limited. Amy then insisted on coloring her hair with the strawberry blond rinse they'd bought. Maybe it was the abrupt change, but the rinse just made everything look worse than before.

When Mari finally emerged with Amy, JD shot them both a hard look. Mari met his gaze, silently warning him not to say a word against Amy's efforts to help them.

JD finally just shook his head slowly. "She could use a hat, not that her hair's so...different. Remind me to buy her one."

It was seven by the time they left, but under the mantle of night they were assured a certain amount of anonymity. "There are two addresses in this quadrant of town. One belongs to an Officer Kyle Romero. He appears twice in the list."

"I met him once," Mari said. "He seemed pleasant enough. Could he be our chunky deputy?"

"Only if he's put on fifteen pounds, but I suppose that's possible, particularly this time of year."

As they entered Romero's neighborhood, JD turned off his headlights, falling behind a procession of cars enjoying the Christmas displays. Santa Claus waved from rooftops and houses sparkled with a multitude of blinking, colored holiday lights.

Mari turned to look at Amy and smiled. The little girl's nose was practically pressed to the window. "Our family used to go out often during the Christmas season when I was little to see the lights," Mari told JD. "That was about the only time we went out together. Both my parents had extremely busy careers."

JD glanced at Amy in the rearview mirror. "I used to walk for hours with Elizabeth and Pat from house to house. We knew it was dangerous to be out so late at night, but it became our special Christmas tradition." He paused. "Sometimes it was the only Christmas we had."

"At least you had each other."

"Were you an only child?"

Mari nodded. "My parents' lives weren't really suited for children." She leaned forward, checking out a house number next to a lighted snowman. "The address we're looking for is two houses down," she said. As they drove past the modest, pueblo-style home, a short, fit-looking man in a tan uniform came out and got into a patrol car. "That's Kyle. I recognize him," Mari commented.

"There's nothing out of the ordinary here," JD said. "Even the light display is nothing to write home about," he added, gesturing toward the set of blinking chili pepper lights that adorned a living-room window. "Of course, if he's part of the gang, that would be the smart way to play it."

"Let's go to the next address. We may get lucky and find something that will give us a possible suspect."

As they drove on, Amy kept calling their attention to the beautiful displays in the neighborhoods they passed.

JD switched on the radio. As "Oh, Holy Night," one of his favorite Christmas carols came on, he glanced at Mari. "I'd give anything if Amy could hear that."

"She enjoys Christmas in her own way," Mari answered. "There are the smells, sights and colors."

As they hit a stretch of road barren of twinkling decorations, Amy leaned down and retrieved something from the floor. A moment later, she held up a radio with headphones. "A new disguise!"

JD glanced at Mari. "I don't get it."

When Mari gave Amy a puzzled look, Amy slipped on the headphones and adjusted them over her head. "Like hearing kids," she explained.

JD cracked up. "Smart move, kiddo. Very smart. Now she's a little boy who's into music. Very ordinary. Won't create any undue attention at all." He studied Mari's short red wig. "I'm the only one who's got limited options."

"Not really. A beard's very effective, and from the looks of it, you'll have a thick one before long. Even now when it's still sparse, it's changed your appearance considerably. You look like a television vice cop."

JD grimaced. "Not exactly an image I've cherished recently."

The second address they checked out belonged to Ricky Estrada. JD pointed out that Estrada had been in the evidence room three times.

"I don't remember ever meeting Estrada or hearing Elizabeth mention him. Do you?" she asked.

He shook his head. "No, I don't."

They entered an upper-middle-class semirural neighborhood. The light displays on these houses were elaborate. One home had decorated their windmill with turquoise blue lights. Its shape was outlined brightly in the darkness.

Amy sat sideways with her head pressed to the window, clutching her teddy bear. "Oohhh! Look!" They passed an enormous twenty-five-foot-tall pine decorated with red and green lights, then Amy pointed to a group of carolers standing on a lighted porch. "Some came to our house last Christmas!" Amy said excitedly. "Do they sound nice?" she asked, glancing at Mari.

"We can't hear them from here, either," Mari replied.

"Oh," Amy said, disappointed. "Then you watch the bright colors and the Santas and the stars like me! Everything's so pretty."

JD slowed to catch sight of one of the house numbers. "It's up ahead." He gestured to his left. "The neighborhood could be explained if his wife has a high-powered job, but take a look at that British sports car in the driveway."

"He didn't buy that on a cop's salary," Mari said flatly.

"This guy's worth keeping an eye on." JD saw approaching headlights in his rearview mirror and a moment later, a patrol car came into sight. "But not now." JD drove slowly to the end of the block, switched on his turn signal, then pulled into the main road. "He was just patrolling, but I didn't want to take a chance."

Mari realized JD was about to head back. "Before we go to the safe house, how about making one more stop? Let's check out a hockshop and find out what kind of market there might be for antique gems. I have a feeling that we'll get some accurate answers if we go to a seedy place. They'll probably take into account the likelihood that the jewels would be stolen."

"How about that place on Central that's always in the news? The owner's been arrested several times."

"Perfect."

As JD drove through the quiet streets, Mari felt a primal desire to soothe all the worry and tension from his face. He was trying so hard to keep them all safe! They needed each other in every way imaginable, and yet theirs was nothing more than an impossible attraction that fate had chosen to taunt them with. He deserved far more than what someone like her, scarred by a painful past, would ever be able to give him.

JD pulled into the parking lot of the hockshop twenty minutes later. "This place is the pits," JD commented. "I don't like the looks of those two guys hanging around the door, either."

"They're punks but I doubt they'd make trouble here. There's too much traffic passing by, don't you think?"

"I don't know. Guys like this are unpredictable. That's what makes them dangerous." JD paused thoughtfully. "I'll tell you what we'll do. I'll go in alone, take a look at some jewelry, then ask a few questions. If he doesn't know, I'll leave. If he does, I'll keep him talking and say I'm buying a gift for you."

"You want Amy and me to stay here?"

"Just keep the car locked. I'll be in and out before you know it."

Mari didn't like it at all, but concern for Amy overrode her instinct to insist on going with him. No way was she leaving Amy alone here or taking her out of the vehicle. "Maybe we should come back during the day."

"No, we'd stand out too much then. It would be even more risky. Hang tight. I'll be right back."

Mari watched him go inside and through the barred glass window, saw him walking around. After speaking to a man behind the counter, he left the shop. Suddenly, one of the men who'd been standing by the entrance came up behind him, holding what looked like a knife.

Without looking at them, JD switched directions, heading to the alley behind the building. Mari felt her heart leap to her throat. She had to do something! They were about to rob him, mug him, or worse. She switched to the driver's side and glanced down, intending to drive right at them and break up whatever was going on. It was only then she noticed that, out of habit, JD had taken the keys with him.

She glanced back at Amy, wanting to stay with her but knowing she had to get help. A second later, a flicker of lights caught her eye and she realized the store owner had closed for the night. There was no time to lose.

"Stay here," Mari signed, threw open her door and locked it shut. She went to the shop's entrance and banged on the window. The owner, probably immune to irate customers, maybe even frantic ones, ignored her. She glanced around. Nothing. No weapons. Then she heard the grunts and thuds of a fight in the alley and knew she had to act now.

The only weapon available, if it could be called that, was a large lidless trash can. She pushed it onto its side. Rolling it in front of her, she ran around the corner. JD was fighting the two men less than a dozen feet away from her. One had pinned his arms, but the kick he gave to the other sent the man reeling backward with a curse.

Pushing the trash can as fast as she could, she aimed it straight at the man holding JD. The loud clatter of whatever was still inside the can caught their attention. As JD's adversary tried to swing him around to face the can, JD shoved his elbow into the man's midsection. Spinning around, JD chopped down hard on the guy's neck, sending him sprawling to the ground.

As the second man scrambled to his feet, Amy suddenly came into sight from the other side of the building. Swinging a jack handle, she whacked the man right on his knee. The man collapsed, falling onto the asphalt with an ear-shattering howl.

JD turned to face the man who'd pinned his arms before he could get to Amy. Seeing the little girl there gave Mari energy and strength she hadn't known she possessed. As the one with the injured knee tried to rise to his feet, Mari raced forward. Before he could get anywhere near Amy, who was standing there with the jack cocked like a baseball bat, Mari landed a right cross directly on his nose that sent him flat on his back.

A second later, JD was at her side. As the hood reached for Mari, JD kicked him hard below the belt. The thug curled up like a coiled spring. Lifting Amy into his arms, JD raced with Mari back to the truck.

They were underway in ten seconds flat. "Are you okay?" JD gasped, trying to catch his breath.

Amy's eyes sparkled and danced in the half-light of nighttime traffic. "We won!" she said.

Mari glowered at JD. "If you *ever* leave us behind again, I'm going to personally break all your fingers." She looked down, opening and closing her hand experimentally. It felt as if she'd struck a wall.

"I'll be sure to remember that," JD replied but winced as he tried to smile. "You've got a mean right cross, Knuckles."

Chapter Nine

JD tucked Amy in that night while Mari cleaned up. The awestruck look in the little girl's face worried him more than he'd ever dreamed possible. Oh, sure, he was human, and terribly flattered that she was seeing him as some kind of superhero who battled crooks, but her reaction also made him nervous. He was an ordinary man with as many flaws as the next guy. He didn't want her to find him out and then see that adoring look turn to disappointment.

Amy seemed to fall asleep the instant her head hit the pillow. He wouldn't be so lucky. His ribs hurt where one of the punks had managed to punch him. But at least the other two guys were in far worse shape. That soothed some of his pride. Having a little girl and a woman come to his aid hadn't exactly boosted his self-image.

He'd never forget the sight of Amy swinging the jack like a bat. Their help had come in handy, he had to admit. Still, he wished they hadn't interfered. They could have been killed. He'd have to have a stern talk with Mari. Then again, maybe not. She'd probably kick him where it would hurt most for taking the keys. He'd deserve it, too.

Mari joined him in the living room a short time later and helped him remove some of the dustcovers from the furniture. "Some evening we've had," she muttered. "A nice and humble 'thank you, Mari, for saving my butt' would be good to hear about now." She dropped down onto the couch.

JD joined her, stretching his legs out in front of him. "You should have stayed in the Bronco. I could have handled those two."

"And got a few broken parts in the process."

He glanced down at her hand. "Speaking of broken parts..."

Mari flexed her fingers. "I'll be sore but that's about it." She rubbed her eyes then took a deep breath. "I'm going to hit the sack. I've had it."

Mari looked exhausted. Sitting there in comfortable-looking wool socks that had been darned at the toe, she looked more vulnerable than she'd ever seemed before. He cupped the side of her head with one hand and gently turned her until she faced him. "Thanks for coming to help me," he said gently. "Not that I needed it."

Mari smiled. "Right. You always have everything under control." She leaned into his hand, enjoying the warmth. The next second, as if aware of her momentary lapse, she moved away and stood.

JD watched her walk down the hall. "Pleasant dreams, Knuckles," he said softly but loud enough for her to hear.

She stopped and turned around. A tiny smile played on the corners of her mouth. Then, wordlessly, she continued down the hall into the bedroom and closed the door.

"You're quite a lady," he said at last and headed slowly toward his own room.

MARI'S BEDROOM WAS STILL enveloped in darkness when she heard an odd rattling sound somewhere outside. Tossing the covers back, she went to the window and peered out through the blinds. An old truck was pulling into the driveway.

Pulling on her jeans and a sweater, she ran out into the hall. Hearing her call, JD came out of the bathroom wearing only jeans. Stripped to the waist, his lean body was classically proportioned like that of a Greek statue, well developed but not overly muscular. An intense familiar heat blasted through her.

"Didn't your mother tell you it's impolite to stare?" he teased.

"I wasn't..." she started, then shook her head. "We've got problems."

"You mean the truck?" JD shook his head. "Nothing to worry about. I know who it is. He's delivering the portable toilets for the crew. He'll be gone in a few minutes." JD checked his watch and added, "And so will we, long ahead of my crew."

"Good. By the way, after we stop for breakfast someplace, I want to make a few purchases. I've got a plan."

"Fine, but cash may be a problem, and using a credit card is out," he warned.

"I brought money with me when we left my house. I had emergency funds in my freezer. It's a habit I picked up a long time ago. Banking hours always seemed to conflict with my work schedule and teller machines are a pain. I always forget to enter withdrawals in my checkbook."

"Okay. We'll get ready to go, then you can fill me in on the road."

As JD turned and walked away, Mari couldn't resist a last look. The change in direction as he went down the hall only improved the view.

Twenty minutes later, they left the house and made their way to the Bronco. Amy carried her beloved teddy bear and Advent calendar, still refusing to be parted from either.

Afraid to stop at anything other than a drive-up window, they settled for a breakfast burrito from a nearby Taco Barn. Amy insisted on a separate children's order of *biscochitos*, or anise cookies, for her stuffed toy, as well.

Eating as he drove, JD glanced at Mari. "Where to?"

"We're going to have a talk with Father Aragon. I need to find out more about the statue and I'm really worried about the Toys for Tykes drive. Without Elizabeth or me pushing it now, I'm afraid there won't be enough donations. I can't stand the thought that there might be a lot of kids in the parish who won't get anything at all at the party Christmas Day. They'll all go there, their hopes sky-high, sit squirming through mass, then some may end up in tears when there are not enough presents to go around."

"Father Aragon has met you. You're going to be putting him in an awkward position. He may feel obligated to turn us in."

"He won't see me. You're going to be the one talking to him. He's never met you, and I've got a plan to keep you from looking like the picture in the paper. I want you to stop at the drugstore. You're going to buy yourself a pair of those inexpensive reading glasses they sell there, just some real weak ones. You probably won't be able to see very well with them on, but they'll alter your appearance somewhat. Your two-day beard will also help. And get some talcum powder. I want to lighten your hair."

"It's still quite a risk. What do you hope to find out?"

"I want you to ask about the jewels. Maybe some of them have flaws or something unique to help identify them. We also need to know if there's anyone who's shown a non-spiritual interest in the Madonna figure lately."

"I want to help," Amy signed.

"All right," Mari answered. "You can come with me and help me keep a watch out for anyone who recognizes us."

They gathered the few things they needed at a large discount drugstore then made the drive to the small mountain community just north of Santa Fe, off Highway 285.

As they drew near, Mari glanced back again at Amy, who hadn't attempted to communicate with them during the entire hour-and-a-half journey. "Are you okay?" she asked, turning around so that Amy could see her.

Amy looked at the Advent calendar on her lap. There were still three more doors to open. The latest door showed Christmas bells adorned with holly. "Christmas," she signed, making an arc and then shaping her right hand to form the letter *C*. "It's almost here."

Mari studied Amy's expression and knew that presents were the furthest thing from the little girl's mind. Amy was worried about her mom and the promise JD had made was the only thing she had to hold on to. Mari forced a reassuring smile. "Yes, Christmas will be here before you know it."

As Mari shifted in her seat, she caught a glimpse of JD's face. Deep-set lines framed his eyes, which had narrowed in response to a pain far deeper than any physical blow could ever be. Her heart ached for him. She knew that the promise he'd made to Amy would continue to weigh heavily on him. They all needed a Christmas miracle badly.

It certainly looked like Christmas outside. The high mountain valleys held snow on their north sides and in the shadows of trees and rocks, despite the unseasonably warm weather. Old corrugated metal-roofed farmhouses and twenty-year-old pickups told Mari of the hard-working farmers and ranchers who eked out a living in this beautiful but impoverished region of New Mexico.

Mari knew it was a combination of strong family ties and faith that sustained many of the old Spanish-speaking families in the area—and the Madonna was a strong part of that faith. They had to make some progress soon on discovering who had tampered with the religious treasure starting here today. This community couldn't afford anything that jeopardized its only symbol of hope.

They approached the simple, mission-style church minutes later. Like most of the older structures, it was constructed of thick adobe walls and roofed in the traditional corrugated metal. Twin bell towers stood above the entrance, the right one still unfinished after a hundred years. The story behind the towers reached deep into New Mexico's history. Churches were not taxed by the Spanish until the work was completed. So, being practical, the church fathers had built two bell towers—one fully working and another that would remain unfinished in perpetuity.

"I can't go in with you," Mari said. "But you know the information we need. Tell him you're a free-lancer for the newspaper and you want to do a story about the Madonna."

"Where will you be?"

"I'm going to walk around the grounds. There's a dozen or so parishioners involved in the toy drive. Some of them, I understand, meet behind the rectory in a small portable building. They clean and repair donated clothes that are going to be distributed to needy families. If I can manage it, I'm going to talk to some of those women and find out how the toy drive is going." Before they reached the church parking area, Mari asked JD to pull over to the side of the narrow road and let her and Amy out. "Father's office is in the rectory behind the church, second door down. I'll be around the back of the rectory when you're done."

Amy glanced at her uncle, then back at Mari, and signed. Mari laughed. "No, I promise."

"What did she say?" JD asked as Amy left the vehicle and walked across the road toward an empty basketball court.

"She said I shouldn't let you fight. You're not very good at it."

JD's mouth fell open, then he clamped it shut again.

Mari laughed. "You do a great goldfish imitation. Now we'll see how good you are passing yourself off as a reporter."

A moment later, Mari stopped in the shadows of some pines and watched JD go inside the rectory. She then turned to Amy. "Stay here. If we go up together we may be recognized."

Amy nodded and hung back as Mari went forward.

Mari could hear sewing machines and women's laughter coming from the tiny building behind the church. Unlike Liz, she'd never met any of the women from the auxiliary. Her meetings had invariably been with Father Aragon, usually to confer about Spanish-speaking tutors assigned to his area.

As the door opened, two preschool children hurried down the wooden steps. Mari watched them for a moment. Both girls were around five years old and filled with energy. A young woman came out a moment later and yelled to both girls, cautioning them to keep their clothes clean. Holding a small dress in her hand, she sat down on the steps and continued stitching a hem.

"Mommy, I want a new doll for Christmas!" the smallest one asked. "Couldn't you tell Padre Aragon? He can ask the Madonna."

"You'll get what you get and be grateful," the woman said firmly. Glancing up, she saw Mari and smiled. "Hi. Can I help you?"

Mari shook her head. "No, I'm just wandering around while my husband works. He's doing a story for the *Albuquerque Voice* about the Madonna and the toy drive."

The woman smiled. "Good! With one of our sponsors in the hospital and the other wanted by the police, we're in trouble. Toy donations are way down. The scandal is threatening to ruin Christmas for the kids. The Madonna has her work cut out for her this year if our kids are to have the Christmas they've been wishing for."

Mari looked at the two little girls playing tag and her chest constricted. "Christmas isn't here yet. Don't give up hope," she said.

The young mother smiled. "That's what the padre says, too. But it's hard, you know, particularly when your own kids are among those who may be disappointed." She shrugged. "Maybe the article your husband is writing will help."

"Everything will work out. I'm sure of it," Mari said staunchly.

Mari walked to the Bronco slowly. Fate was asking a great deal of her. Being with Amy and JD reminded her of the very things she longed for and could never have. Now, on top of that, she felt the weight of all those hopes the kids from this poor parish held for Christmas. The happiness this season would bring them might have to last them all year long.

Somehow she had to make sure that the drive she and Elizabeth had spearheaded wouldn't fall by the wayside. Their promise that the Madonna would be protected from harm had been compromised, and that was failure enough. The thought of so many expectant children walking away empty-handed at Christmas knifed through her. One way or another, she had to make sure that that didn't happen.

She returned to the vehicle and found Amy already inside, clutching her bear. "Is something wrong, honey?"

Amy shrugged. "I could see what the lady was telling you. They think Mommy is to blame."

"They're really not sure what to think, honey. Really." Mari's gaze fastened on the bear's colorful bow and sorrow overcame her. Christmas had now become a responsibility that filled her with a feeling of dread.

Her gaze fell onto the car phone. Impulsively she picked it up. It was time to contact Howard Peters. He was in charge of the trust. The kids would have their toys this season, no matter what. After a few minutes' wait, she heard a familiar voice. She stated her request succinctly.

Peters balked. "Be reasonable, Ms. Sanchez. First you need to come in and talk to the police. I know you're not guilty of anything but there are other factors involved...."

"I haven't been officially charged with anything, and the trust is there for me. You *will* do this, Mr. Peters, or I'll personally see to it that you're replaced."

"If a large amount is withdrawn from the trust—"

"Make it the maximum you feel will not cause the authorities any undue alarm. All I'm trying to do is offset the decrease in toy donations. I want toys purchased in time for the Christmas Day party. I don't want any child to go away empty-handed."

"All right. I'll take care of it. But I certainly hope you intend to be back before it's time to distribute them."

"So do I, Mr. Peters. So do I."

Mari placed the phone back and stared at the chapel ahead, lost in thought. She'd done what she could for the children. As her gaze drifted back to Amy, her throat tightened. Despite all her efforts, she still hadn't helped the one child who was counting on her the most.

JD STOOD ALONE in the large alcove. A statue of Jesus and one of the Virgin stood on either side of the door. This was a lousy place for subterfuge.

Father Aragon, a thin, gray-haired man in his fifties, appeared a moment later. "My housekeeper said you wanted to see me."

"Hello, Father. I'm John Harris. I free-lance for the *Albuquerque Voice*. I wanted to do a piece on the Madonna for the paper and maybe help you publicize your toy drive."

"We can use the help," the priest said, ushering JD into his tiny office. "Our two strongest supporters are now at the center of a scandal that has shifted the focus away from the needs of the children."

JD started by asking about the miracles attributed to the Madonna, hoping to set the priest at ease. Once Father Aragon seemed more relaxed, JD moved on to the tougher, more specific questions.

"What do you estimate the worth of the Madonna to be? Aside from its religious and historical significance, the jewels on the dress must be worth quite a bit."

"You're going to ask me why we don't sell her to raise the funds needed here," the priest answered wearily, as if he'd heard the question a million times before. "The Virgin, you see, belongs to the entire community. She's a part of all that we are, and more importantly, of what we will someday become. The jewels are not really the most important part of the Madonna at all."

"Are you saying that the pieces are simply costume jewelry?"

"Not at all. They're quite genuine. The ruby, for instance, is unique because of its purity. But no one would steal those jewels. They wouldn't dare," the priest said staunchly. "That's sacrilege, and whoever did that would incur the wrath of God."

"Not everyone is Catholic," JD countered gently.

"True, but there's still a great deal of superstition about gifts for the church. It carries over even to nonbelievers. But I'm not overly complacent. When we heard about the thefts from the evidence room, I had our insurance adjuster check the Madonna. He assured me she was all right."

"Can you tell me more about the Madonna? For example, who sewed the original dress and who cut the jewels?"

"Over one hundred years ago now, the Santeiro family donated her to this church. Señora Santeiro was a wonderful seamstress, and Alvaro Santeiro had many businesses throughout the state. He handpicked each of the gems his wife placed on the Virgin's dress. Most of the gems came from collections once owned by prominent families from Mexico. But the pride of the collection he gathered was the ruby. At first, the parish believed that it was an Arizona ruby or a garnet. It was so big and brilliant that Santeiro never said any different.

"But one day his *señora* told the real story to the padre. Santeiro had used most of his wealth to find a cure for his dying child without success. Then he and his wife prayed to Our Lady and the child had a miraculous recovery. He decided to thank Our Lady by having a Madonna hand carved and fitting her in vestures worthy of the Queen of Heaven.

Every gem picked for the dress was nearly flawless in cut and purity. He sold most of his land to purchase the final ruby from a man who'd traveled here from Thailand.''

"Whatever made you agree to let such a treasure out of your parish?"

"The children," the priest said in a sad voice. "They need Our Lady's help. Last year was very tough on our farmers. The late freeze and the dry winter ruined the apples and apricots. Many orchards lost trees, as well. And the summer rains rotted much of our alfalfa. Our parishioners have had to struggle to meet even their most basic needs. There isn't anything left over for Christmas. This is a season of hope and we don't want to disappoint the children."

The priest's words touched JD deeply. He remembered so many childhood Christmases when there had been nothing to mark the holiday at his home, not even a tree. He'd tried hard back then to pretend he didn't care that other kids would be waking up to presents under the tree, to love and joy and some special reminder of the season.

"Thanks for your time, Father," JD said, standing and walking to the door. "I'll do whatever I can to help you make sure the kids have pleasant memories this Christmas. You have my word."

When JD returned to the Bronco, he saw that Mari and Amy were already inside. Amy was lying down in the back, looking at the little open doors on her Advent calendar.

JD quickly slipped behind the wheel. As they got underway, he told Mari what he'd learned. "I'm sure now that those jewels would never go to an ordinary fence. My guess is they'll be shipped out of state, maybe even out of the country, if that hasn't already happened."

"We're no closer to protecting the Madonna than before, or even proving our own innocence. But I refuse to think that the Madonna will allow us all to suffer for a crime we didn't commit."

"Hold onto that thought," JD said softly. "We can't afford to get discouraged or lose hope."

They rode back in silence, unwilling to voice any more troubled thoughts. As they reached the outskirts of the city, JD picked up the car phone. He called Bruce Campbell and arranged a meeting.

Mari watched him, listening. "Are you sure that was a good idea?" she asked after he'd set the phone down.

"What choice do we have? We need his help. So far I've been relying on my memory to choose safe houses for us. He's the only one in a position to bring us the addresses of projects we've been asked to submit bids on that are still pending. I know some of those are vacant houses we could use as hideouts."

Mari shrugged. "I wish you didn't trust people so casually."

"I don't trust people easily at all, Mari," JD answered somberly. "I had to become tough and streetwise very early in life. I also learned to be an excellent judge of character, a skill I've come to rely on. Bruce Campbell is a good man. He's loyal to his friends no matter what comes down. If you're reluctant to believe that, then look at it in a practical way. Bruce needs me to make the company work. He's great with the men but he's a lousy businessman and he knows it."

"He may have learned more than you think and now believes he's ready to solo. What better way to get his big chance than to cut you out of the picture?"

"Hold on a minute, Mari. I won't listen to you talk that way about Bruce. He doesn't deserve it. Besides being my partner, he's my friend, and I choose my friends very, very carefully. That's why I have so few."

JD's loyalty was unquestionable. But life had taught her to be wary. She'd trusted another, too, with all her heart. Yet her faith had only led her into betrayal and a broken heart.

She prayed for all of them now. They were being asked to trust and let go of the lessons of a lifetime of trials. Mari gazed at the giant Christmas star that adorned the roof of a community hall. Then again, maybe it was the spirit of Christmas asking to be received with an open heart.

Chapter Ten

They drove through Albuquerque at dusk admiring the Christmas lights as they were gradually switched on. On the way across town, JD stopped at a large shopping center. "I have to meet Bruce inside, but I don't think all of us should be seen together. Do you want to go inside the mall, or wait for me out here?"

"It's too cold to wait in the car," Mari said. "We'll go in a separate entrance and walk around a bit."

"Meet me back here in twenty minutes, okay?"

"Sure." Mari glanced at Amy and spoke slowly. "No signing inside the mall. It'll give us away."

"I'll keep my earphones on. No one will talk to me then. And I won't talk, either. I know I don't sound like hearing kids," Amy said, hugging her bear tightly.

Mari's heart felt leaden, knowing how that one fact always tugged at the little girl's heart. "Someday maybe you will," Mari said, facing Amy. "But if you want that, you'll have to work at it."

"I want to be like you, help deaf kids," Amy said.

The words were like arrows. They were what she'd always hoped to hear from her own child, a little girl who would have been about Amy's age now, if fate had been kinder. Mari brushed the thought away, concentrating on the present. "Let's go," Mari said, holding out her hand.

"You and I are going shopping." Amy's eyes were bright as she entered the mall. A tall Christmas tree near the entrance sparkled with tinsel, which reflected hundreds of multicolored lights like sunlight on a windswept pond. As Mari saw the look on Amy's face, she wished she could have given the child her own Christmas tree and a safe haven in which to enjoy it.

As they walked down the mall hand in hand, Amy stared with fascination at the window displays filled with pine boughs, holly and figures of elves, but she was careful never to sign or speak. They stopped by a shop whose display incorporated white teddy bears like the one Amy held, only with different bows.

"Mine's prettier," Amy mouthed.

Mari smiled. Up ahead, children chattered happily as they waited in line to see Santa Claus. Amy's wide eyes revealed a quiet longing. Noting it, Mari began to have serious doubts about her decision to come inside the mall. Suddenly her gaze fell onto a jewelry store's window display. A sign announced an ongoing sale of estate jewelry.

What a perfect place for the stones from the Madonna to show up! Cursing herself for not having thought of the possibility before, she hurried Amy toward the store. An elderly man came over to the counter to help them. He glanced at Amy, then shifted his gaze to Mari. "May I help you?"

Mari breathed a sigh of relief. The only emotion that had crossed the man's face had been one of vague annoyance. He obviously didn't like kids in his store. "Yes, I was hoping you could show me your selection of estate jewelry. I'm also particularly interested in gems that have an unusual shape or cut. I'd like something that looks really old-fashioned."

The man shook his head. "What I've got here is all very modern. The older stones just don't have the sparkle or refractive quality of the cuts we use today. You really don't want an old stone. Of course, you could recut them, but then you end up losing some of their weight and that lessens the value.''

"I'm not interested in anything new," Mari insisted pleasantly. "Do you know of anyone who specializes in antique jewelry, or stones that might have historical value?"

The man thought for a moment. "In this area, if you find them at all, it'll be a fluke. There's more of a market for such things back east."

Mari glanced at Amy and had to bite her lip to keep from smiling. Amy was pretending to move around to the beat of the music. She reached out and tapped Amy on the shoulder. "Time to go." She mouthed the words, speaking loudly.

"Kids." The shop owner shook his head. "Those earphones will damage her hearing for sure, ma'am."

Mari led the way back to their vehicle. "You did a good job," she signed as they reached the parking lot.

"But we still haven't proved Mommy didn't do anything wrong."

"We'll just have to work at it harder, that's all."

JD, already waiting inside, leaned over to open the door. "How did it go, ladies?"

Amy smiled. "We played detective."

Seeing the surprised look on JD's face, Mari quickly explained. "At least we know the stones haven't been put on one legitimate market. I worried they might be, since the crooks have taken a lot of care to hide the crime."

JD looked somber. "Those jewels are long gone, I'm sure of it. The best we can hope to do is catch the thieves and then track down what they stole." He glanced at her, then back at the road. "I don't want to discourage you, but I honestly think that's the reality."

Mari said nothing. Things just kept getting worse and worse. Sooner or later their luck would have to change.

They returned to the safe house. It was empty, the workers gone. In the kitchen, Mari opened cans of soup to heat, which she hoped would offset the chill they felt in the un-heated house.

JD came to stand beside her. "I'll be back in a minute. I'm going to the car to phone Pat. She can call the hospital. Maybe she can get an update on Elizabeth's condition."

"Good idea."

He returned a few minutes later. "She'd called a few minutes ago. There's been no change." JD approached the counter. "I'll take care of this. I'm good at warming up canned stuff."

"Wow, a chef!" Mari teased. "In that case, I'm going to take my wig off and see if I've still got any of my own hair left."

Mari went to her bedroom, changed quickly and walked out to join the others. Her hair was fastened in a loose po-nytail at the base of her neck and she felt one hundred per-cent better. As she passed the living room, she saw Amy fast asleep on the couch.

JD came out of the kitchen, then stood looking down at his niece, a mug of steaming soup in his hand. "She looks so peaceful. Should I wake her?"

"She's got to eat something," Mari said, gently awaken-ing the child.

Amy blinked, then smiled. "I'm not hungry. I want to sleep."

"Eat a little, then go to bed," Mari insisted.

Amy took a few sips of the steaming soup as JD and Mari joined her. They sat on the huge, overstuffed couch that dominated the room, all too tired to do much talking.

Finally, JD placed his mug down. "What else is there to eat? I have lots of room for dessert."

"How about a sandwich instead?" Mari suggested.

"Nah. How about a candy bar?"

Mari shook her head. "I didn't buy junk food. I figured that with all the takeout, it was the last thing we needed."

Amy watched him, then smiled. "I saved a surprise for you." Reaching into the pocket of her jeans, she extracted something meticulously wrapped in two paper napkins. "My last two cookies from this morning. For you two." She unwrapped the bundle carefully. Working slowly, she divided the crumbs the cookies had long since become into two equal parts. Sampling a tiny crumb, she smiled. "Mmm. Still good."

"Uh, I don't—" JD began.

Mari cleared her throat and shook her head imperceptibly. If JD turned Amy's gift down, she'd throttle him. Anise cookies were Amy's all-time favorite Christmas treat, even more than candy canes. It must have taken all her willpower to save these for them. She remembered a night at Elizabeth's house when Amy had wolfed down over a dozen of the tiny cookies in one sitting. "Thanks, Amy," Mari said, accepting.

Amy smiled, satisfied, then stood up and stretched. "Good night," she said, giving JD and Mari a hug.

As she walked down the hall, JD stared at the crumbs still in his hand. "Amazing taste these acquired. I wonder what else she had stashed in her pocket keeping them company all day."

"Do you really want to know?"

"No, probably not. Why did you glare at me when I started to refuse? It was no big deal."

"You're wrong." Mari paused, trying to figure out a way to explain. "You see, these are Amy's favorite cookies, so this is her way of taking care of us, just as we're taking care of her. She can't give us anything else. She has few enough possessions at the moment as it is. This was her way of showing us that she cares."

JD nodded, his gaze growing distant. "I know that feeling, wanting to give something, yet having nothing. I felt that way with Elizabeth and Pat many times when we were kids."

"What was it like for you when you were growing up?" Mari asked quietly. She wanted to know him, to see past all the barriers that held her at bay.

"My dad worked hard every day of his life but he barely made enough for us to live on. Mom wanted to help, but Dad insisted she stay home with us. Then, when I was ten, he died. Mom had never worked outside the home before. She had no skills. She ended up working as a waitress, sometimes a housekeeper. Then she got sick. We went from having very little, to having nothing. It was the charity of local groups that helped us keep body and soul together. But even that wasn't always enough. My sisters and I learned what it was like to go hungry in those days."

JD stood and walked to the empty fireplace. "We learned never to count on anything. We were kicked out of so many places, I lost count. We were always late with the rent and when we got too far behind, they'd run us out. We even lived in the car for a while. But eventually we'd find someplace else and the cycle would start all over again."

His expression grew taut as memories blew across the landscape of his mind. "The worst part was dealing with the thinly veiled contempt of others who were better off. The name Hawken was bandied about like a four-letter word, or one that left a bad taste in your mouth. We became examples of what not to be, what not to do. I learned back then that accepting charity always comes at a price."

Pride was the key to everything JD was and had become. Mari had already suspected that for some time. "And now? Are you happy with what you are and what you have?"

"My company has allowed me to earn the respect of this community. I've worked darned hard for that. But, you know, inside I still feel like the kid who has to try harder than anyone else. And now there's this mess." JD gestured to the newspaper. "It's a constant reminder of everything I tried to leave behind—having to move from one place to another, people speaking about us as if we were criminals.

But nothing is as hard as seeing this through Amy's eyes. I don't want that little girl to grow up haunted by loneliness and disgrace.''

"That won't happen," Mari said, placing her hand over his. "As long as you're there for her, she'll be just fine."

"Will she?" JD shook his head. "That little girl is seeing me in a light that makes me very uncomfortable. I'm no knight on a white horse. If she believes otherwise, she's heading for a big fall." He rubbed his neck with one hand. "But it's more than that. I'm afraid of letting her get too attached to me. I can't always be around for her, Mari, even if the unthinkable were to happen to Elizabeth. Don't get me wrong. I'll always provide financially for Amy. She's blood. But to let her get too attached to me would be cruel in the long run.''

"The most cruel thing you could do now is deny her your attention and warmth," Mari said firmly.

"You're wrong. Have you taken a close look at what *you're* offering her? Your friendship is only temporary. Sooner or later you'll go back to your own busy life and where will that leave Amy, particularly if something happens to Elizabeth? I've seen the way she looks at you. Amy depends on you a lot.''

"I promised Elizabeth that I would take care of Amy. As her godmother, I'd be very willing to keep Amy for as long as it takes Elizabeth to recover. I love Amy, JD. I'm praying Elizabeth will be fine. But if, God forbid, something did happen, I won't hesitate for a second to take Amy in permanently.''

"It would never come to that," he said, turning around. His eyes flashed angrily. "I'm responsible for Amy. I won't let someone outside the family come in and take over."

Mari blinked, taken aback by his response. "I'm *not* an outsider and you know it. That's your pride talking."

"Pride? Lady, what do you know about it? Pride gave me the drive to achieve. Without that, I wouldn't have been able to do anything to help my family now."

"I'm not putting down—" Hearing footsteps, Mari turned around.

Amy stared at her, and then at JD. "I'm thirsty," she said, looking at them curiously. "Why are you angry?"

"We weren't angry, honey," Mari signed. "Just having a difference of opinion."

Amy studied their expressions. "You were arguing. I can tell. About me?"

Mari glanced at JD. "You answer her."

Amy looked at JD, big tears rolling down her cheeks. "You wish I wasn't here, don't you?" she asked rhetorically. "I'm deaf and too much trouble."

JD looked as if someone had knocked the wind out of him. "No, honey." He crouched in front of his niece and tried to sign the phrase "I love you."

Mari smiled. He was trying, but by opening his tension-filled hands halfway, he was actually saying something very different. "Close your hands," she said, glancing at Amy, who laughed despite her tears. "That's not the sign for love. That's the sign for bear. As in the animal."

"Bear? No, I was trying to tell her—"

"I bear you, too," Amy signed back laughing, and hugged him.

Mari watched JD walk with Amy back to the bedroom to tuck her in. It would have been easier if she hadn't been able to see past the facade of toughness he projected. Yet she knew him only too well. Behind his granite strength was a man who had been hurt deeply and now wanted to protect himself and those he loved from pain. Her own aching heart yearned to reach out to him, certain that together they could find something worthy of a lifetime.

But no, that was only a daydream. Some things could never be changed and wishing wasn't enough. Numbly, she walked to her own bedroom and shut the door. She wanted no more time alone with JD tonight. Her own instincts for survival assured her that she was heading straight for heartbreak.

MARI WOKE UP EARLY the following day. It was still dark, but some of the things JD had said about her relationship with Amy had made it impossible for her to sleep peacefully. Maybe he had a point, but right now Amy needed them both. Mari just didn't know how she could possibly draw away from Amy at a time like this.

JD, however, was another matter. Being forced to rely on each other was bringing them closer no matter how hard she tried to fight it. Mari had accepted her life, knowing she'd spend it alone, putting all her passion into her work. But these feelings for JD that had come unbidden reminded her how much she'd given up. It was slowly tearing her into pieces inside.

Mari dressed and left the bedroom. Not expecting to see anyone else out of bed yet, she jumped when she almost ran into JD coming out of the kitchen. "What are you doing up?"

"Couldn't sleep, so I decided to put my time to good use. Bruce should be here shortly."

"Has he been able to find out anything?"

"He's been tracking down a few items for us, some things to help us investigate."

"What kind of things?" Mari asked curiously. Before JD could answer, they heard a car coming up the drive. Mari pulled back the curtains and peered outside. Daylight was breaking and she could make out an off-white, medium-sized sedan. "That doesn't look like the kind of thing Bruce would drive. It's too...too..." She fumbled for the right word.

JD peered out. "Ordinary," he finished for her. "You better wake Amy. We have to leave."

With a quick nod, she hurried toward the back of the house. She was halfway down the hall when JD called out to her. "It's okay. It's Bruce driving. I just caught a glimpse of his face." Moments later, JD opened the door to let Bruce inside. "Where did you get the wheels? Don't tell me you finally passed adolescence!" JD baited.

"I was trying to do you a favor. I figured I'd pick up my nice little four-wheel-drive and leave you with this one. It suits your personality more—conservative, sorta blah, the kind that no one would give a second look to."

Mari stood behind them and found herself envying the easy banter between the two men. Her best friend was in the hospital fighting for her life, and without her, Mari felt more alone than she had in a long time.

JD gestured to the couch. "Fill me in."

"Well, let me start with the car. It's rented, but I equipped it with one of my car phones. You can get hold of me anytime you want." Bruce reached into the paper sack and placed a small buttonlike device, a tube of instant glue and something resembling a tape recorder on the coffee table. "Microphone and receiver. This is the most powerful unit I could get in a hurry. Its radius is listed as a quarter mile, but I figure that's without obstructions in the way." He pulled the last item from the bag. "And here's the doll." It was a popular, soft plastic figure of an infant wearing a flannel sleeping gown.

Mari nodded, their plan suddenly becoming clear. "Now I get it. You're going to bug the doll and get it inside the evidence room somehow."

JD rubbed his jaw pensively. "All we've got to figure out is how to do it without getting someone else involved or risking getting caught."

Bruce shrugged. "I'm already involved. Don't give it another thought. I'll drop it in, along with several other toys at the same time. Are you sure it'll find its way into the evidence room?"

Mari nodded. "That's the procedure. All the donated toys are taken there at the end of each day."

"Then what?" Bruce asked. "How are you going to monitor it?"

"I haven't worked out the details yet," JD answered. "But there aren't that many options. We'll have to find a place for the receiver and leave the tape recorder going all the time."

"A listening post?" Bruce nodded. "Yeah, I suppose that's the only thing that makes sense. But you're really going to have to be careful. You'll be playing in the police's backyard, so to speak."

"Don't I know it?" JD muttered.

Amy bounded into the living room before they could discuss specifics. As her gaze settled on Bruce, she suddenly stopped and looked at Mari.

"It's okay," Mari signed. "He's a friend."

Approaching shyly, Amy glanced at the doll and then the tape recorder. "Are you going to tape what the doll says? I don't think Baby Sarah talks."

Mari laughed. "We're going to tape what Baby Sarah hears. We'll put a microphone inside the doll."

"You're going to put the doll with the other toys, huh. Where Mommy works—the evidence room."

Mari and JD exchanged glances. This was the first time Amy had mentioned anything pertaining to Liz's work. Mari sat on the couch with Amy. "Did your mom ever say anything to you about what was going on in the evidence room?"

"The day she was hurt, Mom was worried about the statue," Amy answered. "But she didn't say why. She said you and Uncle JD would help her figure out what to do."

"Honey, I want you to think back. You have to tell us what you remember. When your mommy went to get the mail, what happened?"

Tears appeared in Amy's eyes. "The pickup came very fast and hit Mommy. It knocked her down. Then the bad person got out. I was afraid, so I hid with Teddy Fuzzball."

Mari smiled at the name the toy had been given.

"Then I felt cold air," Amy continued. "I knew he'd opened the door. At first I was afraid to peek out, then I was afraid not to. When I did, I saw him running away. His leg was stiff and looked hurt."

"Did you ever see his face?"

Amy shook her head and tried to wipe the tears from her eyes with the back of her hand. "Is that bad?"

"No, honey, everything's okay." Mari held her tightly for several moments, then drew away slightly so Amy could read her lips. "Let's go into the kitchen. I'll get you some cereal."

As Mari left, JD turned to Bruce. "Do something else for me. Use the company card and buy some toys for the Toys for Tykes drive. I think this mess is making them come out short."

"No problem."

Mari returned a moment later. She faced both men squarely. "They've made that child a target, and she can't even identify the scum who ran Liz down."

"But *they* don't know that," Bruce countered softly. "She's a loose end, like you two have become."

"We're in danger from the police *and* the crooks," JD observed wryly.

"Who may be one and the same," Mari reminded him. "I think it's time we started an all-out offensive. But first we're going to need a few more things." Mari looked at Bruce. "You still in?"

"You bet."

IT WAS ALMOST TWO in the afternoon when Mari and JD gathered up everything in readiness for their most dangerous move so far. The tape recorder had been planted in a nearby parking garage. Bruce had brought them the video camera and the baby carriage Mari had asked for and then left to meet one of the work crews.

As JD drove across town, Mari shifted in her seat to face Amy. "Do you understand what we're going to do?" Mari asked the girl.

Amy nodded. "We're a family. I'm the big sister and we're all going for a walk."

"Some walk," JD muttered. "A video camera hidden inside a carriage, filming through a hole in its side."

"We can view the tape later at our leisure, and maybe we'll be able to identify the chubby sheriff's deputy. Or it could be that Amy will see something or someone to jog her memory."

Mari smiled at Amy. "Between those earphones and that new hairstyle, even your mom wouldn't recognize you."

Mari shifted in her seat and stared ahead. Uneasiness crept through her the closer they got to the station. She didn't mind taking this risk, yet she wished that JD and Amy could have stayed someplace safe. Every person she'd loved and cared about throughout her life had eventually left her or been taken away. If anything happened to either JD or Amy today, she wasn't sure she would be able to go on or how much strength she had left.

Amy pressed her hand against Mari's forearm. "Only us little kids are supposed to be scared," she mouthed.

Mari smiled and shrugged. "I'm okay."

JD parked the sedan two blocks down from the station. "We need to rely on each other now. The odds aren't hopeless."

Mari looked at him, then at Amy. They'd stand together, and together they'd find more strength than any one of them would ever have alone. That was their only edge, but it was a formidable one.

They left the car, unloaded the carriage from the trunk and began walking down the street, camera securely in position and ready. Mari pushed the baby carriage as JD fell into step beside her. Amy glanced at her and smiled, moving to the rhythm of music playing only in her mind.

The shift change at the station began moments later with the usual spurt of activity, and JD reached in to start the camera as if checking on the baby. Mari had to force herself to look away from the officers coming and going from the parking lot. She slowed down slightly, wanting to make sure the camera caught as many of them as possible.

JD casually looped his arm around her waist and she felt the electricity of that contact surge through her. She glanced at him, not wanting to be distracted, and yet finding an inexplicable security and thrill in the warmth of his touch.

Then she saw JD look at Amy. His expression changed from casual to tense. Mari followed his gaze. Amy's eyes were glued on a sheriff's deputy walking across the lot toward a pickup. Mari felt her skin prickle. He was too far away to tell for sure, but he could have been the deputy JD had seen at Elizabeth's house.

Amy whirled to face them, signing at lightning speed.

"No, don't." Mari shook her head and reached out, forcing Amy's hands back down. "He'll know who you are!" she mouthed.

Amy's face crumpled, but an instant later, JD took control of the carriage and maneuvered them all away toward an alley twenty yards ahead.

Mari glanced at Amy. Hurt and shame were reflected in her eyes. "Don't worry. We'll be okay," she assured her, but Amy wouldn't maintain eye contact with her.

JD hurried them into the alley, then took a final look back toward the street. "He saw us, but all he did was glance. I think he may have assumed that Amy was taking a swipe at a bee or other insect."

Mari could tell from his tone that he wasn't at all convinced.

"Sorry," Amy managed with a choked sob, tears spilling down her cheeks.

Mari hugged her, then pulled away slightly so Amy could see her. "It's okay. We all make mistakes."

"But that man. I know him. He was at your house."

"Mine?" Mari asked.

Amy nodded. "I was so scared before, I just remembered. Before you had to hide me because he had a gun, I saw him outside. A car light from the highway showed his face. I'm sure."

JD pulled the video camera from the baby carriage. "We're finally getting someplace! Let's take a look at this guy."

"What are you doing?" she asked.

"I'm going to rewind and play this back through the viewfinder. Let's see what we've got. If we have a close shot of him, we'll have the break we've been hoping for—an eyewitness report and a suspect we can watch."

As JD started to play back the tape, they heard the roar of an engine echoing in the narrow alley. A battered pickup was heading directly for Amy.

Chapter Eleven

JD shoved the camera into Mari's hands and scooped Amy up into his arms. Together they ran toward the other end of the alley as fast as they could go.

Mari, half a step behind, realized that they'd never make it in time. The truck was narrowing the distance too fast. Turning, she faced the pickup and hurled the video camera right at the windshield.

The explosion of cubed glass was lost against the roar of the engine, but the driver instinctively swerved, sideswiping the far wall in passing.

Taking advantage of this opportunity, JD reached for Mari's hand and pulled her toward the safety of a tumbleweed-filled vacant lot twenty feet from the alley. As they reached a sheltered thicket, they heard the truck's squealing tires as it sped out of the alley and down the street.

"We've lost him!" Mari gasped.

"Maybe, or he might come back," JD said, putting Amy down slowly.

"It's my fault," Amy said, sobbing wildly.

"No, honey, it isn't. You're caught in this just like we are," JD answered, his gaze darting up and down the alley in search of any further threat.

"Our camera and film are gone," Mari said quietly. "Right into the cab of his truck. But I had to do something to make him swerve."

"It worked. You bought us the few feet that probably saved our lives."

As their eyes met, Mari sensed the emotions that raged inside him. Fierce protectiveness and the fear of what might have been struggled just behind the calm expression he was trying to present for Amy's benefit. "Maybe we should report what happened. The police should be able to track down which of their officers has a smashed windshield on his truck."

"We certainly can't return to the station to file that report. They won't take us seriously. We've lost our evidence, and to them we're the bad guys." JD led them across the lot and then took the roundabout way back to the car. "Don't walk fast," he warned Amy. "You, too, Mari. Slow down. We don't want to attract attention."

Seeing the haunted look on Amy's face made Mari's heart break. She'd sworn to herself to let nothing happen to Amy and yet something very nearly had. She glanced at JD, who was watching their surroundings. His muscles were as taut as those of a commando in the midst of battle. His jaw clenched and unclenched, and he looked as if he wanted to break something, or someone, in half.

As they approached the car, Mari tried to brush aside the despair building within her. She wouldn't, couldn't let anything happen to either JD or Amy. Like it or not, they had become like a family to her. Through the trials they'd faced together and had yet to see through, a bond had been forged between them. JD hustled them into the car. "Let's get out of here."

"I've got a friend, Jennifer Anderson, who works for the morning paper," Mari said. "I'm going to write her a letter and tell her exactly what happened to us today. She's an investigative reporter and I can guarantee she'll look into it."

"Do you want to go back to the house now?"

Mari weighed their options. "No, not yet. Bruce must have made his Toys for Tykes donation by now. Let's check out our listening post and see if we can pick up anything from the microphone we put inside that doll." Mari turned in her seat, looked at Amy and explained. "Is that okay with you?"

Amy shrugged.

The little girl's response worried Mari more than she let on. If Amy retreated into her own world, the damage might be permanent. Mari couldn't allow that to happen. "Don't give up on us, Amy," she signed. "We need your help in this."

"I couldn't help Mommy and I can't help you," she said, speaking but not signing.

Mari worried that Amy had become afraid to sign, thinking it was bound to give them away. "You *are* helping your mommy and you're helping us, too, honey. You're the one who recognized the officer who'd been outside my house. That was a big help, probably the biggest break we've had so far. You're part of our team. We need each other, Amy. We have to look out for one another because no one else is going to do it for us. But it's more than that. I need you because I love you very much." She avoided looking at JD, knowing that was becoming true with him, too.

Amy looked deep into Mari's eyes, then glanced at JD and smiled. "Yes, you two *do* need me. I see things that you don't."

Mari studied Amy's peculiar little smile and the twinkle in the little girl's eye but Amy refused to elaborate.

JD PULLED INTO the parking garage where they had planted the tape recorder. After he retrieved the tape and put it in the cassette player in the car, he suggested that Amy and Mari take this opportunity to stretch their legs. "I don't think you two should sit in the car with me. Take Amy and maybe get some carryout. It's still warm outside. You can sit in the park next to the day-care center."

"I'm not sure that's a good idea...." Mari paused.

"Nothing's going to look more normal than you having a picnic meal with your little boy," he said.

And having the three of them sit in a parked car was not only pointless, but risky, Mari concluded. It was just unusual enough to be dangerously noticeable. "All right," she agreed as he pulled into a parking space. Mari gave JD one last look. "You know where we'll be if you need us."

Lost in thought, JD watched Mari walk away with Amy. Mari was beautiful, but it was her gentle nature and fierce protectiveness that attracted him most. It made her precious to him, and that was something that went far deeper than the hormone-driven attractions he'd felt in the past. He'd finally found a woman who could make his life truly worthwhile. Only she didn't particularly want him or anything he could offer her. The knowledge knifed at his gut but he forced it aside, concentrating on the sounds the tape had picked up.

MARI GAVE AMY a reassuring smile. "Have you eaten at any of the take-out places here?"

Amy nodded. "Mommy liked the Yellow Submarine Sandwich Shop."

"Then what do you say we get one of their specials?"

Amy's face was drawn with worry. "I want to go back to the car."

"I didn't like leaving him, either, Amy," she admitted, guessing what was on the little girl's mind.

"Do you like my uncle?"

"Sure."

Amy smiled. "Good, because I know Uncle JD likes you. A lot. I see the way he looks at you when you're not watching."

"Your uncle and I are only friends."

"You're just like Mommy."

Mari glanced at her. "What makes you say that?"

"I want a daddy like other kids, but Mommy doesn't go on many dates. She's scared. Like you."

"You think I'm scared of JD?" Mari asked, surprised. Amy was sure doing a lot of talking, something she rarely did in public. Maybe this was a reaction to their almost getting caught earlier.

"Yes. I watch you when you're with him. You're always nervous, not like you are with me."

Mari ordered a small sub for Amy and a large one to split with JD later, grateful for the time to consider her reply. "I don't want to ever get married, Amy, so it's easier not to let a special guy like your uncle get too friendly. Otherwise, things could get very complicated." Mari studied Amy's expression, wondering if she'd understand.

"Mommy says that, too, every time she meets someone nice. But Mommy at least has me. You're all alone. I know you like kids. So why don't you give Uncle JD a chance? He's very nice," Amy insisted.

"Are you playing Cupid?" Mari asked with a chuckle.

Amy smiled sheepishly. "I like you. I like him. It would be nice if we were all family."

"That's not the way it works," Mari answered as Amy picked a spot for their picnic.

As they sat beneath the branches of a pine sheltered from a slight breeze, Amy smiled. "He might make you change your mind."

"No, honey, he won't," Mari said softly. "Some things just aren't meant to happen."

"See? You're sad not being with him. I *am* right. You two need each other."

Mari sighed. This was getting them nowhere. "Eat your sandwich."

Amy watched the children come out of the day-care center and gather around a pine tree in the middle of the playground. The children soon began decorating it with tinsel and brightly painted ornaments they'd made.

Hearing running footsteps approaching, Mari turned her head. JD was rushing toward them. Her heart beating at her throat, she stood up. "What's wrong?"

"I overheard Lieutenant Randall making a date to meet Ruth here during their afternoon coffee break, though I'm not sure what time that is. Have you seen them?"

Amy gestured ahead, past the park sign. "I know Ruth. Look. She's just over there." Mari started to go around the pine when Amy reached for her hand. "No. This way," Amy said, then led her toward a hedge. "We can see their faces," she added.

"Having them looking in our direction isn't a good idea. He's a police officer. And look how tense he is. He's constantly looking around," Mari warned.

"I can tell what they're saying from here. Don't you want to know?"

"You bet we do," JD answered.

As they crouched behind the hedge, Mari saw Colin Randall and Ruth Whitmore, his secretary, whom she'd met a few times after the toy drive had started. The two of them stood hidden from the street behind a cluster of arborvitaes. It was obvious they wanted privacy.

Amy watched them, signing to Mari. Mari translated in a whisper. "Ruth says she's worried. That everything's too dangerous now."

As Randall turned away, Amy expelled her breath in a rush. "I can't see his face." Before either Mari or JD could grab her, Amy dashed forward staying low, and ducked behind the trunk of a cottonwood.

Mari felt her heart lodge at her throat. She started to move when she felt JD's hand on her shoulder. "No." JD kept Mari from going any farther. "Let Amy stay. The tree will hide her, but not us."

Mari stayed where she was as an eternity passed. At long last, she saw the lieutenant walk away. Ruth waited for a few minutes, then finally turned and with a stiff gait that favored her right leg, started walking back toward the station.

"I didn't know she had a limp," JD observed.

"She didn't the last time I saw her. Maybe it's a recent injury or just a touch of arthritis," Mari suggested.

Amy returned and joined them. "I did it! I saw what they said. She said she'll lose her job if they don't stop. He said not to worry. Nobody would know. He wanted to meet her after work today at the usual place."

"After work for the office staff would be around five, but did he say where their usual place was?" JD asked.

"No," Amy said, her shoulders slumping slightly.

Mari fell into step between JD and Amy as they went back to the car. "This could mean something important, like dissension among thieves."

"Or not." JD looked up pensively at the candy cane decorations that adorned the streetlights. "But it's worth checking out."

"Their workday ends in another hour or so. Let's follow him then and see where he goes."

"It'll be tricky, but we'll give it our best shot." Minutes later, he turned eastbound, looking for a place to park where they could watch the station.

Amy leaned forward and placed a hand on his shoulder. "I remember when Mommy saw the lieutenant and Ruth together after work before. Mommy was curious."

JD glanced in the rearview mirror. "When was that?"

Amy pressed her lips together, thinking. "When I was out of school for Thanksgiving."

JD glanced at Mari. "Did Elizabeth ever talk to you about Ruth?"

"She said that she and Ruth were the only women in her office who didn't have fathers for their kids."

"If Ruth is supporting a child, then it's possible her finances are strained. That might give her a motive but it's scarcely conclusive." JD looked in the rearview mirror again.

"Randall's name appears on the list of people who had access to the evidence room. Of course, he's the head of that section, so that's hardly surprising," Mari added.

JD parked a block down from an empty, weed-covered lot dotted with Realtors' signs. "It might be boring, but we can wait Randall out until the shift changes and monitor conversations in the station from here."

Time dragged by. Their monitor picked up nothing except snatches of office gossip and jokes. Mari was grateful that Amy couldn't hear them. Some were X-rated. JD called Pat to check on Elizabeth's condition, but there had been no change. When it was finally time for the office personnel to leave, they were all eager for action.

They'd been waiting anxiously for only a few moments when JD saw Randall's van pull out into the street. "Here we go."

They followed Randall to a flower shop first and saw him emerge with a large poinsettia in a green foil-wrapped pot adorned with a bright red bow. As the lieutenant pulled back into traffic, JD hung back at least a block.

"You think he'll spot us?" Mari asked.

"There's a chance. That's why I'm keeping our distance. He won't be able to make a positive ID. Also it'll give us an edge if we have to make a quick getaway."

Suddenly Randall snapped a turn to the left, tires squealing as the van roared down a side street. JD resisted following and continued past, doing his best to blend with the flow of traffic.

"What the— Did he see us?" Mari asked.

"I don't know, but we're getting out of here." JD continued down the street then drove up the freeway ramp to the interstate.

Mari glanced back. "About four cars behind us is a sheriff's vehicle."

"Randall might have called in for backup. If that's the case, we'll have to make a run for it. Keep an eye on him and make sure he doesn't try to narrow the gap." JD got off at the next exit, watching his rearview mirror carefully. When no patrol car followed them, he breathed a sigh of relief. "I think Randall may have just been taking precautions. He may not have spotted us at all."

"If he's that nervous about a tail, then he must have something to hide."

"Yes, but it may not have anything to do with what we're investigating," JD speculated.

"I have an idea. Let's drive to his house. We've got his address. If we don't catch up to him there, we can try Ruth's. It'll give us a chance to check out his house and maybe hers, too, while we try to find out what they're doing."

JD looked in his small notebook for the lieutenant's address, then began the long drive that took them to the northwestern edge of town. Thirty minutes later, they entered a semirural area. "This isn't good. The houses here are scattered and there are few places we can hide and still keep watch. There aren't enough trees and the terrain's too flat."

"Maybe that's one of the reasons he chose to live here." Mari couldn't deny the feeling of excitement that pulsed through her. Maybe they were finally close to finding some answers.

JD parked behind a cluster of scrub oak about fifty yards away from the gate in the fence that bordered the lieutenant's property. Christmas lights had been strung over it, but no one had bothered to turn them on. There were no signs of activity. "It's possible he pulled the van into the garage, but I really don't think he's there. It looks like he's left the lights on in the front room just as a precaution against thieves."

As the minutes dragged by, Amy's breathing became rhythmic. "She's asleep," Mari said with a smile. "I envy her. Lately I've had problems doing that even in a comfortable bed."

"Maybe it just feels too lonely," JD commented, his voice a husky murmur.

Awareness shimmered forcefully between them. The outdoorsy scent of his clothes, the look of his beard-roughened chin, the way his strong hands idly rubbed the wheel, stirred her imagination and created vivid pictures in her mind. Her pulse picked up its pace almost audibly.

"You feel it, too, don't you?" JD asked, capturing her gaze.

"I don't know what you mean," Mari answered, looking away.

"Why do you deny what we both know is happening?"

"Nothing is happening and nothing will."

"Do you honestly believe our feelings will just go away if we ignore them? You're fighting too many battles, Mari. We don't need to fight each other, as well."

"We don't have a choice," Mari answered sadly. "Let's just concentrate on what we have to do now."

JD said nothing. After another five minutes with no sign of activity, he started the car. "We're getting nowhere," he said in a tone that let her know he'd woven more than one meaning into his words.

"Then let's drive on to Ruth's place," she suggested.

Mari could feel his restlessness as acutely as she felt her own. If only the attraction between them would just vanish! She didn't need this, not now. But he was right. This wasn't something she could just will away. If it was true that mortal danger brought out the real man, then she'd seen someone she'd thought had existed only in her most cherished fantasies and dreams. JD's emotions ran deep. He was capable of great courage and amazing tenderness; her heart ached for the comforts of both.

"Why isn't there someone special in your life, Mari?"

"I've chosen it that way," she said flatly.

"Living alone isn't much of a life," JD insisted.

"You seem to have done okay," Mari answered. "What's good for the goose..."

"But I always saw it as a temporary thing. I knew I'd get married and start a family as soon as my company was on firm financial ground."

"What if you didn't fall in love? That's not an emotion that appears on cue," she said.

"I never placed a lot of importance on romantic love. I planned to search for a woman who needed me and what I have to offer—a compatible mate who shared my commitment to marriage. That's a lot more stable than love."

Mari shook her head. "It's logical, but you'd be cheating yourself out of the best that life has to offer."

"Maybe, maybe not. It's only when you love deeply that you can really be hurt. If you rely on common sense instead of emotions, you may not have the exciting highs and lows, but you'll live longer."

"Unless fate intervenes," she mused.

"Yeah, well, I never expected to be in a situation like this, either. When you stand to lose it all, things take on a new perspective. Everything I value and have worked for may come crashing down around us. I've got to keep that from happening somehow, to be there with financial support and help for Elizabeth and Amy."

His words were spoken without inflection, and that more than anything attested to the depth of emotion behind them. When one struggled fiercely to hide pain, words often lost all color. "We won't fail anyone, including ourselves," Mari assured him in a gentle but firm voice.

"You have your own demons, too, Mari. That's why we need each other." He reached across and covered her hand with his own.

His touch, filled with tenderness, was powerfully seductive. It seemed to break through the barriers she'd built around her heart with the power of love's healing touch. Emotions clashed inside her as she pulled away. "No. What we feel is being confused by many other things, like our love for a little girl who desperately needs us and our own will to survive. How can we be sure what we feel for each other is anything more than a reaction to fear? At best, what we'd really be giving each other at this stage is hollow support."

"You're wrong, Mari. There's nothing false in what we feel. The only lie is in trying to deny it."

Twenty minutes later, JD drove down a street in a residential suburb. Houses stood side to side, all alike in size and shape differentiated only by the type and colors of Christmas decorations chosen by their owners. It was the kind of middle-class neighborhood where everyone mowed their lawns on Saturday morning and washed their cars on Sunday afternoon.

JD parked half a block away from Ruth's one-story pueblo-style home. "I think we're safe parking here at this house. Nobody seems to be at home. As long as we don't stick around for too long, we shouldn't attract attention." Just as he finished speaking, JD noticed Lieutenant Randall's van parked on a side street near Ruth's home. "Bingo."

A poinsettia identical to the one they'd seen Randall pick up earlier was on the front porch. While they were watching, the door opened and Ruth and Randall stepped out. He brushed her face with the palm of his hand in a tender caress. The gesture filled Mari with longing. The scene was so touching and so ordinary, yet it spoke of something Mari would never have again in her own life. "Those two are really in love," Mari said quietly.

Ruth's face beamed as she took Randall's hand and tugged him back inside. Colin Randall laughed and followed her through the door. Mari swallowed hard against the bittersweet lump in her throat. Maybe there was something to seizing the moment after all.

"Her home is in the income bracket you'd expect, and her car is several years old. I think they're a dead end for us," Mari added. "We were right about their having something to hide, though. The department has got a policy prohibiting people who work in the same sections from dating. They could lose their jobs."

JD started the car and they got underway again. "It's time to decide on a more permanent listening post for the recorder. Someone might find its hiding place in the garage."

"Wherever we plant it, we have no assurance we'll ever pick up anything useful, and if anyone finds us checking the machine, we'll lose the only real advantage we may have. It must be illegal to bug the department, and that's another charge they could add to our list of crimes."

"We've got to press on with this," JD argued. "It's our only tool right now. I think I know a good place. There's a house for rent close to the station. It's currently vacant from what I could tell. I vote we leave the machine hidden there somewhere."

"No, if the place is vacant, chances are it's being shown often. That means that almost anyone could come across the recorder. I have a better idea. Let me rent an office nearby. There's that new office complex a block or so away from the station, and the sign says they're ready to lease. It's a two-story building, so if we can get on the second floor, we'll be able to monitor the comings and goings of everyone."

JD considered it. "Okay. Let me get hold of Bruce. We'll need some cash, phony business cards and a good pair of binoculars."

JD's conversation with Bruce was brief and cryptic. Mobile phones used the public airwaves, and it was risky to communicate too much.

"Where to now?" Mari asked.

Before he could answer, Amy woke up and leaned forward. "Did I miss anything?"

"Not at all," Mari assured her. "Did you have a good nap?"

"I dreamed about Mommy. She kept asking to see me but no one would let me in her room. She was sad and crying."

Mari reached over the seat and touched Amy's hand. "It was just a dream, honey."

"No. Mommy needs to know I'm okay. I have to go see her. I just have to!" she cried.

"I spoke to Aunt Pat. There's been no change, honey," JD said softly.

"Please, I have to see Mommy," she said, tears welling in her eyes.

Mari looked at JD, who was shaking his head. "Maybe Amy and I can get in and she can walk past the room quickly. They'll think she's a boy," Mari said.

"Absolutely not. It's too dangerous. Remember all the cops?"

Amy shifted so she could look at her uncle. "I'm tired of hiding and being scared," she said. "Mommy's hurt and I'm angry. If Mommy can talk to us, maybe she can tell us what to do, and then we can go home."

"Your mommy can't talk to us," JD protested. "Not yet."

"Well, we don't actually know that," Mari observed. "The information the desk nurse can give over the telephone is pretty limited."

"Can we go find out how she is?" Amy pleaded.

Mari looked at JD. "We've been taking chances but getting nowhere. Maybe it's time to try a different, more direct approach. We really don't know what Liz's current condition is. There's a possibility that the bad cops have suppressed news of her recovery. They wouldn't want the questions she can raise to hit the papers."

"Or she may still be in a coma, and there's no need for them to suppress anything."

"It's worth finding out for sure. We all need to know, not just Amy. And Liz is one of the keys to this investigation. She could answer a lot of questions for us." Mari adjusted her wig. "My disguise is the best one of all, and I still have the scrub greens stored in the back. I'll go in alone."

JD exhaled softly. "I'll give you twenty minutes. Elizabeth's on the second floor, so it shouldn't take you long to get there and do what you want."

"If something happens to delay me, then go with Amy to the safe house. Don't wait or come after me. If I can, I'll meet you there later." She gestured for Amy to hand her the sack with the disguises.

"Just don't let anything delay you," JD growled. Not long after, he drove through the residential area that bordered the large hospital and pulled into the parking lot near the side entrance. "Be careful," he warned.

"Always. See you both in a little bit," Mari said, getting out of the car and adjusting her scrub greens.

Mari walked inside the crowded hospital lobby quickly. No one seemed to be paying much attention to her. She took the elevator to the second floor. Her hands were clammy and her heart was pounding frantically. Yet as she approached Elizabeth's room, still no one appeared to as much as give her a second glance.

Mari stopped beside the guard posted by the door. "I'm Mari Sanchez," she said softly. "You work for me."

The guard's eyes darted from side to side. A sheriff's deputy stood at the nurses' station chatting amicably with the women there. "You're in danger here, Ms. Sanchez."

She nodded and stepped inside the room. Elizabeth lay motionless on the bed. She looked so pale that Mari's throat tightened. She picked up the chart hooked to the bed railing and skimmed it. "I hired two of you to watch over her. Where's your partner?"

"We each take a fifteen-minute break every four hours. It helps us stay alert."

"That makes sense," she conceded grudgingly. "We've been concerned that perhaps the reports the family has been getting were not accurate," Mari explained.

"You mean you think that the police were manipulating the information that you were receiving?" He shook his head. "No. They can suppress general information given out at the switchboard, but when Ms. Hawken's sister calls, the doctor takes special pains to be accurate. I've heard her speaking to the nurses."

Mari's gaze fell on Elizabeth's face. "Just make sure she's well protected."

"We'll do our job. You can count on it. But at the moment, you're the one in the most danger. You have your own reasons for not wanting to talk to the police. I'd advise you to leave the hospital as quickly as possible."

Mari stood casually at the door, then glanced down the corridor. Another uniformed officer had come in since she'd arrived. "You're right. It's time for me to go." Unnoticed, Mari went down the corridor keeping her pace steady but brisk.

Five minutes after she'd left Elizabeth's room, she was halfway through the entrance doors. Suddenly a window up above exploded into a million tiny shards. Glass rained down around her as flames licked out from a room on the second floor.

Chapter Twelve

JD felt the concussion of the blast slam against the car, rocking it violently. In the moments before chaos erupted, it seemed as if each second stretched out into an eternity. Then, streams of people began running outside screaming.

He unbuckled his seat belt while his other hand lifted the door handle. Amy, however, was on the side of the car closer to the hospital. She threw open her door. With her teddy bear stuffed beneath her jacket, she bolted toward the hospital before JD could get around the car.

Cursing loudly, JD raced after her. Though Amy was less than fifty feet ahead of him, he lost sight of her among the sea of people, some on stretchers. He ran a twisting, turning gauntlet through rows of gurneys and wheelchairs. Mari, Amy and Elizabeth were all in danger now.

Fear gave JD almost superhuman energy. He ran through the side entrance and turned down the hall, looking for the stairs. Shouts and the annoying buzz of the fire alarm added to the confusion. As he rounded the corner, he saw someone who looked like Elizabeth being rolled out of one of the elevators. He strode rapidly in that direction, hoping that Mari and Amy would also be nearby. Less than twenty feet away, he saw Amy. She looked in his direction, but suddenly veered to her right. Once again, he lost sight of her as she disappeared into the crowd. His stomach churned. Had she panicked and gone further into danger? As he ran around the corner, he saw Mari coming out of the stairwell.

She spotted him immediately and ran over. "As soon as I heard the blast, I went back upstairs. Elizabeth's okay. The fire's contained. It was set in an empty room near hers. The guard thinks it was meant as a diversion. Whoever it was took advantage of the few minutes the guard was with me in the room. Both the men will stay with her now, though, while the nurses evacuate the floor and bring Elizabeth and the other patients down here."

"I think Elizabeth was just wheeled out," JD answered. "But we have to find Amy. She ran in here right after the explosion."

"She's in the hospital?" Mari yelled above the incessant clamor of the alarm.

"I saw her a second or two ago but she didn't see me. She went around the corner." JD moved down the hall slowly, his back against the wall as he resisted being swept up by the fleeing patients and staff. "We just went around in a circle! If she followed the same route, she's got to be close by."

"There!" Mari pointed ahead. "Right near the doors. Behind the guards with Elizabeth."

As they watched, Amy grabbed a food cart and pushed it as hard as she could against a man walking away. He stumbled against the wall, but kept to his feet and ran toward the exit doors.

"What the—" Dodging around people with the agility of a football star, JD raced directly for Amy. He caught her a second later just as she aimed another cart at the man, trying to knock him down. "What are you doing?" JD asked, scooping her up in his arms. Amy struggled wildly for a second, then realized it was JD and settled down.

"She's after that man for some reason," Mari said, catching up to them, "but we've got to let him go. It's too dangerous in here. We'll talk once we're out of the building."

They made their way around the Christmas tree that had been knocked to the ground by the fleeing crowd and stepped out into the cold night air. As soon as they were outside, Amy reached for Mari's hand and fingerspelled *danger.*

"Explain," Mari asked quickly, allowing Amy to continue fingerspelling.

"What's she saying now?" JD asked.

"The man she attacked was the one who ran Liz down," Mari translated. "We have to warn the guards!"

JD looked around for his sister. "I think that's Elizabeth over there, halfway between us and the portable building. Where's the guy Amy saw?"

Undeterred by the confused and angry voices surrounding her, Amy broke away from JD's grasp, jumped to the ground and hurried through the crowd toward her mother.

Before Mari or JD could catch her, Amy suddenly switched directions and headed toward the parking area behind the portable hospital building. As they emerged from the crowd, JD saw the man Amy was pursuing. "She's chasing the guy in the blue jacket. I'm going after them!"

"There's a TV camera from the evening news! Don't let them film you!"

"Go back and make sure Elizabeth's safe! I'll take care of Amy!" JD spun back around and ran after his niece. More than anything, he wanted to catch, or at least identify, the man responsible for the living hell his family was going through.

As JD reached the end of the brightly lit parking lot, he caught up with Amy who was about to spurt across the street. Intent on the fleeing man on the median strip, she didn't see the fire truck heading their way. JD dived forward, sweeping Amy up with one arm as she stepped off the curb. As they tumbled back onto the sidewalk, he caught a glimpse of the figure they'd pursued, hopping into a beat-up truck in a doughnut-shop parking lot. A breath later, the truck and their quarry were gone.

"No." Amy struggled, fighting to get away.

JD held Amy with shaking hands until she calmed down. Finally he eased his hold, keeping her at arm's length and forcing her to meet his gaze. "You could have been killed! Don't do that to me again!"

Amy watched him for a moment, then, with a broken little smile, hugged him hard. "I'm sorry," she said. "I love you."

JD held her, wishing he had the answers to put an end to this nightmare. But the only things he had were questions and the determination to keep this little girl, and the women who loved her, safe. He scooped Amy up into his arms and walked back. As they reached the edge of the crowd, he caught bits and pieces of conversations around him.

"It was deliberately set," one woman told another. "That's what I heard the firemen saying."

"The TV reporter said something about a witness in protective custody."

JD saw Mari talking to one of the guards. Several yards behind her, a sheriff's deputy was making his way through the crowd, heading in her direction.

Amy wriggled in his arms. "I'm short. The policeman won't see me because of all the grown-ups. I can get Mari."

JD set Amy down, then faced her toward him. "Just let her see you then come right back. Promise?" Amy nodded, then wove through the adults, heading for Mari.

JD turned sideways to the officer and watched, confident that Amy would be able to do what he couldn't. Then, in mute shock, he saw the officer increase his pace as the crowd before him thinned. It was impossible to tell if he'd recognized Mari, but he was walking right in her direction.

JD rushed forward to grab Amy before she got any closer to them, but she ducked behind a large Dumpster, unaware of him. She bent down to pick up something from the ground then rose to her full height. It was a rotting piece of fruit and JD realized Amy had come up with a way to divert the cop. Amy hurled the projectile then ducked out of sight, running around the Dumpster.

As JD edged past a group of patients and nurses, he saw Amy heading toward Mari. The officer was wiping something unbelievably viscous from his jacket with a handkerchief. The mixture clung to his fingers and his hands in long strings. Searching for his attacker, the deputy walked around the Dumpster but, seeing no one, shifted his attention back to his jacket.

A second later, Amy reached Mari. JD moved back, watching them weave their way back to him, deliberately going through the thickest part of the crowd. Once all together, they quickly returned to the car.

Moments later, they were on the road, heading away from the area. JD's hands were moist with perspiration despite the cold. "I want a promise from both of you right now." His voice was calm and although not abrasively commanding, brooked no debate. "You two are going to *stop* trying to give me a heart attack. You'll both be perfect ladies and let me take care of you. No more cowboy tactics."

"And let you have all the fun?" Mari countered, giving Amy a wink. "Never."

JD glanced at Mari. In the intricate pattern of light and shadow the passing streetlights and holiday decorations cast, her face looked as if it were aglow with the flame of phantom fires. Pride and determination were etched into her features. But even more, there was love, as fierce as his own.

JD reached for her hand, then drew back as he saw Amy watching. There was a little grin on her face that told him she knew far too much about his feelings.

Silence descended around them, welcome after the chaos of the past fifteen minutes. Despite his efforts to mask his thoughts, JD was vividly aware of everything about Mari.

Her hands, small and delicate, rested on her lap. Despite the uncertainty and fear they'd all experienced at the hospital, she now sat as calmly as if they were on their way to see a movie. Mari had the grace of a grande dame who'd spent a lifetime of practicing poise and exuding confidence.

It was this reserve that tempted everything male in him. He wanted to feel her beneath him, absorbing him, surrendering to everything he was and could give her. The sensual images that played in his mind blasted him with a shock wave of heat.

He gripped the steering wheel tightly and forced these thoughts into the deepest recesses of his mind. The way he already felt about this woman made making love to her out of the question. There'd be no turning back after that. Their union would forge a bond that would be impossible to break.

They arrived at the safe house twenty minutes later. Bruce was already there, nervously waiting. JD turned to Mari before they got out of the car. "We're moving again tonight. Pack our things and be ready to go as quickly as you can. I'll talk to Bruce."

Mari nodded. "You're right. We shouldn't stay in any place for long. Even one person knowing where we can be found increases the danger."

As Amy and Mari gathered their belongings, JD met with Bruce.

"You look like crap, buddy," Bruce commented. "How can I help you?"

"You're doing it," JD answered. "Things would have been a lot tougher without you."

"You'd have managed," Bruce countered. "You're the only person I know who really doesn't need anyone else."

JD looked off into the distance. "And look what happens when I get too close to someone," he said, almost to himself.

"Your sister's always been the wild card in your life," Bruce commented. "Now you're not only in trouble, you've got others to protect, as well. For a loner, that's got to be some version of hell."

"It makes some things tough, but other things easier."

"Hey, do I see a softening in that reinforced-concrete heart of yours?"

"Softening?" His voice held a warning edge, but Bruce either didn't notice or didn't care.

"Yeah. Mari Sanchez is some woman. Don't tell me she's getting under your skin," he baited.

JD took a deep breath and let it out slowly. "I'm tired, and I haven't had much sleep. If you don't want to have to crawl to your car, then I suggest you drop this."

Bruce grinned. "Oh, so I *am* right!"

JD glowered at him. "Enough talk. We're leaving now."

"Let me know if there's anything else I can do to help." Bruce handed him a list of several addresses and a set of keys. "These are some homes we're scheduled to work up bids on. Their owners are away on vacation so they're all vacant. Any one would make a suitable safe house. All the other contractors up for the jobs have already completed their estimates. We're the last in line."

"Thanks. I owe you in a major way."

"You bet," Bruce said good-naturedly. "And I intend to collect. I may even ask you to fix me up with Mari Sanchez once you get this mess cleared up."

"Keep dreaming," JD countered, watching as Mari and Amy transferred their luggage and supplies into the car and climbed in. "Looks like the ladies are ready to go. Thanks again for the help."

"Stay in touch."

JD approached the car and glanced at Mari, who was busy writing by the glow of the dome light. "What's that?"

She tore off a sheet from the pad of paper, then placed it in an envelope. "It's the letter for Jennifer Anderson. I want to get it off as soon as possible."

JD nodded in approval then glanced at Amy, who was cuddling her bear on the back seat. "How's she doing?"

"She's still worried about her mom."

"What have you told her?"

"Not much. Despite what I'd hoped, I didn't find out much at the hospital. There just haven't been any new developments."

"I figured as much when I saw those tubes and lines hooked up to her," he admitted. JD switched on the ignition as Bruce's taillights disappeared into the night. "We're going to a house that's not too far from here." He glanced at Amy, who'd sat up and edged forward to lip-read. "It's adobe, a historical landmark dating from the turn of the century. Very elegant and classy. I think we deserve someplace attractive and comfortable. It's the holiday season after all."

Amy nodded. "It would be nice to stay someplace pretty," she admitted.

"This one will. I remember viewing it last week. The owners left only a few days ago and will be back the day after Christmas. That gives us four days."

The trip took fifteen minutes but only because Mari insisted on finding a mailbox first. The moon came out from behind the clouds just as they arrived at their destination. JD drove slowly up a long winding driveway that was hidden from the road by a stand of tall pines. Each turn seemed to welcome them further into a circle of protection that would shield them from prying eyes. "I've always liked tall trees," JD said. "They're a sign of stability and endurance."

"I lived in a place like this while I was growing up," Mari mused, "but I never saw it in that light."

"This is the kind of home I've always dreamed of having for myself someday. It has grace and a history." He felt Mari's gaze on him. "It's important, you know. Everyone needs roots of some kind. I didn't realize how much until recently."

"Particularly children," Mari added in a soft, pensive voice.

JD glanced in the rearview mirror and saw Amy curled up in the back seat, checking the unopened doors on her Advent calendar. "Yes, insecurity is even worse for them. And some memories never fade away."

JD saw Mari's eyes close against the pain of the memories she kept locked tightly inside her. He wanted to find a way to reach past her defenses, to erase the old hurts with the strength of his love. Nevertheless, he held himself in check. At the moment, his future gave new meaning to the word *bleak.* He had nothing to offer Mari except stolen moments. She deserved more than that.

Amy stirred in the back seat, diverting his attention. "Hi," she signed, noting his eyes on her.

"Hi yourself." JD smiled. "Tired?"

Amy nodded. "But I'm glad I got to see Mommy and help her out," she said drowsily.

"You did a great job, honey," JD answered.

"I can be lots of help without having to be like hearing people."

"You're special, Amy, because of who you are. What you can or can't do has nothing to do with it," JD asserted vehemently. "Don't you ever forget that."

After Amy drifted off to sleep, Mari looked at JD. "That was good advice. Maybe you should remember it yourself."

JD smiled sheepishly. "Don't have to. I think I've found someone to remind me."

MARI PASSED THROUGH the blue wooden gate. The courtyard beyond was private, enclosed by thick adobe walls
bordered with piñons. The smell of pine filled the air, wel-
coming them with its Christmassy scent.

JD retrieved the keys Bruce had given him from his jacket
pocket, opened the heavy wooden door and led the way into
the traditional *sala,* or living room. Santa Fe-style furniture, with its thick, carved wooden sides, gave the old hacienda an air of elegance.

As JD switched on the lights, an antique chandelier in the
center of the room illuminated everything in a soft glow.
Amy, standing a few feet behind them, gasped, and Mari
turned around instantly. Seeing Amy's gaze was fixed on
something across the room, she shifted to look.

A huge spruce Christmas tree, bedecked with traditional
New Mexican decorations like hand-sewn animals and red
chili peppers, sparkled with holiday cheer.

"It's beautiful," Amy signed.

Mari felt a lump form at her throat as she realized how
much this child had needed a touch of normality in her life.
"Plug in the Christmas lights," Mari asked JD.

"I don't know if that's a good idea. Someone might see
from outside...."

"The tree faces the backyard. We can keep the curtains
drawn." Seeing JD hesitate, she added, "Amy needs this."

"Maybe you're right," he conceded, glancing at Amy.

Amy stood by the tree touching the ornaments with the tip
of her fingers in awe. As JD plugged in the lights, she
jumped back and clapped her hands. Amy pointed to the
angel at the top of the tall tree. "Mommy said angels were
always looking after us. And that angel is so pretty! We'll
be safe here. The angel will protect all of us now," she said
aloud.

JD saw the unspoken hope of his Christmas promise in
the sparkle that touched Amy's eyes. Pain and regret
stabbed through him as he remembered all the broken

promises of his own childhood. "Mari and I will bring in our things. You can stay here and enjoy the tree until it's time for you to go to bed."

"Can I sleep out here on the couch?"

JD nodded. "Sure, honey. We'll leave the tree on as a night-light until you fall asleep."

An hour later, after showering and changing clothes, they met in the living room. Amy curled up on the couch with a sandwich. Mari covered her with the thick crocheted afghan that had been draped over the back of the couch. An atmosphere of peace descended over them as they basked in the serenity of the old hacienda. JD read a magazine he'd picked up from the coffee table, and Mari tucked her legs beneath her and sewed a button back onto one of Amy's shirts.

Within a half hour, Amy drifted off to an easy sleep. JD tucked the afghan in around her, then switched off the Christmas tree. Signaling for Mari to follow him, he grabbed his coat and stepped out into the courtyard.

The breeze was brisk and Mari wrapped her jacket snugly around her. "Is something wrong?"

"No, I just thought we could watch the stars. You and I haven't had a chance to unwind since this whole thing started," he said.

"We've had it rough, but it's been especially hard on Amy."

"I'd give anything if we could have spared her this but today I realized something else. She needs to be given the opportunity to take a more active part."

Mari nodded. "Amy needs to know she's valued. She was feeling useless because she wasn't contributing. It's easy to be overly protective with her, but that's not what she needs."

"I know all about feeling useless, believe me," JD admitted. "When my dad died, I wanted to take care of Mom, Elizabeth and Pat, but I was too young to do much good. The only job I could get was a paper route. So I ended up watching Mom work herself to death while Elizabeth pretended she was tougher than she was.''

"Believe me when I tell you that money isn't a hedge against pain. I know what it's like to feel useless, too, and in a way so total I'm not sure anyone except a woman could ever understand.''

"Tell me what happened," he prodded gently.

"I was married once, a long time ago. Our parents said we had it all. We each had promising futures and were secure financially. We lacked nothing and thought we owned the world. Tragedies happened to other people, but not to us.''

"But then something did go wrong," he observed.

"I gave birth to a little girl, and we loved her dearly. She was such a good baby, smiling and good-natured from the beginning. Then one night she simply stopped breathing. Sudden infant death syndrome, they called it. Crib death. No one can possibly understand the pain of burying your own child unless you've gone through it yourself." A shaft of agony pierced Mari. "I had failed at the one thing that mattered to me most. I hadn't been able to keep my child safe in her own home." She lapsed into silence, overcome by loneliness and grief. A vital piece of her had been taken away and there was nothing that would ever change that.

"I don't know much about that specific problem, but I do know that it's something that just happens sometimes. It wasn't your fault.''

A sob rose in her throat but Mari held back the tears. "Maybe. But I lost the most precious gift life had ever given me. Michael blamed me and I blamed him. We both needed a culprit, some direction to vent our anger and sorrow. After the anger passed, the sorrow remained, but it was impossible for us to look at each other without remembering. We drifted farther and farther apart until finally we divorced.''

"The past can't be changed, but we've got the present and the future. All you have to do is open your heart to the possibilities."

"I found a new direction for my life. One that made life bearable again and gave me a sense of purpose. I don't want anything more."

JD drew her gently against him. "But your heart does." He leaned down and captured her mouth in a gentle kiss.

Mari was incredibly attracted to his tenderness. It was what she'd yearned for. But she couldn't allow herself to give in. Mustering the last of her willpower, she stepped back. "No, you're wrong."

JD eased his hold only slightly. "We each have pasts that dog our footsteps, love, but there's one thing I know. We've been brought together for a purpose. If there's such a thing as destiny, then this is ours. My feelings for you are the only thing that have made perfect sense to me since all this began."

"This is too crazy," Mari protested weakly, allowing herself to be drawn back against him.

"It isn't crazy. It's the one sane thing we have to hold on to. I need your softness and your love, and if you let it, my strength can comfort you."

His mouth coaxed her lips apart and she felt a thrill race through her. She'd been alone for so long! Even if only for a short time, it would be wonderful to lean on him. She needed the safety of JD's arms, to feel herself encircled by his love.

JD lifted her as easily as if she weighed no more than Amy, and carried her inside. As Amy slept, he went past the *sala* and into the den. Starlight filtered through the curtains in tiny slivers, filling the room with light like blue velvet.

He eased himself down onto the sofa, placing her on top of him. His strong, rough hands slid beneath her clothing, unfastening and touching, but with a tenderness that made her ache all over.

Mari felt him shudder at her touch. She stroked the flat, hard surface of his chest, finally tugging his sweater away and stripping him to the waist. She kissed him slowly, learning about his body, exploring to discover what pleased him, enjoying the feel and taste of him.

As she gave him pleasure, he caressed her body with infinite tenderness, touching intimately and drawing response after response from her. There was a delicious languor about his pace. Mari felt hot and melting, like chocolate left in the sun. She wriggled against him, urging him to take more.

Chuckling softly, JD imprisoned her in the cradle of his thighs. "No, love, let's not rush. We've both been through so much. Life hasn't been kind. But tonight it will be. Let it happen slowly. Think of each second as something you want to capture for all time."

She felt him undo the fastening on her jeans. He slipped his hand beneath her clothing, pushing the material away. Then his fingers caressed the center of her, coaxing and stroking. Stars exploded and she thought she would dissolve, but his arm remained firm around her, holding her close, letting her know she was safe.

As her breathing slowly returned to normal, a tear spilled down her cheek. He looked down at her and kissed it away gently. "Why are you sad?"

"I'm not," she managed. "I just never knew it could be like this . . . so beautiful . . . so loving and gentle."

"That's the way it's meant to be for us," JD murmured, brushing her forehead with a kiss.

He held her all through the night, refusing to let her rush what they both knew would eventually happen. The rest of their clothing was eventually discarded and they lay naked together. Intimacy and desire left her weak with needs and longings that went beyond the physical.

It wasn't until the first rays of dawn filled the room that he finally possessed her. The feel of her satin skin against his tore at his restraint, but his passion was tempered with the need to cherish and protect her.

Mari felt him push inside her, his love touching her soul even as his body claimed hers. With each thrust, her heart soared, the union taking everything and giving everything in return. She felt treasured, wanted, and so very loved.

Gentle emotions wrapped around her, filling her and renewing her strength. She found her heart again in their affirmation of life. The need to love and be loved had never died as she'd thought. It had only lain dormant waiting for the right moment to come to life again. And that knowledge was perhaps the most precious gift JD had given her.

Though they hadn't slept much, she felt totally refreshed that morning. After fixing a large breakfast for all of them, she felt ready to tackle the challenges that lay ahead. Finding a short, blond, curly-haired wig in the master bedroom, she decided to borrow it. Fifteen minutes later, she emerged wearing her new disguise.

JD started as he saw her, then grinned. "Some look."

"You like it?"

Amy giggled and signed. "Who are you?"

"The point of a disguise is to look different, right?" Mari answered confidently. She looked at JD with determination. "Let's go rent that office space and set up a listening post. It's time for our luck to change. Let's give the bad guys something to worry about from now on."

They arrived at the professional building twenty minutes later. JD took Amy with him to retrieve the recorder. Using Vanessa Vanderstoop's name and claiming she was about to open a typing service, Mari rented the smallest available office facing the sheriff's station, paying the security deposit in cash. Then she went downstairs to wait for JD and Amy and escort them to her new office.

JD placed the receiver with its sound-activated recorder on a cardboard box next to the window and prepared to play the previous day's messages. "Now all we can do is wait and hope for the best."

"It'll work," Mari assured him. "It has to," she added, with a glance at Amy.

JD stared pensively at the station. "I wonder if the morning news will have footage of the hospital fire last night."

"There was at least one camera crew there," Mari responded. "I suppose they'll run the film as often as possible. TV stations love to air stuff like that."

"The morning news should be coming on soon. You go ahead and listen. I'll go to the café next door to see what's on the broadcast."

"You want to see if you showed up on film?" Mari asked.

"Well, there's that, but what I'm hoping is that the footage includes the man who eluded us."

"Good thought," Mari agreed.

"I'll be back."

Mari watched JD leave, then realized Amy was staring at her, a big grin on her face. "What are you looking at, young lady?" she asked, unable to suppress a smile of her own.

"Me? Nothing at all!" Amy said with a wide-eyed look of innocence.

Mari started to answer, then thought better of it and started to play the tape. Yesterday's entries were few and far between, but when she reached what had been picked up early that morning, it sounded more interesting.

"I want you to check and double-check all the entries. We need answers," a man ordered. Mari thought it sounded a bit like Lieutenant Randall, but she couldn't be sure. "Pearline, I know you always got along with Elizabeth, but this department is taking a lot of heat. Don't hold back anything you find."

"I've been at this all morning, double-checking each entry on the computer." Pearline's voice came through distinctly. She sounded tired.

"Well, stay on it."

"I'll keep working until lunch, but then I'm signing off. If I don't use my leave now, I'll lose it anyway."

"You're free to do that, but I would strongly encourage you to come back right after lunch."

"What if the answer you're looking for isn't there to find?"

"Then that'll be my answer, won't it?"

Mari heard a door slam, then a woman curse. Nothing else was said after that.

She switched the receiver to broadcast as well as record, in the hope that something more might be happening now. As she leaned over the receiver, intent on listening, JD came back in quietly. "It was on the morning news," he said quickly. "I couldn't see a face, but he's on film. I spotted him in the background, walking away from where the guards had Elizabeth."

"Now all we have to do is identify him and then prove to the sheriff's department that this is a clue worth looking into."

"No small task, but it's got to be done."

JD looked like a mass of compressed energy about to burst. His hands clenched into fists, then unclenched, in an endless cycle. "Is there something else you're not telling me?"

"Near the end of the footage, I saw someone I recognized standing near the hospital entrance. It probably means nothing," he said, turning to meet her gaze, "but it bothered me."

"Who was it?" she prodded impatiently.

"My partner, Bruce Campbell."

Chapter Thirteen

Mari stared at JD, stunned. She'd felt guilty being suspicious of Bruce, but maybe she'd been right all along. Sympathy filled her now, seeing the confusion mirrored on JD's face. "He may have been there to check on Elizabeth for us," she said in the interest of fairness.

"I thought of that, and since there's been no change in her condition, he may have decided not to worry me. Or he may have had business of his own there. When Bruce thinks something is private, he doesn't talk about it. But it still bothers me that he was there because it raises so many questions. And while his sprained ankle is better now, he was limping at the time Elizabeth was hurt."

Mari's doubts about Bruce remained, though for JD's sake, she tried to downplay them. "Just to be on the safe side, let's not tell him too much about what we're doing."

"So far, I've only told him enough to get whatever it is we need. Don't forget what he's done, Mari. Without him, we would have been out of cash by now and without the list of safe houses that can't be easily traced back to our company."

"We'll do without his help if we have to." Mari reached into her purse and pulled out the list Elizabeth had placed in Vanessa's safety deposit box.

He glanced down at the paper. "What are you doing?"

"Pearline Gutierrez is the last name on this list of Elizabeth's. She's a friend of Elizabeth's. I've met her a few times, and in fact, I taught her son a few years ago. I think we should go talk to her. Let's go by her house. She's usually home for lunch. It's worth a try." She played back the conversation on the tape recorder for JD. "She should be willing to give us the benefit of the doubt."

"And if she turns us in?"

"We'll hedge our bets. She's not expecting us, and we'll try to catch her alone. While we're there, we'll make sure she doesn't use the phone. After we're gone, it won't matter. Even if she calls in, it'll take time for them to respond, and by then we'll be out of the area."

JD considered the plan carefully. "I think you're right. This is definitely worth a shot. Pearline's right in the midst of whatever's going on in the department. She's in a unique position to help us if she decides to cooperate."

JD and Amy went back to the car first, with Mari following shortly thereafter. By the time they were underway, Mari felt more hopeful than she had in a long time. "I think we're close to finding answers. We just have to hang in there a bit longer."

"There's something we have to do first. That film segment the camera crew took has to be protected. It's evidence. Only I'm not sure how to go about it. If I just call in, they may think I'm a crank. And if I identify myself, they'll want to follow up on this and could end up putting the entire force on alert. We'll never track down the jewels or find the person behind the theft."

"I'll contact Jennifer Anderson," Mari decided. "She's the investigative reporter I told about the sheriff's deputy who tried to run us down. She's painstaking and honest. Jennifer won't go to press until she's one hundred percent sure of her facts. She'll know what to do to get hold of that film and protect it."

JD considered Mari's plan. "I've seen her pieces in the paper. She's good. But we have no way of knowing if she followed up on what you sent so far or not."

"I can try calling her directly and see what, if anything, she's done, but I probably won't get anywhere. She came to speak to one of my classes on career day last semester. I remember Jennifer emphasizing how she never lets anyone know what she's doing until she's ready to make a definite move."

"She's our best chance for now," JD agreed after a moment. "We'll go with your plan."

Mari picked up a pad from the glove compartment and wrote a quick note. "This should do."

JD noticed the time and switched on the radio to tune in the hourly news. News of another fire was the lead story. As Elizabeth's home address was read over the air, JD glanced at Mari, but was careful to keep his face neutral to avoid frightening Amy.

Mari sneaked a glance at Amy, but she seemed absorbed in the bright rows of tinsel the city had wrapped around the street lamps. "Do you think they were worried that Liz had stashed some evidence there, like the photocopied list? If they'd come up empty after searching, they might have opted for something more drastic." Mari asked him to pull over at the newspaper office and dashed in to drop off the letter. Moments later, she sat back, relieved to know it was on its way. "I told Jennifer about the attacker's limp, but I asked her not to mention it in any story she writes. That could make Elizabeth's assailant all the more determined to remove us as witnesses." She gave Amy a quick glance and was relieved to see the little girl's attention was still diverted. "Let's not talk about the house anymore. We'll deal with that later."

JD made his way around Old Town to Pearline Gutierrez's home. Several snowmen made out of tumbleweeds decorated the sidewalks. At last they found the cottage at the end of a long, narrow driveway between two shops. A single car was parked out front.

"Good. She's home," Mari said, recognizing the figure that strode quickly past the Christmas tree in the living-room window.

"Do you want to go in alone?" JD asked. "Woman to woman, you may have a better chance of getting her to talk openly to you."

Mari smiled, knowing that the offer was a sign JD trusted her to call the shots. For a man like JD, who liked to be in control, that was a large leap of faith. "In some cases that would be the best way to handle it," she conceded, "but Pearline is very traditional and a great believer in family. By now, she must have heard a dozen times that we're working together. If I go in alone, Pearline might think you don't trust her and that might just make things worse. This way you can make it clear you're defending your family and I'm helping out. We need for her to *want* to help us, too. To do that, we have to earn her trust by showing that we're willing to trust her."

They parked by the end of the drive. Mari took off her blond wig, fluffed out her hair, then walked to the front door. Forcing herself to relax, she knocked on the door.

Pearline answered a moment later and her eyes immediately widened with recognition. She stepped aside, gesturing for them to enter. "You're all taking a terrible risk coming here. But I don't suppose you have too many options."

The distinctive aroma of *posole,* a hominy, pork and chili stew simmering in the tiny kitchen, filled the room with the flavor of a New Mexican Christmas. When Mari looked over at JD, she saw he was smiling and sniffing the air appreciatively, too.

Mari studied Pearline's eyes. There was sympathy in them as she welcomed the couple into her home, but no fear. "We need some information. I hate putting you in this position, but I think you know that neither Elizabeth nor any of us are guilty of anything.''

"I know Elizabeth would never do what she is accused of, so I believe you. Come in and sit down." Pearline was about fifty pounds overweight, but she moved with grace and a fluid agility that seemed incongruous with her bulk. She faced Mari squarely. "Now tell me your side of the story."

Mari told the woman what had happened, omitting very little. "We're trying desperately to keep Amy safe."

"I had no idea things were this bad." Her gaze fell on Amy, who was walking around the small piñon Christmas tree looking wistfully at the tiny silver bells hanging from its branches. "I've suspected a cover-up at the station," Pearline admitted, "but I have no proof of anything. I just know they want answers fast and sometimes that means finding an easy scapegoat." Pearline saw the wonder in Amy's eyes as she looked at all the presents beneath the tree. Each was wrapped in glitter-flecked tissue and tied and decorated with red-and-green plaid ribbons. Pearline walked to the breakfast bar and picked up a tray of candy canes. "How about some of these?" she offered Amy. "Take as many as you like."

Amy smiled and took three.

Pearline returned to her easy chair. "I guess I've known something was wrong at the station for a while now. Things just don't add up."

"Like what?" Mari asked.

"It's crazy to think that Elizabeth, or any other person for that matter, can steal something from the evidence room. Security is very tight. Even our chief is searched before leaving that area. It's been that way for years."

"Then how do you explain the missing evidence they reported?" JD asked. "Somebody said my sister was responsible and that's a lie."

"I know. Elizabeth's in charge but it's my job to keep all the records in order. Our files show some missing Rolex watches and jewelry but I never saw merchandise of that kind in there." She shrugged. "I just can't explain it. The only items that go in without paperwork and will eventually leave the same way are those toys for the padre's church. It's a shame donations have dropped off so much since Elizabeth's accident.

"What about the other civilians or cops in that division. Is there anyone who dislikes Elizabeth and might want to see her framed?" JD asked.

"Elizabeth doesn't have many close friends but she also doesn't have enemies. She's real independent but you know that. Oh, it's common knowledge that she and Lieutenant Randall have had some spectacular fights but Colin's a good man. He really cares about the department. I'm sure he really suspects Elizabeth was involved in something shady. That's why he's had officers breathing down everyone's neck and people checking on every move Elizabeth ever made. It's not some kind of vendetta. He's just trying to be a good cop."

"What's your theory? What do you think is going on?" Mari asked.

"To be perfectly honest, I think it's all a mistake in records. Someone forgot to delete something or maybe entered the wrong thing."

"Can the records be deliberately altered?" JD prodded.

Pearline considered the question for a few moments before answering. "Anyone who knows how to use a computer could do that, but you'd need some knowledge of how our system works."

"How specialized is that knowledge?" Mari asked.

Pearline exhaled softly. "Not very. When I first started to work there I had no one to teach me the system. I figured out things by myself and I'm no computer genius." Pearline met JD's gaze. "I know you're going through a very tough time and I'm very sorry. You and I both know your sister is not guilty of anything, but someone is sure trying hard to make it look like she is. I know you probably have no faith left in the system but Colin Randall isn't so bad. At the moment, he's under a lot of pressure to find evidence implicating Elizabeth, but he won't railroad anyone. He'll keep digging until he finds the truth."

Amy looked wistfully at the candy canes in the dish then took one more and placed it in her pocket, looking up at Pearline.

Pearline laughed. "I'll give you a bag of those to take with you."

"May I use your phone?" JD asked.

"Sure." Pearline waved him to the hall. "It's on the table."

JD WAITED UNTIL THEY WERE all in the kitchen checking the *posole,* then dialed. He needed to get hold of Bruce Campbell. He trusted his partner, but the discovery that he'd been at the hospital during the fire continued to prey on his mind.

JD allowed the telephone to ring several times. He was about to hang up when he recognized his partner's breathless voice. "It's me," JD said without identifying himself.

"Yeah, I'm at one of the sites and I was away from the car phone. What's up? Is there a problem?"

"I wanted to ask you a question. You've heard about the hospital fire?"

"Yeah, sure, I was there. And don't worry, Elizabeth was being well cared for."

"I appreciate you checking on her," JD said. "Is that why you went?"

"Well, I *had* planned to stop by her room and see how she was doing, but that wasn't the primary reason I was there. My mother's been hospitalized. She's got a bad heart."

"I'm sorry to hear that," JD answered. Bruce and he seldom discussed personal matters. That wasn't the nature of their relationship. The last time he remembered Bruce mentioning family at all was when his father had died about a year ago.

"Listen, while I have you on the telephone, I'm having some trouble with a few of our contract jobs," Bruce said.

"What kind of trouble?"

"Our two largest jobs have been canceled and three pending deals have fallen through. Bad publicity is catching up with us."

JD felt his gut clench. Everything he'd spent his lifetime working for was in danger of unraveling and the worst part was knowing there was nothing he could do about it. "Whenever we have signed contracts, take a firm stand. Threaten them with legal action unless they honor the agreement."

"I can do that, but we really don't have the funds to take this all the way to court."

"Nor can we afford to have people back out of deals. Have our attorney write a few letters and then let's see how it goes."

Insecurity and uncertainty, those demons from his past, nipped at his heels. JD hung up the phone, frustration tearing at him. His dream of financial security, his own view of himself as a provider for his family, all were being challenged.

As JD joined the others in the kitchen, Mari picked up a photo of a sheriff's deputy in uniform from the breakfast table. "Good-looking man. Anyone you want to talk about?" she asked, giving Pearline a teasing smile.

Pearline laughed. "That's my brother, Ricky. Did you ever meet him? Ricky Estrada?" Seeing Mari shake her head, she continued. "I've wanted to fix him up with Elizabeth, but then he started working vice. He's changed since then."

Mari recognized the name. He was the cop with the expensive sports car. She glanced at JD then back at Pearline. "How did he change? You mean his appearance?"

"That, too. He has a new image, drives a fancy car and all that as part of the job, but he's become really guarded and edgy all the time. I wish he'd get out of vice but he likes the action." Pearline gave Amy a bag filled with Christmas treats, glanced at her watch and turned the *posole* down low. "I have to go back to work soon. But I do want to help you. I'll tell you what I'll do. If I find something that can clear you, or some information I think you need to have, I'll contact you. Is there some way for me to get hold of you?"

Mari hesitated. "We'll call you," she said, planning to call on Christmas Eve a couple of days away. Phone lines would be incredibly busy then. Hopefully that would make it just that much harder to trace anything. "Okay?"

"That sounds fine."

Mari thanked Pearline for her help then hurried back to the car with JD and Amy. Several minutes later, on their way back through the city, JD glanced over at Mari. "I didn't mean to take so long on the phone. Did everything go all right?"

"I had to divert some questions, but that's about it. I didn't want to discuss the Madonna, or what we suspect, in any detail. That would place Pearline in danger. Who did you call?"

"Bruce. He said his mother's in the hospital, so that explains what he was doing there. We talked a bit about business, too."

After he lapsed into a lengthy silence, Mari grew worried. "Is something wrong?"

"Some of our biggest clients are getting nervous. If this continues much longer, I'm likely to lose the company. Then I won't be much good to Elizabeth and Amy, or to myself."

"You place way too much emphasis on money," Mari said firmly.

"You've never known poverty, have you?" JD asked slowly, then saw her shake her head. "I have." He glanced at Amy in the rearview mirror but she was busy looking out the window. "It's especially bad for a child, believe me. You can't imagine what relying on charity does to a kid's self-esteem."

"Was it money that was really at the heart of what you were missing?"

He shrugged. "My mother did her best, but she had to work at whatever jobs she could find. When she came home she was tired then later she was sick all the time. That affected us, too. I'm sure had we been on firm financial ground, she wouldn't have had to work herself into an early grave. Our lives would have been different."

Mari sighed. She wasn't going to convince JD to see things any other way. "Well, it doesn't matter what it costs either of us. Amy needs us now and we have to see this through."

"Are you worried about your job?" JD asked.

"Not the job—the kids," she answered. "There are some students who really need me. They've become used to working with me, and they may not accept a substitute easily."

"You think my quest for financial security is too consuming and that I've locked myself out of relationships. Yet, in your own way, you've done the same. Although you work closely with the kids, you keep a professional distance. Your heart is safely locked away."

Mari started to protest then decided against it. This wasn't something she wanted to discuss. She glanced at the rear seat and saw Amy staring at a young family strolling down the street. A little boy was eagerly pointing out a Santa Claus who was standing on the corner. The look on Amy's face told it all. Mari reached over the back of the seat and touched Amy. "You okay?"

Amy nodded, but then looked out the window again.

A vague disquiet settled over Mari. Amy's bright smile had vanished and she hadn't tried to become part of the conversation. She was withdrawing in her own way. Maybe it had been happening slowly all along, only she'd been too distracted to see it. The signs all pointed to one thing—a loss of hope. Christmas was just around the corner and it didn't look as if Amy's mother would be home to share the holiday with her.

JD followed Mari's gaze. "I think we need to take a few hours off for her sake. How would you like to take her to one of the malls and let her look at all the displays and Christmas decorations? That'll give me time to make a call to Pat and hopefully get some further news on Elizabeth's condition."

"Better yet, let me make that phone call. I'll talk directly to the guards instead. And I can try to reach Jennifer Anderson, too. In the meantime, you can take Amy with you and buy her a little gift. Maybe help her choose something for her mom. I saw her looking at the presents under Pearline's tree with the saddest little look. I think she misses all the normal things she would have been doing with Elizabeth this time of year."

JD glanced at the rearview mirror. Amy was staring at the Advent calendar on her lap, her bear clutched tightly against her. "I'll see what I can do."

"It doesn't have to be an expensive gift," Mari reminded him gently. "Get her something that shows you care about her. Maybe you could even get her a present for her bear, Teddy Fuzzball. I bet she'd love that."

"She's really attached to that stuffed toy, isn't she?"

"It was Elizabeth's gift to her, and Amy's using it as a way of holding on to her mom."

JD pursed his lips. "I'm worried about my sister, too, you know. I'm worried about all of us."

Mari touched his hand then drew away. This was not their time. The moments they'd shared the night before had never carried the promise of forever. Yet she couldn't deny that love had touched her and opened her heart.

She closed her mind to those thoughts as an intense long-ing left her aching inside. She should have known better. Love had always come at a high cost for her. Memories and new yearnings that threatened to break her heart would now become her constant companions.

Chapter Fourteen

JD walked through the crowded mall with Amy. Mari had stayed by the public phones near the entrance.

As they strolled slowly past the shop windows, Amy's eyes were glued to the red, green and blue lights that sparkled with the joys of the season. In one store, a train circled a small Christmas tree, stopping at a station filled with one-inch-tall passengers carrying brightly wrapped presents. Seeing his niece's eyes light up made him wish he could have bought the entire display for her. A touch of sadness filled him, too, as he remembered his own empty childhood. A set of trains had been his dream, an impossible dream. To this day, he still loved toy trains. He had a room devoted to them at his home.

Amy was all smiles as they went from one window display to the next. As they reached a children's clothing store, her eyes grew wide. A six-foot bear wearing a red-and-green stocking cap sat in the center of the window surrounded by children's clothes.

"You want another bear to keep your friend company?" he asked, knowing he would find a way to get it for her if it was what she wanted.

Amy glanced at him as if tempted, then shook her head. Instead she pointed to her head.

"The stocking cap?"

"Two," she signed.

"Ah, I get it. One for you and one for your friend."

Amy nodded.

"Well, let's go pick them out. From what I can see, there are several designs to choose from."

JD stayed by her side as she sorted through the stack of brightly colored Christmas stocking caps. Finally, Amy settled on two that were filled with images of the season. She then picked up two bright red scarfs. "For Mari, and one for Mommy."

After JD paid for them and they walked out of the store, Amy glanced up at him and smiled. Though she seemed more relaxed, tension still lingered in her. JD's heart felt like a rock. Maybe it was easier for him to sympathize with her because he'd been there himself. He knew how easy it was for Christmas to turn into nothing but heartbreak.

Mari greeted Amy with a hug then glanced at JD. "Liz hasn't come out of the coma. The guards say her doctor is worried because the longer she stays in a coma, the more it tends to indicate that there won't be a quick recovery. But that's not certain. There are no hard-and-fast rules."

JD nodded and tried to keep the rage he felt hidden deep within him. If his sister didn't wake up and recover, and his business failed, then where would that leave all of them? Frustration tore through him and he silently cursed those who had forced them into this nightmare.

After they were back in the car, Amy took the smaller stocking cap and placed it on the bear. Satisfied, she put on the bigger one, adjusting it until it fit comfortably around her ears.

Mari turned around to look at Amy. "Perfect. It's not only pretty, but it'll add to your disguise. And I like the designs on it, too."

Amy pointed to the image of a toy soldier holding a brightly lit candle. "My favorite," she said. "Like us."

"How like us?" Mari asked, signing.

"We're like soldiers," Amy said. "And the candle keeps away the dark."

JD glanced in the rearview mirror. "I wish you didn't have to live like this, Amy. I really do."

Amy shrugged. "Christmas will be here soon. Mommy will be with us then and everything will be okay."

JD saw his niece avert her gaze. Maybe she was beginning to doubt the promise he'd made her. Unable to confront that doubt in her eyes, he concentrated on the road.

"By the way, I also checked on something else while I had the hospital on the line," Mari added. "I thought I'd find out how Bruce's mom was doing." She hesitated. "But it seems there are only two patients listed under the name Campbell and both are men."

JD stared directly ahead. He wasn't sure what to make of this. "Maybe it hasn't shown up in the computer records yet because she was admitted recently. Or maybe there was a clerical error."

"Or Bruce's mom may have passed on," Mari added. "But I thought you should know."

JD remained silent. As a kid, he'd often envisioned his future as the wise head of the family, a "Father Knows Best" type, who'd provide in every way for those he loved. He was falling way short of his dreams on every score. "Let's check on our bug and see what the recorder has picked up, then we'll go to the safe house."

They arrived twenty minutes later and Mari set the machine to replay the recorded conversations. The transmission was filled with static and she couldn't recognize either of the voices. "They're saying something about the Madonna, I think."

JD listened, then turned up the volume. "Let's hope the transmission will clear up in a minute. If it does, maybe we can figure out what was said at the beginning by what was said at the end." JD held the recorder between them, both listening without daring to breathe. The voices were soft, conspiratorial and unrecognizable.

"We're getting close...to date... It's time," one voice began.

"The transfer has to be made."

"The Madonna will have to be returned to the church and..."

"That's already covered."

"...meet tonight?"

The transmission became a maze of static then abruptly cleared up. They heard the rest plainly.

"All the jewels have to be accounted for. No loose ends."

"Okay. We meet tonight to work out the details of the final phase. Nine o'clock at One-Eyed Dan's."

They heard a door slam, then silence followed. Mari looked at JD. "We've got to be there. Even if we never get close enough to hear their plan, we'll be able to identify the players. I think I should also call Jennifer Anderson. She should be in on this."

"No, not yet. Once we learn who's involved and photograph the meeting, we'll have a good chance of tracking down the jewels. From that conversation, I get the strong feeling that they're still in the area."

Amy came to join them. "What did you hear on the tape?"

Mari explained. "We're going to have to find a way to see what they're up to."

"If they talk outside, I could help. I saw special binoculars on the TV news once. You could see in the dark with them, only everyone is green. If you can get a pair like that, I could tell you what they're saying."

JD smiled. "Yeah, those things exist, but they cost a fortune." He paused. "We'll need to pick up a camera and some fast film."

"And we'll have to stake out the place," Mari answered. "It'll be risky."

"Yes, but we have no choice. Think of the return if everything goes right. By tonight, we may have enough evidence between the photos and our tape to clear ourselves."

As JD WENT INSIDE a convenience store for sandwiches, Mari inserted two quarters and pulled a newspaper from the box outside on the sidewalk. A triumphant smile was etched on her face when he slipped back into the driver's seat a few minutes later. "I told you Jennifer Anderson would come through for us!" She showed him the article at the bottom of the front page.

JD read it quickly. "So she did track down the rogue cop who tried to run us down!" he said with a grin. "She wasn't taken in by the sheriff's department's assurances. When she didn't find anyone who fit the description and had a vehicle that matched, she kept digging. The guy turns out to be a civilian volunteer, what they call an auxiliary officer. They're the ones who assist and wear regular uniforms but have reduced authority. His name is Jerry Romero. His brother's a deputy."

"Kyle Romero, maybe? He's one of the deputies on Elizabeth's list," Mari said thoughtfully.

"Could be," JD answered. "It also says here that the hospital fire was arson, and she mentions the person in the coat and cap as running from the scene."

Mari pulled the story continuation from page three. "Look! They've run a photo taken from the news videotape. But his face is blurry. I think he may have a mustache, but I can't be sure. There's a good caption below the photo. It reads, 'Visitor or Villain?'"

"Let's go back to the safe house and get ready. Jennifer's done a lot for us, so let's see what happens tonight before we commit her to a wild-goose chase."

Mari glanced at a brief piece pleading with people to donate toys for the drive despite the scandal. She was glad now that she'd called the head of the trust from the mall. The toys had been gathered and stored according to plan.

They arrived at the safe house an hour later. Amy set her Advent calendar where she could see all the open doors, then curled up on the couch by the Christmas tree and played with her bear. Mari looked for coffee in the kitchen. JD joined her there and spread the newspaper out on the table. "There's even some things written here about you."

"What's it say?" Mari asked, filling the coffeepot with water.

"It details some of your more impressive successes with handicapped students. Then it throws in a few surprises." His voice suddenly grew hard. "At least, they were surprises to me."

Mari heard the tension in his voice. He was angry but she couldn't quite figure out why. Dreading the thought of new accusations in print, she forced herself to walk around the table and read over his shoulder.

"There were a few things you forgot to tell me about yourself," JD said, his voice low and hostile. "Now I understand why money doesn't matter to you. How very convenient."

Mari stared at the article. Her principal and several other administrators and teachers had spoken highly of her. Then, as if trying to point out that she was beyond corruption, one of them had mentioned her family. Mari felt her stomach sink.

"You play the dedicated teacher," JD said, his eyes ice-cold, "but I see that's an easy role for you. If I had millions in assets and never had to work again, I wouldn't worry so much about losing my job, either."

Mari couldn't believe his words. "My parents left me money when they died, okay. But what exactly is it that you resent? The fact that you don't have as much money, or the fact that I chose not to tell you? For your information, I didn't tell you because it's none of your business. It has nothing to do with what's been happening. If you still think that money is the answer to everything, let me remind you I'm hip-deep with you in this mess.''

"Yes, but you have an edge. If I lose my company, I have nothing. If you lose your job," he said with a shrug, "it's just an inconvenience. You could build your own school.''

Anger shot through her with an intensity that left her trembling. "My *job,* as you call it, is more than just work. It's been a lifeline for me. Stop judging the importance of everything by weighing it in dollars and cents. If that's all you learned to value from your childhood, I feel sorry for you.''

Mari took a deep breath, then continued. "When my baby died, my life dissolved into an endless parade of minutes that had no meaning. Life has colors, but for me there was only gray. It took me a very long time to crawl out of that darkness. Money couldn't replace what I lost. Teaching was what gave my life meaning again.''

"I understand that you've known pain...." JD said, his voice gentler.

"Known it? For a year it was the only emotion I was capable of feeling. It was the only sign I had that I was still alive inside. Then I met one of my neighbors. Her little boy was mentally handicapped. She'd been told there was no way he could be taught even the simplest of tasks. Trying to pull myself together again, I started making time to see him, to talk and work with him. I had my teaching certificate by then but I hadn't done much with it. After a few months he was retested and they discovered that he was capable of learning far more than anyone had suspected. I knew then that I had something to offer. I could help other children, though I hadn't been able to save my own.''

"Can you have other kids?" JD asked softly.

"Yes, but I'll never try again. I've found a new direction for myself and I'm at peace. I guess you can say I'm married to my job." Mari took a deep breath. "My only real personal relationships nowadays are with Elizabeth and Amy. There's nothing I wouldn't do for either of them.''

"There's something more driving you now, isn't there?" JD observed.

She nodded slowly. "I lost one child in my care. I won't allow anything to happen to Amy. I'll give up my own life first." She'd also risk her life to keep JD safe, but that was something that could never be said. Not now, not ever. "I don't want to talk anymore. We need to get some rest if we're going to be alert tonight."

"I have to go find the equipment we need. Why don't you stay with Amy and see if at least you two can get some rest."

Mari nodded. "That's probably best."

She was getting too used to being with him. Unfortunately, when she looked into the future, all she could see was heartbreak. Once the danger to Amy had ended and their names were cleared, they'd each go back to their own separate lives.

For a brief moment, as she stood by the window and watched him drive away, she envisioned the lifetime of cold, lonely nights stretching out before her. The prospect left her feeling desolate, trapped by a grief that would never relinquish its hold.

JD TOOK THE FREEWAY, heading across town. Speed suited his mood. He'd spent a lifetime nurturing a dream; he wanted a home of his own, children in the yard, a dog, barbecues on Sunday. Yet he'd fallen in love with a woman whose vision of the future did not include any of the things he held dear.

He loved Mari. He was as sure of that as he was of his own name. She was caring and compassionate and gentle. And that's where the biggest problem lay. Mari was a rescuer. She needed to be needed. That's why if she'd turned to him now, with his business crumbling and Elizabeth in a coma, he'd never be sure it was solely out of love. Even the chance that he'd suddenly become her latest charity case was enough to make him keep his distance. He wanted her to respect and love him for the man he was. He wanted her to feel she could lean on him, not see him as someone else who had to depend on her.

JD pressed hard on the accelerator, knowing the police rarely stopped people on the interstate crisscrossing the city. At least speed gave him a feeling of strength and control. It also numbed caution for a while. Forced to concentrate on the traffic, he tried to quiet his thoughts. Yet, as the miles stretched out, Mari's image remained in the foreground of his mind.

He took the exit into Central, then drove down searching for a camera store. He found one less than two blocks from the freeway exit. The place was small but he was sure it would have what he was looking for.

JD emerged ten minutes later with the items he needed. He now had a camera with a fast lens and high-speed film. As he got underway, he picked up the car phone and dialed. He recognized Bruce's voice when he answered on the second ring.

"It's me," JD said without identifying himself more specifically.

"What can I do for you? Is something wrong?"

"No, I just thought I'd check in with you. Anything new happening?"

There was a brief pause. "I sure wish things would get back to normal. I need you at the office."

"How are things going there?"

"Not good. Business really slows down when your partner's a fugitive." Bruce moaned. "Maybe you can talk Mari into a loan after all this is over."

The suggestion struck JD almost like a physical blow. He took a breath and struggled to keep his temper in check. "We'll handle our own problems."

"Easy for you to say," Bruce grumbled. "You haven't seen the books."

"How's your mother?" JD asked, switching the topic to the reason he'd called.

"She's hanging in there."

"Will she be released soon?"

"I doubt it. They said she'd probably be in for two weeks, and she's only been there for five days so far."

"I'll keep a good thought out for her."

"And I'll do the same for you, buddy. Stay in touch."

JD placed the phone back. The discrepancies between Bruce's story about his mother and the hospital records made no sense, yet it wasn't like Bruce to lie. He'd have Mari check with the hospital again later. It had to have been an error in admitting.

As JD drove away, his partner's jest about the loan stayed in his mind. He tightened his grip on the wheel. There was no way he'd ever ask Mari to bail him out financially. He'd sell the company first.

Slowly another thought formed. Was that the way people usually saw her, as someone they sought out for cash, giving little need to the special woman she was? Though people were sometimes quick to ask for help, many less fortunate eventually grew to resent the ones in a position to give it. Maybe wealth had isolated her in a way he hadn't realized until now. A new understanding filled him. All she'd ever wanted to do was live a normal, ordinary life. But from the looks of it, she'd been thwarted at every turn.

MARI SAW JD PULL UP and park. She was glad he was back. At least she knew he was safe for now. He came in a few seconds later, a thirty-five millimeter camera in his hand. "We've got all the equipment we need. Give me a moment to load the film, and then we'll be on our way."

Mari saw Amy come to join them and smiled. JD was avoiding looking at her, and she him, so Amy was a welcome distraction.

Amy's gaze darted back and forth between JD and Mari. At long last, Amy went to stand beside JD as he loaded the film. "Who'll take the pictures?" she signed, mouthing but not vocalizing the words.

"We'll be taking the photos after you tell us what's going on, if you can." JD held up the camera with the heavy, expensive lens attached and showed her how to hold it up to her eye.

Amy looked through the viewfinder across the room and laughed. "Funny," she signed to Mari and looked at JD.

"Is something wrong?" Mari asked her.

Amy shrugged. "My throat hurts. You translate for Uncle JD. Talk to him."

Mari felt Amy's forehead. "Temperature's normal. Maybe it's just a little cold." She wasn't convinced. Intuition told her that there was something more going on. "Can you still help us tonight?"

Amy nodded and signed quickly to Mari.

"She'd like for us to go outside now that it's dark, and then stand close together. She wants to see if she can make out what we're saying in the moonlight."

JD accompanied Mari out into the backyard while Amy stood in the doorway of the darkened house, bracing the camera on the back of a chair JD had moved for her. Moonlight filtered through the clouds, painting everything in shades of silver.

JD smiled. "Amy's a big help. I don't know what any of us would do without her."

The delighted squeal from the other side of the yard made Mari smile. "Ah, I think she's found that the lens works just fine."

Amy set the camera on the chair carefully then dashed toward them, signing.

"Whoa! Slow down!" Mari said with a chuckle. Amy started again and Mari translated. "She's ready to go. Amy says we're too slow."

JD laughed. "Oh, great, an eight-year-old slave driver. We've created a monster."

Amy made a face and went to her uncle's side. She edged close against him, forcing him to move closer to Mari.

JD glanced at Mari. "What's she up to?"

Mari shrugged.

As they loaded what they needed into the car, Mari speculated. It was possible that Amy had sensed the tension between them. The thought depressed her. She'd wanted nothing else to worry Amy. The girl already had enough to contend with.

Mari shifted in her seat and gave Amy a reassuring smile. "Remember that tonight we're all counting on one another. We have to stay alert so we can keep each other safe."

Amy toyed with the camera, bringing the camera into focus as she'd been taught. "I'm going to practice some more now," she said, her face serious. As they pulled to a stop by the light, Amy stared at a nearby driver and passengers, watching to see if they spoke as she rested the camera on the car seat.

"I think she senses division between us," Mari warned JD. "For her sake, we can't let our emotions affect the way we act around each other. She needs both of us now, JD."

"You're right. She doesn't need anything else to worry about." JD wove through traffic, then slowed down as they approached One-Eyed Dan's. The parking area of the popular night spot was filled with cars. "It'll be easy to get lost in that crowd. Undoubtedly that's why they picked this place. But it'll work for us, too."

As JD circled around to the back of the parking lot, Mari spotted three men near the Dumpster beside the building. "What do you think? Is that them?"

JD watched the trio for a moment. "Maybe. Two of them look like cops. Here comes another one."

Mari heard the abrupt change in his voice. "What is it?"

"It's the chunky sheriff's deputy. I'm almost positive."

Sitting in a darkened car gave them some protection from prying eyes, but it also restricted their field of vision. "I think you're right but I can't be sure."

She saw JD reach over to pick up the camera from the back. "I'm no photographer, but we'll see what I can do with this thing." JD snapped a few shots. He then glanced back at Amy and held the camera out, supporting it with his arm so she could look through the viewfinder. "Try to make out what they're saying," he asked.

Amy watched carefully, moving the camera slightly as she changed her aim. "I don't understand," she said at last. "It's hard to read. They talk real fast."

JD placed a hand on her shoulder to get her attention. "Just do the best you can to repeat what they're saying."

Amy peered through the camera again. "Buyer wants a sample. But... seek your tea is tight."

"I think she means security," Mari said with a rueful smile.

Amy continued. "I can't get them out with all the sir cheese."

"Searches?" JD speculated.

"We better get the—something with an *o*—in your ant's papers."

"Insurance papers?" Mari suggested.

"We have to destroy them before someone starts making come pear sons," Amy added.

"And they don't want comparisons. Maybe the 'o' word was 'originals'?" JD said pensively. "So they don't want any comparisons to the originals?"

"The man with the beard is walking away!" Amy said. "I can't tell what he's saying, but he's waving his arms and I think he's angry." Amy edged forward, straining to see through the lens. Suddenly she cried out, "He can see us!"

Mari turned around and saw a man approaching their car from behind, crouching low. "Get us out of here, JD!"

JD floored the accelerator and they fishtailed out of the parking lot in a flurry of dust and gravel. As he reached the end of the back alley, a car moved in to block their path.

Chapter Fifteen

JD slammed hard on the brakes and shifted into reverse. With tires spinning, he rocketed in the opposite direction.

He saw two men at the opposite end of the alley, guns drawn, running to block his escape. Without hesitation, he pulled back into One-Eyed Dan's parking lot and blaring the horn to warn startled patrons out of the way, barreled through until he reached the street.

Mari clutched the dashboard. "I think I recognized one of those guys. The headlights caught the one at the very end of the alley for a moment. I'm almost sure it was Al Stuart's assistant, Larry Wright, from the insurance company."

"Officer Kyle Romero, who we saw walking out of his very ordinary home, was one of the other ones," JD said.

As they rounded the corner, they passed a police car heading in the opposite direction. In the rearview mirror, JD saw the car switch on its emergency lights and do a one-eighty in the road.

JD cursed loudly. "I had a feeling one of the guys back there would phone in a report. All they would have had to do was say they saw us and put out an APB."

"We can outrun one car, but how are we going to outrun their radios? Everyone will be after us now." Mari could see the police car racing after them.

"We've got to ditch this car the first chance we get. But before we can do anything, we've got to get a little more room to operate." JD slammed on the accelerator, cutting across the pavement onto a gravel road which paralleled the street. Suddenly he veered sharply to the left and cut across the rugged desert of the west mesa.

Mari grabbed the edge of her seat, checking to see if Amy was okay. "What are you doing? We can't outrun them across the desert!"

"I know this area. Up ahead is open country, criss-crossed with arroyos and a big escarpment. People go up there to shoot, unofficially. It's state land, and not nearly as rugged if you know where you're going."

They bounced along a faint track which was almost indiscernible on the uneven ground. The only things keeping them from repeatedly smashing their heads against the roof of the car were their seat belts. Mari glanced back at Amy but no fear shone in the little girl's eyes, only excitement. At that moment, Mari fervently wished she could see through the eyes of an eight-year-old. To Amy, this was probably like some television movie. The flashing lights of the cop car, a quarter of a mile behind, only added to the illusion.

Blood sang in her ears and her skin felt clammy despite the cold. The track crossed another just ahead. JD turned out his lights, let his foot off the gas pedal, then turned sharply, braking. They inched along slowly as JD picked his way across country. Mari glanced at the path behind them, but somehow the police car had disappeared from view. "Where is he?"

JD grinned. "I thought making a turn in that spot would take care of him. Guess I was right." He gave her a thumbs-up. "There's an area back there that's littered with sharp rocks jutting out just above the sand. You wouldn't see them readily because of the brush but they're there. I knew enough to turn just before we reached them. He didn't. I figure he either blew a tire or ripped out his oil pan."

"Now what? I'm sure he's called in for help."

"No doubt. But we're going to reach the highway soon, about a mile south of the bar. They won't expect that. Then I'm going to find another license plate and get rid of the one on this car. You and Amy crouch low. It'll make us look different if there's just one person in the car."

JD took a slow, circuitous route back. Fifteen minutes later, he emerged at a parking lot shared by a shopping mall and two restaurants. He pulled up beside a car that was almost a duplicate of the one they were driving, near the rear entrance of a hair salon. Switching plates took only a few seconds.

Minutes later, they were on their way back to the safe house. "That'll confuse them and give us a little more time. I'll get hold of Bruce and ask him to bring us a new set of wheels."

Mari bit her bottom lip worriedly. "We've assumed that one of the guys at the bar called in. But what if we were wrong? Could we have been followed to the bar?"

"No way. I've been alert every step of the way."

By the time they arrived at the safe house, Mari was exhausted. Every bone and muscle in her body ached from weariness. From the looks of her, Amy felt the same way. Mari helped Amy to bed on the couch, then tucked her in. "Sleep well," she signed, then kissed her on the forehead.

Amy smiled, snuggling down into the covers, hugging her bear tightly in her arms, the Advent calendar propped up on the coffee table. "When we see Mommy, will you tell her how I helped?"

"You bet, honey."

"We'll all be together soon," she signed. "Christmas is in two days." Amy pointed to the calendar.

"That's right," Mari signed, then glanced at JD as he came into the room. "Now go to sleep."

JD left the tree lights on for Amy, watching her from a corner of the room. He seemed to be lost in thought. "We do have one win," he said at last. "I was able to take a few photos before everything went sour. I'll drop off the film at a developing place tomorrow."

"Maybe it's safer to send the roll to Jennifer Anderson with the tape recording."

He nodded. "We'll take it to the newspaper office tomorrow morning."

Mari carried a few things from her bag into the rear bedroom. Remembering the night before, her flesh prickled with awareness. She didn't want to sleep alone—not tonight, not ever again. She yearned for JD's touch and for the tender fires she'd found in his arms.

He came down the hall and stood in front of the room she'd chosen as hers. "Tomorrow we're going to have to find a way to get into the insurance agent's office. From what we learned tonight, I strongly suspect they're hoping to mask their crime by altering the appraisal and insurance papers on the Madonna."

"Reasonable assumptions." She tried to brush aside the longing that ribboned through her. Taking a deep breath, she continued. "There are usually two sets of originals, one for the insurance office and one for the policyholder. Elizabeth might have had one once since she took out the policy, but we have no chance of finding it now. Maybe that was one of the reasons they burned down her house. They weren't able to find it in Liz's disaster of an office but figured it must have been there someplace." She paused consideringly. "Well, they've left us no choice. We'll have to take theirs."

"I think you're right," JD agreed. "That'll be our proof that they tampered with the jewels on the Madonna's dress." JD held her gaze for a long moment. A sorrowful understanding flickered in his eyes before he turned and walked away.

After he left her, sadness filled Mari's heart. It was time to let go, but some dreams were tenacious and refused to yield easily to logic. As she lay down, she prayed that at least some of the pain would stay with her always to remind her about the high cost of dreams.

MARI AWOKE ABRUPTLY, feeling a hand on her shoulder. Jackknifing to a sitting position, she blinked furiously in the dark.

Slowly, shaking out the cobwebs of a dream, she recognized Amy. "What are you doing up?" Mari signed, trying hard to clear her vision. Her mind was smothered in thick, fuzzy clouds that made clear thinking impossible.

Amy signed, pointing to her nose. "Smell."

Mari caught a faint whiff of the odor of rotten eggs. As a cold breeze hit her, she shuddered and turned her head toward the window.

"I opened the window," Amy signed. "There's a man in the kitchen working. The oven door is open. Awful smell."

The reality of what was happening hit her full force. Mari bolted out of bed and taking Amy's hand, ran to JD's bedroom. He was either fast asleep or unconscious. The blankets were pulled down around his narrow hips. A thrill coursed through her at the memory the sight aroused. "JD, wake up," she whispered.

He smiled groggily and reached out to her, pulling her onto the bed with him.

She disentangled herself. "Will you wake up!" Mari turned to Amy. "Open the window," she signed. As fresh air streamed into the room, she shook him again. "Come on, wake up!"

JD took a breath and coughed harshly. His eyes focused on her face and he sat up quickly. "What's going on?"

She held a finger to his lips. "Shhh. Someone got into the house and they've turned on the gas."

JD's nose crinkled. "Turn around, both of you," he said, motioning with his hand so Amy would understand.

Mari and Amy turned their backs to him, but as a flicker of movement caught her eye, Mari stole a glance in the mirror. JD stood naked, looking powerful and strong, like some proud jungle cat whose territory has been invaded. Muscles rippled across his shoulders and his buttocks were taut.

A wave of heat washed through her. Then, to her chagrin, his gaze caught hers in the mirror and he winked. She felt her face burning as she averted her gaze. "Hurry," she whispered.

JD pulled on his jeans. Walking to the window and glancing outside to make sure it was safe, he signaled for Mari and Amy to crawl outside.

Amy went through it and hopped to the ground easily. Mari straddled the windowsill and glanced back at JD. He was a foot or so away, pulling on a crewneck sweater. "You *are* coming with us, aren't you?"

"No, I'm going after him," JD muttered.

"But—"

"Go. Take care of Amy."

The words made her realize she had no choice. Amy needed her. As she hopped down, Mari saw JD disappear into the darkness of the hall. Her heart felt as if it had broken loose and sunk down into her stomach.

JD HEARD LIGHT FOOTSTEPS heading toward the back door across the brick floor. The smell of rotting eggs was stronger in here, but the creep had left a door half-open to avoid gassing himself in the process.

He wanted to catch this guy. He needed answers, but something primal inside JD hoped that their intruder would resist providing them. That would give him an excuse to break every bone in the jerk's body. Frustration and helplessness belonged to the boy he'd been once but not the man he was now. He was an adult, who up to very recently had been in charge of his own life and future. Someone would pay for what they'd done to him and his family, and to the woman he had grown to love.

As the intruder stepped out into the moonlight, JD ran forward after him. Just then, the man turned around and JD saw his face clearly. It was Officer Kyle Romero. Instantly, Romero darted forward and leapt over the hedge. He was in remarkably good shape. JD also cleared the hedge easily, but by then his quarry had reached an old pickup. In the blink of an eye, Romero was racing down the street at full throttle.

JD spat out an angry oath. He'd moved too soon and lost the one chance he'd had. He turned and ran back to the house, thoughts of Mari and Amy crowding his mind. At least they were safe for the time being. They'd come close, too close, to death tonight. A moment later, JD found them huddled in some brush by the fence that bordered the property. Mari held Amy tightly against her. "You two okay?" he asked.

"Yes, we're fine," Mari replied. "When I heard the truck drive off, I went back in and turned off the gas. Once it clears out, we'd better get our things and put them in the car. We can't stay here anymore."

JD nodded. "We'll go by my office and I'll take one of the company trucks. Bruce'll know who took it, so he won't say anything."

TEN MINUTES LATER, they were in the car, ready to leave. "How did they track us here?" Mari asked. "Have you given any thought to that?"

"I don't know. I suppose someone could have trailed us from a distance."

"I didn't see anyone following us, did you?" Seeing him shake his head, she continued. "I realize that doesn't mean they didn't, but there's another possibility that worries me. What if they've figured out where we're staying through a process of elimination? Maybe someone else has a copy of the houses your firm's bid on."

"No one but Bruce has that information."

"What about your office staff?"

"We only have one full-time secretary. She's been with us for years."

"After we take one of your company's trucks, I think we should put the rest of this night to good use."

JD grinned slowly. "What did you have in mind?"

"Not what's on yours," Mari retorted, unable to suppress a smile. "We have some work to do that shouldn't be postponed. We need to break into Al Stuart's office."

His eyes widened slightly. "How? I'm sure there are alarms in that building. If we set one off, we'll have half the police force down our necks."

"There's a lobby there. We don't have to go in an outside window."

"There's a guard in the lobby."

"He can't be everywhere at once."

"No. I don't like it."

Mari lapsed into a thoughtful silence. "We'll need those original appraisals if we're to prove, before it's too late, that a crime was committed. Without that evidence, we won't be able to convince the authorities that Elizabeth was framed and that whatever's turned up missing in the evidence room was only part of a cover-up. We have to break in."

"Let's get over there. If there's a way in, we'll find it. I know most maintenance crews around here go in during the wee hours before the office staffs do. Right now most buildings downtown are gearing up for our coldest month, which is January. If I play it right maybe I can pass for a worker."

"But what about Amy? We can't leave her alone in the car out there. It's just too dangerous."

"She'll have to come in with us." As they arrived at Thunderbird Construction, JD circled the block to make sure no police officers were watching the building. Then he parked by the gates, got out and unlocked them. Moments later, they were inside. "There's a truck beside the supply building. It's not fancy, but it's in good shape. We'll use that one."

JD led the way. He wasn't sure how long Amy and Mari could go on facing one failure after another. Sooner or later they'd start to lose faith in him. The thought felt like cold steel in his gut.

JD took a deep breath. For now, he'd just worry about getting them out of here safely. "Okay. Here's the truck." He produced a key from his pocket, then stowed their gear inside the light blue extended-cab pickup. They were underway moments later. JD felt the tension coiling through him as he thought of what lay ahead. "If we don't have a clear, safe method of entry, we may have to split up. Be prepared for that."

Twenty minutes later, after stopping to drop off their evidence and a note for Jennifer Anderson, they drove around the back of the building. The door had been left ajar with a rock, but no one was around. JD parked next to an all-night coffee shop a block away. Staying in the shadows, they went toward the adobe structure. Amy clutched her little white bear tightly to her chest.

"I'll get in closer and scout things out," JD said. "If everything's clear, then you guys can follow me in. If I don't come out and signal you, go back to the truck. Give me twenty minutes, then drive around the building. I'll find you. But if you see any signs of trouble, get out of here fast."

"I'm not going to abandon you," Mari protested. "If you're in trouble, we'll find a way to help."

"No. You'll only end up under arrest, too. If I get caught, believe me, I'm going to do my best to get away. I'll have a better chance if I know you two are already safe someplace else."

JD moved forward cautiously, mingling with the shadows. There was a maintenance truck up ahead. He saw a man go in through the back door, then it shut. Taking a chance, he waited a moment then followed the man in. He was about six offices down from Stuart's when he heard the maintenance crew walking in the hall around the corner. The heating was obviously off in the building which gave him an idea.

JD glanced up and studied a heating and cooling vent. If he could gain access to an office and squeeze through the vent, that would be the safest way to move through the building. He noticed a real-estate office ahead, its door open. A minute later, a man stepped out, toolbox in hand, and walked to a thermostat on the wall.

While his back was turned, JD quickly slipped inside the office and hid inside a closet. The maintenance man returned just as he pulled the door shut. JD watched the gap at the bottom of the door. It seemed like forever, but eventually the lights in the room were turned off. Then he heard the door lock as the man left. JD came out of hiding quickly, knowing twenty minutes had already passed. If Mari did as he'd asked, she would return to the truck.

It took him less than three minutes to unfasten the grille over a vent and crawl through the ducting to the next office. Pushing out the barrier covering the vent over Stuart's office, he slipped down onto a desk and then to the floor. He moved fast, going to the cabinets and searching through the files. It took longer than he expected. Each minute felt like an eternity. Finally he found what he needed under the name of the parish.

JD wanted to make a photocopy of the papers, but when he turned on the copy machine, it made so much noise warming up, he shut it off again. He'd have to take the original. He went to the door and listened. Everything was still quiet. Opening the door a crack, he verified no one was around, then stepped out into the hall, closing the door behind him.

As he started toward the rear exit, JD saw the security guard coming down the hall. There was no place and no time to hide. Pressing into the shadows of a doorway, he waited.

Chapter Sixteen

Fear clutched at Mari's heart as she looked around. Twenty minutes had gone by and five minutes ago the back door had been shut and locked. Sneaking in was no longer an option. She glanced at her watch. He was more than over-due, but she couldn't bring herself to go back to the truck and simply hope for the best. There had to be some way to figure out what was going on. She circled the building with Amy. The lobby, open all night because it contained an ATM, stood empty. She could see a security guard walking down one of the corridors.

Deep in thought, she was startled when Amy tugged at her sleeve and gestured ahead. "Look," she mouthed.

Mari nodded absently, at first only aware of the tall, glit-tering, white-flocked tree that stood in the lobby. Then Mari saw JD ducking out of an office, and at that precise mo-ment, the guard turned and started heading in that direc-tion. Mari felt her heart skip several beats, then speed up. An idea formed quickly in her mind and she signed to Amy at lightning speed. For once, she was glad that American Sign Language was like abbreviated English.

Amy nodded, understanding, and ran into the building. Mari stuck her hands into her pockets to make sure no one would see them shaking, then followed Amy inside. Amy's footsteps were heavy, and the guard, hearing them, stopped and turned around. Amy stood inches from the tree, touching the simulated snow that created a glowing background for each colored light that decorated the branches. Mari saw the guard's expression change from wariness to a relaxed smile.

"Wait a minute there, little girl. What are you doing here at this time of night. Don't tell me you have a bank card?"

Mari came through the door just then, making a show of having just caught up with Amy. "Oh, I'm so very sorry. She got away from me!"

Amy hid her face against Mari's side, pretending a sudden attack of shyness.

"Forgive us. My daughter doesn't mean any harm, but the decorations on the tree caught her attention all the way from the end of the block. She thought it was real snow and just wanted to feel it. We've never decorated ours like this. I had no idea that she'd run in here."

The guard smiled as Amy clutched her bear tightly, her face hidden in the folds of Mari's coat. "No problem, ma'am. If she wants to look at the tree, let her. That's what it's there for, and this, after all, is a season for children."

Mari took Amy's hand, and as the guard watched with a smile, they slowly circled the tree. As they got halfway around, Mari caught a glimpse of JD sprinting across the back hallway. Convinced that he had made his escape, Mari thanked the guard and then led Amy back into the street. "Well done, Amy!"

Amy placed the tips of her fingers against her mouth, then moved them forward, signing thank-you.

"Now let's go find your uncle."

As they walked past the building, they saw JD coming toward them as if he had also just gone for a walk. He beamed a grateful smile at them both. "I thought you'd agreed to go back to the truck and wait for me there."

"Yeah, well . . . aren't you glad I don't always listen to you?"

He grinned. "Maybe this time."

"Did you get what we needed?"

"I've got the original appraisal inside my jacket pocket. But when they find out, they'll come after us with a vengeance."

"True, but we still don't have anything to clear ourselves of all suspicion. The department may not have enough to convict us, but they can ruin us anyway. We'll have a cloud hanging over our heads for life."

They quickly returned to the vehicle. "Let's go to our listening post and see if there's anything new. We can decide what to do next after that."

They arrived at their rented office a short time later. After making a bed of blankets for Amy, they played back what they'd managed to record.

A man's voice came through clearly. "The final move is tomorrow afternoon at around one. Can't say I'm sorry. I wish it had been much sooner."

To Mari's surprise, Pearline answered. "There was no choice, Ricky. There's no other way to get them out safely except like this. Is the van ready?"

"Yeah, it's all taken care of. The transfer will be a piece of cake."

"Good thing I take care of the computerized records. It was easy to frame Elizabeth by adding a few items that never existed. Too bad I couldn't fix you and Elizabeth up. You could have planted 'stolen' evidence in her house that would have sealed the frame."

"I asked her out, but she just wasn't interested. That woman never trusted me."

"You're too pushy, that's why."

"Naw, I just don't have your innocent face. That's why I'm working vice. You played her brother and his girlfriend like a violin. You even had them arrange to check with you. We'll find a way to nab them then and we'll be heroes. What a joke!"

JD clenched and unclenched his fists but remained silent. Ricky Estrada was a sheriff's deputy gone bad, one who'd brought his sister along to share in his crimes. Or was it the other way around?

"They're fools, I told you," Pearline returned. "Neither JD nor Mari Sanchez were ever a threat to our operation. In fact, they worked to our advantage. Having them on the loose as suspects suited our purpose perfectly."

They heard the sound of something being slid across the floor.

"This is heavy. It's going to be difficult to move."

"So get some help. This is turning out better than I expected. No one will ever guess what's hidden in here."

Suddenly a burst of static covered up their conversation. It continued for several minutes, then the sound of voices came through clearly again. "Okay. It's boxed, taped shut and ready to go."

"I suppose you two have some real work to do today?" another voice interjected. "Or do you plan on running a charity in here the rest of the month?"

"Lieutenant, we were just..."

Mari looked up at JD. "Randall?" she mouthed.

"Okay. I see you're done with that now. So get back to work. Our butts are on the line in this department. We can't let up for a moment."

They heard the door close, then silence.

Mari glanced at JD. "I don't get it. What were they talking about, and is Randall in on this? It didn't sound like it."

"I don't know, but we better put it all together fast. I have a feeling we're about out of time. Christmas is in two days," JD noted, his gaze straying over Amy's sleeping figure. "I'd hoped she'd have a regular Christmas, one filled with love and laughter, not one on the run," JD added, his tone filled with gentleness. "I'd give anything if I could do that much for her."

Mari paced around the room. "Replacing the gems on the Madonna shouldn't have been difficult for them in the evidence room. You can buy glass or plastic gems at craft stores and no one could have walked in on them in there without warning. They could see anyone who was signing in. The real trick would have been to get the real jewels out of the evidence room. Everyone's searched coming out. Smuggling them out one by one would have increased the risk significantly. I can't see them doing that, but I haven't been able to think of any other way."

"They've gone to a great deal of trouble to divert suspicion from the real nature of the crime. Maybe that's a clue."

"I just don't see how everything ties in," Mari answered.

JD searched the table for his keys. "Well, let's think about it later. For now, let's find some place to spend the night. I don't want to stay this close to the station. It'll be too easy for someone to trap us in here. We'll sleep in the truck somewhere off the road where we can make a quick getaway." JD glanced around, feeling inside his jeans for the keys. "Where did I put them?"

Mari picked up his jacket from the floor and went through the pockets. "Here you go, Mr. Detective," she teased.

He stared at the keys as she handed them over. "I just had a thought."

"I bet it's lonely all by itself up there," Mari quipped with a smile.

JD grinned back. "I've got the answer," he said, his voice taut with excitement. "Those jewels are still in the evidence room somewhere. I'd bet my last dime on it. It's the ideal place to hide them indefinitely. If they'd been discovered missing, it wouldn't have been difficult to get them back onto the Madonna's gown on short notice. In fact, maybe that's what happened when Randall had others check on the Madonna."

"This has been meticulously planned right from the beginning," Mari observed, leaning back against the wall.

JD's gaze fell on Amy and he smiled. "I'm glad she's got that bear. Little girls need something to hug. Big girls, too, though they don't always admit it," he teased, looking directly at Mari.

"That's it! You've put your finger on it, JD!" Mari's eyes grew wide.

"No, arms... you need arms to hug, not fingers," he answered, giving her a totally perplexed look.

"Don't you see? You're absolutely right that the best hiding place for the gems was in the evidence room. And where? In the toys from the Toys for Tykes campaign! That's how they're planning to smuggle the gems out. No one's searching the toys." Mari was almost shouting.

"Only one flaw with your theory, Sherlock." JD smiled wryly. "The toys will be taken directly to the parish from the evidence room tomorrow at 1:00 p.m. Then they'll be wrapped and given out at the party Christmas Day. That doesn't leave any time for someone to sneak into the rectory and take the gems out of the toys. And there's no way an adult can get out of the church holding a toy or that a kid could be guaranteed to get a specific toy. There would be too many people wandering around there to do anything in secrecy."

"But what if the toys never make it to the parish? What if the entire shipment is hijacked?" Mari knew she had it figured out now, and the knowledge was depressing. "Taking the jewels from the Madonna is bad enough. Smuggling them out in those toys, and then robbing the children of Christmas, is like piling desecration on top of desecration." She weighed what she'd just deduced. "And here's a worse thought. Let's assume that the shipment goes through, that they plan on stealing only specific toys that have the contraband. They couldn't do it during the party so it would have to be afterward. Any child who receives a toy with one of the Madonna's gems inside could be in mortal danger."

JD's expression grew hard. "We can't let that happen."

"The problem is, we can't just go to Jennifer Anderson now. There are several department people involved that we know of, but there may be others we haven't identified. If the paper blows the whistle on the department, they'll be alerting the criminals. It would only take one person left undiscovered to cover up the crime. We'd be right back where we started from and Elizabeth and Amy will remain loose ends for the gang. Then they'll be in mortal danger and so will we."

He nodded. "You're right, but we've got to stop the gang."

"We have to make sure we cover all the bases. We need two plans. One in case they're going to hijack the whole truckload of toys, and another in case they're planning to steal specific toys from the kids after the party."

"How? Covering both contingencies would require us to be at the church's Christmas party. And if they're going to keep track of where certain toys go, then that means they'll be there, too. They'd place us under arrest before we could warn anyone."

"They'd have to recognize us first," Mari said slowly. "And they won't, not if we go as Santa Claus and his two elves."

"Costumes are going to be tough to find this close to Christmas."

"For most people, yes, but I always help out during our school's winter carnival. I still have my key to the building where the fund-raising costumes are kept. There are elf costumes in various sizes and a Santa Claus costume, too. One of our teachers dresses up each year for the gift exchange. We'll borrow what we need, then bring everything back." She glanced at Amy, who was still sleeping peacefully. "I hate to wake her, but this is the best time for us to get those costumes."

"I'll take her," JD said.

The tenderness JD showed as he lifted Amy took Mari's breath away. He had so much love to give! Her heart ached with longing to accept his gift.

Mari walked with him to the truck and helped him settle Amy into the back seat. "I'm glad she didn't wake up. She needs to rest."

"We need rest, too," he replied, his voice betraying the intense weariness he felt. "After we find the costumes, we'll park off the road, maybe in the foothills, and get some sleep."

"Anywhere is fine with me," she said, yawning. "I could sleep on a rock."

"How about in my arms?"

A searing warmth spread through her. "No. You're too much of a distraction."

He grinned. "You find me that disturbing even when you're exhausted? My ego and I both thank you."

Mari laughed softly. Neither of them could let the situation get to them. Joking around was nothing more than a smoke screen to keep fear at bay. They'd hit a point where it was all or nothing. The next twenty-four hours would determine if they were capable of clearing themselves and helping Elizabeth and Amy—or not. There'd be no more opportunities.

"We can't fail, and I'm so afraid we might," Mari admitted in a whisper-thin voice.

JD reached for her hand and covered it with his own. "We'll do whatever we have to. We can accomplish miracles together, you know we can. In many ways, we already have."

Maybe he was right. They'd both changed. His humanity had tempered his pride and her heart had known love again. They'd already been blessed with gifts that would last a lifetime. "It is a season of hope," she agreed. "I guess we'll have to hold fast to ours."

They arrived at the portable building adjacent to the school forty minutes later. Moonlight filtered through the thin clouds but the darkness was pronounced. JD parked in the deepest shadows on the west side.

Leaving Amy in the truck, they ducked inside the building. "The Christmas costumes are over here." Mari led the way to an adjacent room. Mari took a Santa Claus outfit from the rack and held it up against JD. "It's way too large for me. It'll be a tight fit for you, but I think you can squeeze into it."

JD eyed it skeptically. "What about costumes for you and Amy?"

Mari picked out a small green elf costume with matching hat and a beard in Amy's size and one for herself. "We'll be perfect!"

"Aw, no miniskirted Mrs. Claus?"

Mari chuckled. "Can't afford to give the lecherous Mr. Claus any ideas at the wrong time."

"Implying there might be a right time? What a wonderfully tempting thought."

Mari shoved him gently out the door. "Come on, you dirty old man." As they got underway, Mari rubbed her eyes. They felt like sandpaper. "After we get a few hours of rest, it'll be daylight. Then we'll have to work fast. We'll need to find our own red van, like the one the local Ford dealership is lending to the parish to transport the toys. Then we'll have to buy some toys, at least enough to fill the tops of some large cardboard boxes."

JD nodded pensively. "You're hoping to switch vans, or at least the toys," he observed. JD took a deep breath, then let it out again. "That's a tall order."

"A driver from the parish will be driving the van with the toys. He won't be expecting trouble. I realize it'll still be really risky, but if we get the chance, we'll have to take it. If

not, then we'll just follow behind in case the gang attempts
a hijacking."

JD paused consideringly. "I suppose we can rent a van in
Socorro. The town's far enough away, we may be able to get
away with it. Of course, they'll ask for a driver's license, and
if they check it out right then, we'll be in trouble."

"It's a risk. I know that. But we need the van. I'll rent it
under my name. In New Mexico, it's a far more common
one than yours. You can go buy the toys. Get as many as
you can. The sales will be going strong by now. Use your
company card. By the time they track the purchases, our
plan will have either worked, clearing us, or we'll be in jail."

"Comforting thought," JD muttered. "What a way to
spend Christmas Eve."

IT WAS A LITTLE BEFORE four in the morning by the time JD
pulled off the highway, then continued across the rugged
desert terrain. They'd left the city far behind them. Now he
had to find a low spot where their vehicle would be hidden
from the highway. He wanted to make sure no state cops
would spot them and come check out the car.

JD drove into a narrow canyon, then stopped. From this
spot, the highway was out of sight. "We'll be safe here for
a few hours. That's all the time we'll have to rest, though,
if you want to try to see if we can switch vans right after the
toys are loaded at one this afternoon."

"Like I said, the driver from the parish won't be expecting trouble. His guard will be down. And the department
would never believe we'd try this right under their noses.
That's the only advantage we have."

JD bundled his coat into a pillow then leaned back against
the door. They'd placed several blankets in the truck in case
of emergencies. "You know, there's not enough space in
here for both of us to rest comfortably, so I have a suggestion. If you're willing, you can lie against me, then we can
both stretch out and pull the blankets over us."

The thought of lying in JD's arms filled Mari with an intense yearning. She wanted to feel his heart beating against hers, the warmth of his skin, his arms embracing her protectively. Everything feminine in her needed the comfort of his rugged strength.

Mari moved toward JD and his arms welcomed her. His body was hard, but the safety she found in his embrace was intoxicating. He shifted and her legs slipped between his, her lower body nestled into the cradle of his thighs.

JD let out his breath in one long, shuddering sigh. "You belong in my arms, Mari, whether you admit it or not," he whispered in the darkness.

JD's voice was so kind and gentle, it made her want to cry. No matter what the future held, she'd always have this time to remember. The memories would remain tucked away in her heart because she'd found the kind of love that came only once in a lifetime.

He caressed her tenderly and when she whimpered, he kissed her deeply. "Let me touch you. I want to memorize your body, the way you tremble, your sighs against my neck. This may be all the time we have left."

"But Amy..."

"If she wakes up, you'll be under the blankets, clothed, and I'll stop," he assured her, his voice deep and gentle. JD stroked her breasts then unzipped her jeans. His hand slipped down and began stroking the feminine core of her. Her hands clutched at his shirt as he continued, drinking in her cries with his mouth. "Let go, love," he murmured. "Trust me."

Her body seemed to melt and then shatter as his fingers wove magic all through her. As she shuddered, all her tensions and fears vanished. In that sweet instant, she was totally at peace. It was as if she'd finally reached home after a long absence.

Mari shifted slightly in his arms and felt him rock hard beneath her. "But you..." she whispered.

"I loved you the only way I can right now. Accept the gift."

Her eyes fluttered closed. In the warmth of his embrace, nestled against him, she drifted off to a tranquil sleep.

Chapter Seventeen

Mari awoke as sunlight streamed through the pickup windows, melting the light frost that had crystallized on the glass. JD's gaze rested on her. "Did you get any sleep?" she asked, immediately concerned.

"Some."

His beard was thick now and she liked his new look. She moved away reluctantly, wishing that they could have taken time to enjoy the sunrise. Taking a peek over the seat, Mari heard Amy lightly snoring, curled up like a ball in her blankets.

JD started up the truck and turned on the heater after the engine was warm. He placed the truck in gear and drove back to the highway. "No matter what happens, I want you to know that you're a part of me forever, Mari."

She wanted to tell him that she loved him but held back, knowing that much needed to be resolved before promises could be made. The next few hours would test their courage and everything they wanted to believe about themselves. They had to see this challenge through first. Neither would be free until their debts of honor were paid.

After a quick take-out breakfast, they drove south to Socorro. JD dropped Mari off at a car rental agency. "Good luck."

With a wave, Mari walked inside the small field office. Offering a silent prayer to the Madonna asking for her help, she walked up to the desk.

JD WATCHED MARI WALK through the door, then forced his attention back to their plan. He didn't want to leave her here, but time was critical.

Amy crawled up to the front seat and they got underway. "You like Mari," she said, trying hard to speak clearly for his benefit.

"Yes, I do."

"You two getting married?"

JD took a deep breath then let it out again. "I don't know. It's up to her."

"You asked her?"

"Not yet."

"Why not?"

JD laughed. "I don't think she's ready to be asked."

Amy seemed to consider it. "She loves you. I can tell."

"That may not be enough," JD explained. "She has... other plans for her life."

Amy shook her head. "She's scared. Like Mommy. You have to make her not scared."

"I can't. It's up to her to find that courage. But when she's ready, I'll be there."

"Grown-ups always make easy things hard."

JD smiled. "You may have a point."

JD wove through the maze of unfamiliar streets, heading to a small toy store at the end of Main Street. He pulled into a parking space. The business had opened early to catch the last-minute shoppers. "Let's go in and pick out a variety of toys. We'll need enough so that they'll spill over the tops of cardboard boxes we're going to stuff nearly full with newspaper."

Amy nodded. "So we can switch them for the other ones that'll go to the parish."

JD and Amy spent the next two hours going from store to store, never buying too much in one place to avoid attracting attention. Finally JD stood with Amy and studied all the boxes of toys crammed into the extended cab. "Nothing else is going to fit in there. Not even a marble."

"Yeah, but it looks really neat, doesn't it?" Amy said, eyes sparkling.

JD gazed at his niece, glad for the opportunity he'd had to get to know her, in spite of the circumstances. She had captured his heart and taught him about the gentler side of love. Between Mari and Amy he'd learned how all-encompassing love could be. He couldn't imagine life without them anymore.

They got into the truck and drove across town to meet Mari at their rendezvous, an arroyo south of the city. Now it was time to begin the final phase of their plan.

Amy's face lit up as Mari joined them. "Look!" She waved at the boxes in the truck. "Neat, huh?"

Mari smiled, then helped them transfer the boxes over to the rented van. "No matter what else happens, we'll make sure the kids get their toys. They'll have the kind of Christmas they've been wishing for. We'll see to it."

JD brought out the costumes. "We'll leave my truck parked here. It's time for us to head back to the city. The van will be leaving the station at around one and by then we have to be in place and ready to follow them. Let's get into our costumes now."

Mari gave Amy the small elf costume and smiled as she saw the gleam in Amy's eyes. "You'll look great."

Amy gestured toward Mari's other hand. "And we get to wear beards!"

Mari and Amy went behind a cluster of junipers and changed clothes, helping each other into the costumes. The transformation didn't take long. Mari studied the little girl and laughed. Between the beard, the green pants and smock and floppy elf hat, no one would recognize either of them.

Amy giggled. "You look great!"

"So do you!"

"Where's Santa Claus?" Amy asked, looking around for JD.

Mari heard JD grumbling from behind the van and smiled. "Can I help?" she called out.

"No, it's just this costume. The top is fine, but these pants are too short. And too tight."

"The boots should cover up any problem with the length," she said edging around, eager for a peek.

"Yeah, but these pants..." He stepped clear of the van so she could look.

Mari saw him and smiled. He was right. The pants fit very tightly, clearly outlining the male contours of his body. Awareness of that maleness made her body tingle and burn.

"You keep looking at me like that and I'm going to be an X-rated Santa."

Mari gave him a nervous smile. "Once you put on your top, it'll be much better." Mari helped JD with the jacket then fastened the black belt in place at his waist. "There. That's better," she said, her mouth as dry as the desert.

"Doesn't feel much better," he scowled. "Sitting down without splitting these pants is going to take a miracle."

"We're due for a miracle about now," Mari observed.

JD slowly eased himself behind the wheel of the van. The pant seams held, but a traffic snarl on the interstate forced them to crawl along at a snail's pace. As soon as they reached the city, Mari had JD take a freeway exit and pull into a gas station.

"We can't afford the delay. We have plenty of gas," JD protested.

"We're going to need some way of substantiating everything that happens from this point on. We have to take another chance. I'm calling Jennifer Anderson. I'm certain she won't break the story prematurely and blow what we're trying to do. She'll help us protect the Madonna's jewels and make sure the kids all have a safe Christmas. She's the only ally we've got besides Bruce Campbell. We can't afford to trust him right now unfortunately, so we need her.''

"All right.''

They stopped by a pay phone so Mari could make the call. Thirty minutes before the van was scheduled to leave for the parish, they arrived at the police station. They saw the red parish vehicle parked near the side entrance. Through the driver's side window, which was rolled down, they could see into the back of the van. The toys had already been loaded. No one was around at the moment.

JD's muscles tightened. "I'm going to drop you two off here. Then I'm going to park next to the van and switch vehicles. If I get caught, I'll say that our van holds an extra, last-minute donation." He grinned through the phony beard. "They'll believe Santa.''

"I don't know...." Mari hesitated. "What if the keys aren't in it?''

"I'll hot-wire it. It's a little skill I learned from one of my younger employees. Trust me," JD said, and winked. "Nice girls are supposed to trust Santa.''

"Okay. If any deputies come out, Amy and I will distract them. We'll dance a little jig or something.''

JD groaned. "Heaven help us all. I think this is a Christmas none of us will ever forget." He let them out by the entrance to the parking lot, then drove in beside the other red van.

Mari watched from the sidewalk, praying no one would come out. She rehearsed a little speech in her mind and went through a dance routine in her head. They'd wing it if they had to. She glanced at Amy, who was seated on the curb, reassuring her with a smile.

Amy still held her Advent calendar and her bear, her most cherished possessions, bundled close under her jacket. "We'll be okay," she mouthed. "Santa won't get caught.''

Mari chuckled. This, coming from an elf. "I hope not, honey."

Mari saw JD park next to the Toys for Tykes van, another red Ford vehicle like their own. In a flash, he left one van and ducked into the other, disappearing from view. For an eternity she couldn't see what he was doing, her view blocked by the rental vehicle he'd driven in. She felt herself counting the seconds in heartbeats. Then the parish van started up. A few more heartbeats later, JD pulled up beside them.

Mari and Amy practically dived inside. As Mari's gaze shifted to the Santa Claus behind the wheel, she shook her head in despair. What was the world coming to when Santa had to resort to grand theft auto?

JD grinned at her. "Ho-ho-ho, Merry Christmas!" he said in a rich baritone voice, pulling out into the street and driving away from the station.

Mari burst out laughing. "Excellent, Santa."

As JD glanced at her, his eyes sparkled with an inner fire that even tons of bushy fake white eyebrows couldn't hide. "If I'm a good Santa, then why don't I get any of the perks that go with it?"

"Like giving out toys?"

He shook his head. "No. More like having cute girls on my lap, tempting me to make wishes come true."

Mari laughed. "Oh, great, a lecherous Santa. What a terrible example to set for your tiniest elf." Mari glanced back at Amy but she seemed preoccupied with the toys in the back of the van. Mari reached back and touched her, getting Amy's attention. "Is something wrong?"

"The Madonna isn't here. The kids won't get the toys and the Lady won't be back for Christmas Mass. So many people are going to be sad!"

"They probably weren't planning on carrying the Madonna out until they were ready to leave. She'll end up in the other van, don't worry. We'll find a way to get the Lady and the toys to the parish on time. The kids will have their Christmas. I promise."

They parked at the end of the street and waited. Moments later, they saw the other red van leave the station and drive past them. Mari sucked in her breath.

"That's Lieutenant Randall holding a big box in his lap and sitting next to the driver," Mari said. "So he *is* involved in this!"

"Sure seems that way."

"Hang back," Mari warned. "Randall is a seasoned cop. He'll spot a tail a mile away."

They headed north on I-25 in the direction of Santa Fe. A sense of epiphany hung in the air, adding to the tension between Mari and JD. If they made a mistake now, the Madonna wouldn't be the only one compromised. But at least they'd rescued the toys so the parish children wouldn't be cheated out of Christmas.

They continued north past Santa Fe, then turned up the winding mountain road leading to the village where the church was located. "If anything's going to happen, it's got to happen on this stretch," JD said, slowing down.

He'd barely completed the sentence when they saw a Jeep pulling up beside the red rental van. It slammed hard against the vehicle's side, forcing it off the road into a Forest Service area. Kyle Romero and Ricky Estrada rushed out from the Jeep a moment later. After hauling the startled parish driver and Lieutenant Randall out of the van at gunpoint, they forced them down to the ground. Al Stuart emerged as they were being tied up.

JD turned up the adjacent hill, driving cross-country to avoid being seen, and parked. "Stay low," he whispered, getting out.

They crawled to the edge of the hillside and looked down. "They've got other company besides us," Mari said, gesturing ahead. Near the curve of the road, hidden among some trees and barely discernible, was a tan sedan. A man holding a video camera with a telephoto lens stood a few feet away from it.

"Jennifer did come through for us," JD observed.

"I told her the route we'd be taking but I bet she followed Kyle Romero. Remember she ID'd the civilian volunteer who tried to run us down. We wondered at the time if he could have been Kyle Romero's brother. My guess is she found out he was." Mari shifted her gaze as the rear of the van was opened and the toys were unceremoniously pushed out onto the dirt. "What the heck?"

They watched the men sort out all the teddy bears wearing bows, then with systematic precision, began gutting them with knives. Stuffing flew into the air like puffs of snow.

"They hid the gems inside the teddy bears!" JD exclaimed.

Mari's gaze fell on the bear that Amy was holding. "Honey, where exactly did your mom get that bear?"

"I don't know. Mommy had it under the blanket in our van. I thought it was a Christmas present for me."

"May I borrow it for a second?" Mari took it from Amy's reluctant hands and studied the construction. "The seam at the bottom has been resewn." Mari moved back from the edge of the hillside and sat behind the cover of some bushes. Working slowly, she forced her fingers through the loose stitching. "There's something hard here in the stuffing."

Trapping the marble-size object between her fingers, she worked it slowly out of the bear, forcing it past the opening her fingers had created. A large, bloodred ruby gleamed as it dropped into the palm of her hand.

"No wonder they wanted us so badly! Elizabeth, either knowingly or not, took the prize of the collection."

Suddenly a shout came from somewhere below. Mari ducked and crawled back to their observation point. Several black-uniformed state police officers came out of hiding and surrounded the two vehicles.

"Way to go, Jennifer!" Mari exclaimed. "Seems like she covered all the bases!"

JD motioned them back to the Toys for Tykes van. "It's time to come out of hiding." He drove slowly down the hill and parked behind a squad car. As they stepped out of the vehicle to identify themselves, another black and white came in off the highway and pulled to a screeching halt beside them.

Chapter Eighteen

JD tugged at the Santa Claus beard but part of it was tangled in his own whiskers. Mari quickly unhooked her brown elf beard from her ears then stepped out of the van slowly. A state police officer had his shotgun pointed at them.

"Jennifer!" Mari called out loudly, looking for the one person who'd recognize her and vouch for her helpful involvement in the case.

Jennifer arrived breathlessly from across the highway. The middle-aged brunette had a no-nonsense air about her that commanded attention despite the distracting presence of her film crew. She stepped toward the officer, motioning him to lower his weapon. "This is the woman who tipped me off. If it hadn't been for her, none of us would have been here for the capture of these thieves."

JD took Amy aside, trying to keep her out of the view of the cameras. "Go to the crooks' van and watch out for the Madonna," he said, opting to send her away from where the arrested offenders were now stretched out, facedown on the ground. "We'll come get you in a minute." Until the gang members were all handcuffed and taken away, he wanted her out of their sight.

After Mari recounted the entire story, Jennifer gave her a long, steady look. "Have you ever considered going into investigative reporting? I think you have a knack for it."

Mari laughed. "No thanks. I'd miss my students too much. I'd rather work with kids than crooks."

"Well, 'Santa And His Elves Rescue Christmas' will make a great headline for our Christmas edition."

Stuart, the insurance man, turned and cast Mari an icy glare as he was led away in handcuffs to a police car. "Anyway, at least it's over," she muttered. "I'm sure these guys will turn state's evidence to lighten their own sentences and the police will soon round up the others."

"The tape and photos you sent me will be corroborating evidence, I'm sure," Jennifer added, "even if the tape was illegally obtained."

Mari cast a worried glance at the Toys for Tykes van. "Those gifts really need to be taken to the kids at the parish. For most of the kids, those toys are the only Christmas gifts they're going to get. And the toys we bought are in the other red van and not evidence of anything. They should be sent to the parish as soon as possible."

The driver, a badly frightened elderly volunteer from the parish, joined them. "She's right, Ms. Anderson. If everything including the Madonna is taken away by the police, there'll be lots of broken hearts this Christmas."

"I'm not sure what I can do. It's all evidence," Jennifer said, "but since only the teddy bears are in question, maybe a little public pressure will help."

As Mari looked toward the van, absently checking on Amy, she saw someone step out from behind a cluster of junipers and climb into the driver's seat. Mari recognized Pearline, but as she called out a warning, the vehicle roared to life. The van with Amy inside slipped out between two police cars and sped away in a cloud of dust and gravel.

JD dived into the closest police car, Mari half a step behind him. The keys had been left in it. The police officer was still several yards away when they shot out in pursuit. "We've just stolen a car. We stayed out of trouble for all of two minutes," JD muttered, looking back in his mirror at the cops who were running to their vehicles.

"Forget that. Can you see any sign of Amy?"

"She must be in the back with the Madonna. I stupidly told her to keep an eye on it. All I was trying to do was make sure the camera didn't show her face all over tomorrow's newspaper."

They drove at breakneck speed south down the interstate, darting in and out of traffic as they tried to keep the red rental van in sight. Mari found the control for the emergency lights. The siren helped clear the way for their pursuit as traffic pulled to one side, letting them pass.

The van took an exit just outside Albuquerque, probably anticipating a roadblock ahead. JD followed along Rio Grande Boulevard, almost losing their quarry in the gathering darkness. Traffic was already heavy with people coming to see the city's *luminarias*. Small sacks filled with sand and illuminated by a single candle lined the driveways, streets and rooftops, adorning entire neighborhoods on Christmas Eve. Tradition said *luminarias* would light the way of the Christ Child and elicit a blessing on each household that took part in the annual tradition.

Mari's eyes remained glued on the van ahead. Pearline veered sharply, taking a left toward the city museums and running a stoplight. JD followed as Pearline whipped the van through traffic with amazing ease, staying ahead of them.

Several blocks down, Pearline made a sharp right and ran into a section of heavy traffic. "I think Pearline has just made a fatal mistake," JD said. "We've got her now." He followed her up the residential street southeast of Old Town.

"Isn't this one of the areas in the official *luminaria* tour?"

Before he could answer, they encountered a slow-moving stream of bumper-to-bumper traffic. Cars crept along the street, headlights off, enjoying the *Noche Buena,* Christmas Eve, displays.

"I can see the van six or seven vehicles ahead," JD said. "She can't pick up speed here or make a turn. But, then again, neither can we."

Suddenly the doors at the back of the van flew open. Amy, still in her elf costume, began waving and throwing toys at the cars following behind. Everyone's attention became riveted on the Christmas elf who was busy sharing the spirit of the season. People crossed into the street from the narrow sidewalks and others left their cars, catching toys in midair.

"Way to go, Amy!" Mari cheered. "They'll mob the van and Pearline'll be stuck!"

"I'm going to pull over to the curb," JD said quickly. "We can catch them on foot now!"

As he parked the police car, JD saw Pearline do the same just ahead. She appeared in the back of the van before Amy could climb down and yanked the girl away from the doors. Amy screamed, grabbing at the object nearest her. The Madonna came free of the box and Amy clutched it against her as Pearline forced her out the passenger door. In the blink of an eye, Pearline and Amy had disappeared down an alley between two large buildings. People closed in around the van and a police officer ran toward it.

"That van's not important anymore," Mari said quickly, joining JD on the sidewalk. "We've got to find Amy. Circle around the building to the right. I'll take the left. That alleyway's only about a block long. We'll head them off." JD nodded and took off.

Mari ran faster than she'd ever dreamed possible. Amy's frantic cries had touched her soul. As she emerged on the street west of the alley, she encountered another slow-moving crowd. People flanked a couple playing the part of Mary and Joseph in the yearly ritual of the *Posada.* The man acting the part of Joseph led a burro on which a woman sat. The pair would go down the street asking for lodging, reenacting the first Christmas. They would be turned down until they reached the last house. There, the celebration would begin.

Mari tried desperately to push through the crowd, but there were too many people gathered to allow quick passage. Then, as she turned the corner, she saw Amy struggling against Pearline, who was dragging her away from the procession.

All of a sudden, three men wearing cloaks appeared from the edge of the crowd closest to the old mission church. Pearline was pushed away and one of the men scooped Amy into his arms and ran into another alley.

Mari's feet barely touched the ground, fear and love urging her forward. Although she reached Pearline in a heartbeat, Amy and the two other men had already vanished. Pearline scrambled to her feet, cursing. As the woman tried to escape from Mari, JD suddenly ran around the corner, remnants of his white Santa Claus beard flying in the breeze. In full costume, he blocked Pearline's path. The deadly intent on his face contrasted sharply with the benign image of Santa Claus. Taking advantage of Pearline's hesitation, Mari reached out and grabbed the woman, holding her fast. JD reached them a second before a uniformed officer arrived. Pearline was handcuffed, then two other officers appeared and handcuffed JD and Mari, too.

"You can't take us in! Amy's still missing," Mari said, trying frantically to spot the child. "We've got to find her!"

"Our people will take care of finding the child. Right now, you're all going in," the senior officer said flatly. "You've got half the state looking for you and a stolen police car. Don't make it any harder on yourselves than you already have."

IT WAS TWO MORE HOURS into Christmas Eve before the police questions had been answered and Mari's attorney was allowed to post bail for both of them. Mari arranged for the toys the trust had purchased to be delivered to the parish. The toys JD and Amy had purchased had also been released. Yet all the ones that had come from the evidence room remained at the station, marked as evidence.

To make matters even worse, Amy and the Madonna statue had not been located despite a city-wide search still underway. Hopelessness and black despair filled Mari. "We'll keep searching until we find her. I don't care how long it takes."

"The police are looking, too," JD reminded her. "If they haven't found her yet, what chance do we have?"

"I don't know, but we aren't giving up. We'll start where she was kidnapped and ask every person we see. Someone else must have seen something. People don't always talk to the police, but they may talk to us."

The streets were nearly deserted and most restaurants had closed by the time they returned to the spot where they'd last seen Amy. Mari walked up and down each little street, searching for people to question.

As they moved toward the center of the plaza in front of the church, Mari took a shortcut through a narrow alley. As she glanced down, her heart leapt to her throat. Choking back a sob, she picked up the hat that belonged to Amy's elf costume. "She was here. Look!" Mari held it up for JD.

JD's eyes narrowed with pain as he gently wrapped his arm around Mari's waist, supporting her. "We'll find Amy. Those men probably were trying to help her. They pulled her away from Pearline, didn't they?"

"What if they were part of the gang, hoping to get Amy and the Madonna to use as ransom?"

"That's not likely. How could they have known that she was coming here, prepared disguises and appeared at just the right time and place? And why take her away from Pearline, if she was part of their gang?" He shook his head. "No, they were trying to help her."

"What if Amy couldn't make them understand? A deaf person's speech isn't always clear to those who aren't used to it."

"If they cared enough to help her, they won't just abandon her. She's okay, I'm sure of it. Hold on to that hope, and don't let yourself doubt it for one minute. We *will* find her."

They continued walking the streets, even after everything had grown quiet. The empty sidewalks echoed their footsteps, the sounds accentuating the emptiness inside her.

"We've lost her." Mari wrapped her jacket tightly around her. A cool wind had risen from the north, spitting flakes of snow that swirled in the glow of the street lamps. "It doesn't seem right. This could be the first white Christmas we've had in a long time, yet it will be filled with more disappointment and sorrow than any I can remember."

"Let's keep looking. We know she's around. Sooner or later, we'll find her," JD insisted.

Time dragged on. They heard the church bells announcing the end of midnight Mass. Cars clustered then thinned as the service finished. Mari walked past the church, watching the last of the worshipers leave. She stopped for a moment. "Do you mind if we go inside for a minute?" she asked quietly.

"No, I think that might be a good idea."

Mari went to the front of the church and knelt by the altar in a silent prayer. To her surprise, JD knelt beside her. For several moments, neither moved. Finally Mari stood and led the way back out.

She stopped on the front steps as the icy breeze hit her and wrapped her jacket even more tightly around her. Fighting tears, she stared absently at the life-size Nativity display on the tiny lawn. Tears weren't needed now; answers were.

Mari took a deep breath then let it out again, her eyes still on the manger. "Something's not right over there. What's odd about that Nativity scene?"

"It seems okay to me. There's Joseph, Mary, the Baby Jesus and the Three Wise Men," he said. "Wait. Those Wise Men aren't dressed right. Shouldn't they be wearing cloaks?"

"Yes, like the trio who carried Amy away."

JD and Mari exchanged quick glances, then hurried toward the display. As they drew near, they heard the soft rustle of cloth, and then a yawn. JD and Mari peered around the wooden partition of the mock stable. A man in need of a shave gazed at them questioningly, then raised a finger to his lips and pointed to a bundle of bright pieces of fabric.

Mari caught a glimpse of Amy, curled into a ball beneath the festive cloaks, the Madonna cradled beside her.

With a cry of pure happiness, Mari rushed toward Amy. The little girl's eyes fluttered open. Seeing Mari, Amy threw her arms around her and hugged Mari tightly. "You're back!"

The tallest of the three men smiled. "We weren't sure what to do with her. She couldn't tell us where to find her parents and she was terrified. We figured she'd be safe at our place," he said. Seeing the look on JD's face, he shrugged and waved his hand toward the manger. "Nobody else is using it and the statues don't mind. It keeps us out of the wind."

Mari crouched on the straw-covered flooring, one arm wrapped tightly around Amy. "You kept her safe. I don't know how we can thank you."

"No thanks needed," the oldest man answered. "It's Christmas." His weathered face was lined with a deep-set weariness that spoke of daily hardships.

JD pulled a card from his wallet, then handed the men some cash. "This is for food and warm clothes and a place for you to spend the night. The card will guarantee you jobs if you want them. Just tell my foreman that I sent you."

"Thanks to you, we've been given our Christmas miracle," Mari added.

Amy held the figure in one arm and smiled brightly. "It's Christmas Day! It's finally time to go see Mommy!"

JD glanced at Mari, sorrow and apprehension clouding his features. "Amy, about that promise I made you—"

"It's too early to go to the hospital right now, honey," Mari interrupted. "But since we have the Madonna, we should take it back to Father Aragon right away. At least it'll be there for morning Mass. Let's do that first. After we return the Lady, then we'll go see your mom."

Mari phoned the parish. Father Aragon answered on the first ring. Mari told him they were on their way to see him with the Madonna. She heard the smile in his voice as he replied, "This parish owes you a great deal. We received the toys the trust donated late last night, and our auxiliary is still here wrapping them. We'll be waiting for you when you arrive."

The trip to the parish along virtually empty roads was quicker than usual. They found Father Aragon at the church's recreation hall, wrapping presents alongside the women's auxiliary.

The priest's eyes grew wide as he saw the Madonna in Amy's arms. "She's back!" he managed in an emotional whisper.

As the women continued wrapping toys, an elderly woman with gray hair tied in a bun approached them. "I'm Rosa Perez, the president of our women's auxiliary." She gave Mari a warm hug. "You've done so much for this parish. We will never be able to thank you enough."

Mari smiled. "No thanks are necessary."

Mrs. Perez crouched before Amy, facing her squarely. "We would like to give you the honor of returning the Madonna to her shrine. You brought her back to us and we think she'd like for you to do that."

Amy smiled widely and nodded, then followed the woman inside the chapel through a side door. All eyes were on Amy as she approached the carved stand. A single red rose had been placed on top.

Amy stopped and turned to look at the priest.

Father Aragon looked at Mrs. Perez who shrugged, puzzled.

Father Aragon stepped around Amy and picked up the rose. It was obvious it hadn't come from any florist. The stem was shorter than the ones sold commercially, yet it had been grown to perfection. Each petal was flawless and the leaves shone with a deep green luster. "This looks like the prize of someone's greenhouse, but no one around here has a greenhouse. They cost too much." The priest stared at the rose pensively. "I think it's our Lady's Christmas gift to you," he said at last, looking down at Amy.

"Then I'll take it to Mommy. It'll be a Christmas gift from both of us."

Father Aragon helped Amy put the Madonna back on the stand, then handed her the rose. "We'll say a prayer for your mother at Christmas Mass. Will you stay?" he asked, looking at Amy, then at JD and Mari, who were still in costume. They had been unwilling to waste time changing earlier when Amy was missing. "We could sure use your help at the Christmas party later. Not all the kids are going to receive toys, and you might be able to entertain them so their disappointment won't be as great."

"The police didn't release any of the toys that had been collected for the drive?" Mari asked.

"None. What you sent has helped, of course, but it won't be enough, even with those Bruce purchased as well."

Mari glanced at JD. "I had the trust send some toys."

JD grinned. "I figured you'd do something like that."

"But it isn't enough," she sighed softly. Mari felt crushed as disappointment and sorrow mingled inside her. "Father,

I'm so sorry. I don't know if I can do anything more to help, but I'll try my best. The Christmas party is at noon?"

"A little after, more like one-thirty, after noon Mass."

Amy tugged at the jacket of Mari's elf costume. "It's time to go see Mommy."

Mari saw the pained look on JD's face. "Yes, honey, it is. We'll go now."

The drive back to town was quiet as they each remained in the silence of their own thoughts. Tension so thick it was almost a visible force hung in the air.

They arrived at the hospital shortly after ten. Fear wound its way through Mari as she entered the lobby and walked alongside Amy. This didn't seem to be a Christmas slated to bring smiles to many children's faces. Her heart went out to Amy whose face was radiant with hope. Her gaze was drawn to the rose in Amy's hand and suddenly and inexplicably, her fears seemed to wash away. The Lady was safe; the rest would follow.

JD's misery, however, was etched plainly on his face. Mari felt for him. His promise had been a reckless one, but now it seemed even more so. As they rode up the elevator, Mari touched Amy's shoulder gently. "Honey, just remember we're right here with you."

Amy looked at Mari, then smiled reassuringly. "Mommy's okay."

Mari felt her chest constrict. "Yes, she's being taken care of and she'll have the best of everything."

Amy glanced away from Mari and looked at JD. "We'll stay with her if she can't leave, right? Nobody should be alone on Christmas."

JD nodded. "All right, honey."

Mari gave JD a worried glance. To dash Amy's hopes now seemed cruel, but so did allowing her to get her hopes so high. She was still debating the best course of action when the elevator doors slid open. Bruce Campbell was standing outside.

He smiled at them in surprise. "Hey, it's great to run into you guys here! I heard on the radio what happened. You're not fugitives anymore. Congratulations!"

"What are *you* doing here?" Mari asked.

"Visiting my mother. Not that she needs me," he added wryly. "Her new husband has been right there for her the whole time. Ever since Dad died, I've been really worried. But two weeks ago she up and married Charlie. Now, with him in her life..." He shrugged. "But enough about me. I assume you've already heard the news here."

"About what?" Mari asked quickly, her heart beating frantically against her ribs.

"Elizabeth woke up about two and a half hours ago." Bruce grinned.

Mari looked at the rose in Amy's hand. Two and a half hours ago... about the time they'd returned the Madonna to the church.

ELIZABETH LAY IN BED, propped up by an extra pillow, and listened as Amy told her about their adventures. The rose had been placed in a vase and still looked as fresh as when they'd found it. "Well, I'm very glad you're all here and safe now," Elizabeth said at last.

Her gaze fell on Mari, then shifted to JD. "I knew I could count on you two." She studied their expressions. "But something's happened between you guys. It's written all over your faces. I can tell."

Amy nodded enthusiastically. "They're in love, but they aren't going to tell anyone."

Elizabeth gave her brother a long look. "You've changed, JD, and I think it's for the better. Maybe being in love suits you. You seem more mellow and your outfit proves it." She grinned widely. "*You* in a Santa suit?"

JD laughed. "Yeah, love does strange things to a guy."

Elizabeth, noticing a pensive look on Mari's face, asked, "What's wrong, Mari?"

"The Christmas party is only hours away, and all the toys donated for the drive are still stuck at the station."

Elizabeth's face clouded. "Isn't there anyone you can call, something you can do?"

Mari worried her bottom lip, considering her options. "Maybe if Jennifer Anderson agrees to do a story on the Christmas party, the department will be under extra pressure to release the toys. They desperately need some good publicity now, with so many of their officers in jail."

Elizabeth pointed toward the telephone on her bed table. "Try to get hold of Jennifer. Do whatever it takes. I know you, Mari. You can move mountains." Mari pulled a slip of paper with Jennifer's number out of her back pocket and dialed. As she turned away, phone in hand to make the call, Elizabeth glanced at JD. "Love's finally touched your heart and melted all those walls you've built up around it. About time," she teased gently.

JD smiled. "Some things happen when you least expect them. That's what miracles are all about."

Mari replaced the receiver a few minutes later. Leaning over the bed, she gave Elizabeth a hug. "I'm glad you're okay. Merry Christmas, Elizabeth." She glanced at JD. "But now it's time for you and me to get going. We have a Christmas to save."

"I'm going, too," Amy said. "We started together and we can finish together."

Elizabeth smiled. "I've heard that tone before. You might as well do as she wants. Besides, a hospital is no place for a little girl to spend Christmas."

THEY MADE IT to the station in twenty minutes. As Mari, JD and Amy went inside, they saw Jennifer Anderson already there, waiting.

To their surprise, Father Aragon was also in the lobby, frantically trying to get Lieutenant Randall to listen.

"Without those toys, Christmas at the parish will be a disaster! You can't do that to our kids!"

"Padre, you don't understand."

Determination shone in the priest's eyes. "You must release those toys. They don't belong in a storage room. They belong to the children of my poor parish. In your heart you know that." He met Randall's gaze. "Please." Raw emotion reverberated in the one word.

"A little cooperation will give this department some great press," Jennifer Anderson promised. "I guarantee it. On the other hand, I could write a story about how the department played Scrooge on Christmas."

"Think of those kids who've been looking forward to this day all year!" Mari added. "What kind of Christmas would you want members of *your* family to have? The kids of the parish have no presents waiting at home. They have one chance, and that's at the Christmas party the church holds. Don't take that away from them!"

"Keep all the teddy bears from the shipment that contained the contraband and take photographic records of the rest," JD suggested. "There's no jury that wouldn't understand why it had to be done that way. Think of all the people who donated toys in good faith, hoping to brighten some child's Christmas. I don't think they'll be very sympathetic to regulations that cause children so much sadness."

"The department needs to restore the community's faith in them, particularly after this scandal," Mari insisted. "You're being given a chance to undo some of the damage."

"You're all ganging up on me," Randall said, his eyes narrowing.

"You bet," Mari replied. "Is it working?"

"I'll see what I can do." He went into the adjoining office and closed the door. Minutes ticked by with agonizing slowness. Finally he emerged. "Okay. We'll release the toys,

all except for the teddy bears that were in the evidence room.
Some of those still hold stolen evidence and gems."

Father Aragon smiled. "Thank you. May the Madonna
bless you and yours." He glanced around quickly. "I have
to find a telephone. There's much for the auxiliary to do
before the children's party!"

Randall glanced at the clock on the wall. "Are you going
to have enough time? It's almost nine-thirty. The trip alone
will take more than an hour."

"Don't underestimate us, young man. The Madonna has
accomplished miracles for our parish before, and she's particularly fond of children. She won't let us down now."

THEY MADE THE TRIP BACK to the church in less time than
it had ever taken any of them, including the priest. The police escort helped. The van was nearly filled to capacity.

The women's auxiliary met them at the church's recreation hall, ready to wrap the toys. As they got busy, Father
Aragon approached JD, Mari and Amy. "Santa, I assume
that you and your two elves will stay for our Christmas
party?" he asked with a broad smile.

"You bet, Father," JD said, grinning. "Not that I believe you'd take no for an answer."

"You're right, son, I wouldn't," Father Aragon admitted happily.

THAT AFTERNOON, AS KIDS streamed inside the recreation
hall, Christmas spirit filled the air. Mari couldn't remember ever being this happy. This was what it was all about,
seeing the joy in the small faces as they walked away with
their toys.

While press photographers crowded around them, Santa
and his two elves distributed the goodies that filled Santa's
giant red bag. Not one child left empty-handed.

After the presents had all been distributed, JD stood and
gently led Mari away from the kids. "Amy's had a ball.

There's a hearing-impaired child she's taken under her wing," he said, gesturing across the room. "In fact, I noticed she made sure the little boy received the biggest truck in Santa's bag."

"Everyone's happy," Mari sighed contentedly.

"Isn't anyone going to ask what Santa wants for Christmas?" JD asked, placing his finger under Mari's chin until she looked up at him.

Mari felt the love in that gentle touch flow all through her. "Santa, why do I get the feeling you're asking me a loaded question?"

"After all we've been through together!" JD clicked his tongue in disapproval. "Santa deserves your trust!"

"You're absolutely right," she said. "So tell me, Santa, what's your Christmas wish?"

JD put his arms around Mari and pulled her close. "Santa wants his number one elf to marry him."

"Elves always do Santa's bidding."

"Oh, I'm going to like this," he said, chuckling. As JD leaned over to kiss her, they heard the kids laughing and cheering.

"We're standing under the mistletoe," Mari said, glancing up.

"How appropriate," he replied, and covered her mouth with a kiss.

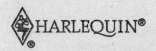

Fifty red-blooded, white-hot, true-blue hunks
from every State in the Union!

Look for MEN MADE IN AMERICA! Written by some
of our most popular authors, these stories feature fifty
of the strongest, sexiest men, each from a different state
in the union!

Two titles available every month at your favorite
retail outlet.

In December, look for:

NATURAL ATTRACTION by Marisa Carroll
(New Hampshire)
MOMENTS HARSH, MOMENTS GENTLE by Joan Hohl
(New Jersey)

In January 1995, look for:

WITHIN REACH by Marilyn Pappano (New Mexico)
IN GOOD FAITH by Judith McWilliams (New York)

You won't be able to resist MEN MADE IN AMERICA!

This holiday, join four hunky heroes under the mistletoe for

Christmas Kisses

Cuddle under a fluffy quilt, with a cup of hot chocolate and these romances sure to warm you up:

#561 HE'S A REBEL (also a Studs title)
Linda Randall Wisdom

#562 THE BABY AND THE BODYGUARD
Jule McBride

#563 THE GIFT-WRAPPED GROOM
M.J. Rodgers

#564 A TIMELESS CHRISTMAS
Pat Chandler

Celebrate the season with all four holiday books sealed with a Christmas kiss—coming to you in December, only from Harlequin American Romance!

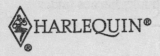 **HARLEQUIN®**

Weddings, Inc.

The proprietors of Weddings, Inc. hope you
have enjoyed visiting Eternity, Massachusetts.
And if you missed any of the exciting Weddings,
Inc. titles, here is your opportunity to complete
your collection:

Harlequin Superromance	#598	*Wedding Invitation* by Marisa Carroll	$3.50 U.S. ☐ $3.99 CAN. ☐	
Harlequin Romance	#3319	*Expectations* by Shannon Waverly	$2.99 U.S. ☐ $3.50 CAN. ☐	
Harlequin Temptation	#502	*Wedding Song* by Vicki Lewis Thompson	$2.99 U.S. ☐ $3.50 CAN. ☐	
Harlequin American Romance	#549	*The Wedding Gamble* by Muriel Jensen	$3.50 U.S. ☐ $3.99 CAN. ☐	
Harlequin Presents	#1692	*The Vengeful Groom* by Sara Wood	$2.99 U.S. ☐ $3.50 CAN. ☐	
Harlequin Intrigue	#298	*Edge of Eternity* by Jasmine Cresswell	$2.99 U.S. ☐ $3.50 CAN. ☐	
Harlequin Historical	#248	*Vows* by Margaret Moore	$3.99 U.S. ☐ $4.50 CAN. ☐	

HARLEQUIN BOOKS...
NOT THE SAME OLD STORY

TOTAL AMOUNT	$
POSTAGE & HANDLING ($1.00 for one book, 50¢ for each additional)	$
APPLICABLE TAXES*	$ _____
TOTAL PAYABLE (check or money order—please do not send cash)	$ _____

To order, complete this form and send it, along with a check or money order for the
total above, payable to Harlequin Books, to: **In the U.S.:** 3010 Walden Avenue,
P.O. Box 9047, Buffalo, NY 14269-9047; **In Canada:** P.O. Box 613, Fort Erie, Ontario,
L2A 5X3.

Name: _____
Address: _____ City: _____
State/Prov.: _____ Zip/Postal Code: _____

*New York residents remit applicable sales taxes.
  Canadian residents remit applicable GST and provincial taxes.   WED-F

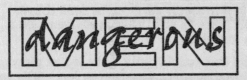

Where do you find hot Texas nights, smooth Texas charm and dangerously sexy cowboys?

Crystal Creek reverberates with the exciting rhythm of Texas. Each story features the rugged individuals who live and love in the Lone Star state.

"...Crystal Creek wonderfully evokes the hot days and steamy nights of a small Texas community...impossible to put down until the last page is turned."
—*Romantic Times*

"With each book the characters in Crystal Creek become more endearingly familiar. This series is far from formula and a welcome addition to the category genre."
—*Affaire de Coeur*

"Altogether, it couldn't be better." —*Rendezvous*

Don't miss the next book in this exciting series. Look for
THE HEART WON'T LIE by MARGOT DALTON

Available in January wherever Harlequin books are sold.